THE
SECRET GAME
OF
POWER

To Dimitri,

Hope your political enthusiasm
will never be the same again.

Thank you for helping me
so much.

Regards,

Florin

10 - March - 2014

THE
SECRET GAME
OF
POWER

FLORIN LUPUSORU

authorHOUSE®

AuthorHouse™ UK Ltd.
1663 Liberty Drive
Bloomington, IN 47403 USA
www.authorhouse.co.uk
Phone: 0800.197.4150

Published by AuthorHouse   02/13/2014

ISBN: 978-1-4918-9523-8 (sc)
ISBN: 978-1-4918-9524-5 (hc)
ISBN: 978-1-4918-9525-2 (e)

CONTENTS

INTRODUCTION

This book might upset many people, especially those privileged individuals with *great* CVs, such as politicians, celebrities, superstars, superheroes, super-rich people, scientists, bestselling authors, artists, charismatic leaders, and any kind of "high achievers." Sadly, those lucky individuals who think they have reasons to believe they are great, amazing, and wonderful, might imagine that they possess fantastic qualities and talent, and thus deserve everyone's attention and admiration.

It's amazing to see the huge amount of garbage, so-called "theories of success", that has invaded our lives aggressively and incessantly in the last few years. Such contradictory theories, developed frenetically at the speed of light and supported arrogantly by the greatest experts in the world, claim, against all the evidence, that we are in control of our destinies. And of course, in this world of experts, it would be difficult to admit that great people can't exist without great opportunities.

Having a great CV might be useless in and of itself. We also have to consider having the *right* skills at the *right* time and in the *right* place, which of course must have the *right* political landscape and the *right* economy. Lastly comes the most important bit: having the *right* connections . . .

In a society so ridiculously obsessed with having perfect CVs, discussing the purpose of a CV, the lies behind it, and the lies behind success can invite social stigma. No wonder so many people seemed to be absolutely outraged by the content of this book, and trying to discuss such an incendiary subject offered me plenty of embarrassing moments. I am emboldened, however, to present a set of suggestions to the reader.

This book is definitely not on the required reading list for those individuals who are rather successful people and entirely comfortable with their lives. Such people have every right to tell everyone how great they are and ignore any contrary opinions.

People who have not reached the dizzy heights of success yet think they are on a sure way towards this pinnacle, or even close to dazzling achievements, had better allow this volume to merely adorn their bookshelves. They are in danger of losing their self-esteem and endangering a comfortable overconfidence and pride.

For those who are neither successful nor on their way towards success but admire someone successful, perhaps it is better for them to ignore this book. Their admiration for that person might simply fade away.

Anyway, to progress reading this book definitely requires a high degree of irony, openness to controversial issues, and some strong coffee. People more prone to heart attacks might wish to avoid both this book and the coffee, since a combination of both could be fatal.

A sense of outrage will possibly see the reader through some of the arguments of this book, and I would not be surprised if some people accused me of either jealousy towards successful people or anarchic intentions, or both. Nevertheless, I believe that the evidence presented by such people will not support their accusations.

In this writer's humble opinion, success is nothing more than political decisions combined with average skills and some great opportunities.

However, above all, soliciting the attention of powerful people, if lucky enough to attract their attention and support, can be more decisive for one's success than incredible talent and a whole life of sacrifice. It is no wonder that references and recommendations have become the most important part of every CV and thus the secret formula for success. Nevertheless, this can be a distressing thing to admit, especially for high achievers.

It appears that the equation of success has two distinct parts: On one side, there are some arbitrary advantages—in fact, too many of them—such as genetic inheritance, parents' social status and wealth, and a combination of other lucky accidents. On the other side, there is a process called "soliciting attention and favours", or more exactly, begging for a job, with your CV in one hand and your unconditional submission in the other.

Depending on the political landscape, this process of begging can be accomplished by either using bribery on a large scale or making use of something more *democratic,* referred to as "references and recommendations". Both systems have the same goal: lobbying in someone's favour. But the secret machinery of lobbying only works after one has taken an oath of allegiance and solemnly promised eternal loyalty and gratitude to the benefactor.

Not surprisingly, the *right* combination of the *right* advantages and opportunities is qualified as "success". However, the equation of success might have no solution if one fails to find the right benefactor or fails to capture that person's attention.

In academic language, the ability to solve the equation of success is referred to as "having strong references". For people who struggle to understand such great scientific terms, it simply means "kissing the right arse".

I have to confess that writing this book has been challenging, having to do the entire work alone and unsupported, with very few opportunities to discuss such an incendiary subject. This is a language endeavour as well, for it has only been five years since I learnt my first words in English. As such, I am the only one to blame if some mistakes are found. I hope there are not that many, however.

CHAPTER 1

The Secret Game of Power

Playing the **Game of Power** could result in so much fun! The participants in this pyramidal scheme agreed that there was nothing more exciting than playing with people's destinies.

This game was only accessible to superstars, superheroes, super-rich people, super-powerful people, and to everyone lucky enough to be one of the super-influential individuals that occupied the top of the social pyramid. They were the world's elite, and mentioning their names would be too dangerous.

This privileged society that moved at a different speed than everyone else decided that *everyone else*, meaning all the "losers" out there, could be a great source of inspiration and entertainment.

Two players were selected from the people present by drawing random numbers used in playing the game. Higher achievers in the world of finance or politics were also rewarded, giving them the chance either to play the game or to preside over it. The person destined to preside over the game was called master of the **Game of Power**, or simply the master.

There was a special requirement that a game couldn't start until a list was completed.

People on the list were different from people present at the game. In fact, the members of this exquisite organisation were those who decided the destinies of those on the list. For every new game, there was a new list of people chosen randomly from all the CVs available. On this list would be found the expected desperate people who never had jobs, and they would be complemented by engineers, artists, students, politicians, and so forth. A list could only contain 240 people, men and women from all around the world, mixed together without any connection to each other. To each of them, a number was then assigned, from one to sixty, with one colour out of the four available. When the list was complete, it was kept far from a pair of selected players.

When a new game started, the players had to be separated from the spectators. The two players sat in front of a big screen, closely watched by the master and his assistants. When everything was ready, the game could start.

The game was played on a table, but it was instantly converted and projected on the screen. A huge triangle could be seen, with 120 dots forming smaller triangles. At the triangle's base were *coins* arranged in many columns in front of each of the two players. Each player had 120 pieces, with one colour on one side. On the other side, there were two different colours, with numbers from one to sixty.

Each player played one piece at a time, but he or she could lose a turn to the adversary if unable to pick up the right piece. This way, no one knew who was going to play the last piece. This last detail was not very important during the first phase of the game but was extremely important within the second phase since the whole purpose of this game was relevant to the last played piece.

There were two games played at the same time, with no apparent interconnection. First was the game between the two players, with the aim to make as many points as possible. Second was the **Game of Power**, in order to select a "winner" arbitrarily. The real fun started when the last piece was being played, the one at the top of the pyramid. At this point, a name on the list corresponding to the colour and number of the piece was declared the winner. All the others suddenly became losers, and no one cared about them anymore.

The atmosphere became hilarious when someone read the winner's CV. Of course, all the positive adjectives characterizing this person must be revealed to the public, along with the skills, qualifications, experience, and references. The above-mentioned CV was then examined with great interest by the audience, who couldn't stop laughing, and everyone came up with his or her own diabolic plan of how to make the "winner" (a loser, of course) a real winner in this crazy world.

On one particular night, the winner was a certain Lee N, a person who'd just graduated from the university with a degree in journalism. He lived alone, struggling to pay his rent and unable to find a job. Looking for further information about this person, it came out that he was also a failed writer who'd just published a book that nobody wanted to read.

"Yeah, we've got our new bestselling author!" shouted someone from the audience with a triumphant voice when they learned this.

"Let's make this loser a celebrity!" shouted another. "His crappy book can find an honoured place among other crappy books."

"Just look at his CV. I bet that in a few months his CV will completely change," said another person, laughing uncontrollably.

"Our superhero will then offer *expertise* and advice to all the losers around him," added another person, stressing the word "expertise" in such a way that some people found themselves rolling on the floor with mirth.

"*Expertise*," repeated someone else, starting a new round of laughing.

"I guess this idiot will come to imagine that he possesses unique and spectacular skills . . ."

"Like all the losers out there," continued somebody else.

"What about his book?" someone asked with curiosity.

"Just the same ridiculous story written by losers about superheroes," someone said, looking into the file with all the information about the winner. "There are plenty of similar stories like this on the market, and I'm not surprised that nobody wants to read it."

"But is his superhero at least going to fall in love after punishing the bad guys?" asked the same curious guy.

"Punishing the bad guys? Ha ha ha."

"Those losers have great imaginations . . ."

This time, the conversation seemed to be moving towards unqualified hilarity. Everyone was laughing, and nobody was listening any more. Conversation was almost impossible. Even the minimum sign that somebody was trying to say anything about the fantastic skills *possessed* by the winner was enough to provoke more uproarious laughter.

This merriment continued for more than an hour. They finally agreed upon a plan of action, and a few people were selected for this mission.

"You know what to do?" the master asked them.

"Yes, sir!"

"How long will it take you to finish this mission?" the master asked.

"Probably a few days," said one of the selected people. "Just a few phone calls and some appointments with the right people . . ."

"Good. Follow the plan. I want to see this loser a bestselling author as soon as possible."

Minutes later, all the people vanished as mysteriously as they had gathered. The objective of that night was to change the life of a loser and get that person on the path towards success.

The Winner

A few months before, Lee had had a normal life, with many problems and very few friends. This might not sound normal at all. Nevertheless, for him it was a normal life, if compared to what would follow next. He was struggling to pay the rent like everybody else, struggling to get a decent job, struggling to make friends, and struggling to be accepted by society, with all his weaknesses and failures.

He was a complete failure at everything, and anything he touched used to fall apart. Publishers rejected his book multitudinous times, and Lee consequently lost the courage and hope of any possible change. Every time he received a new professional rejection letter from publishers or job agencies, it made him feel lonelier and more miserable. His few remaining friends started to avoid him, inventing unexpected duties and obligations.

Perhaps I should never have written that book, he thought, *and instead dedicated more time to my friends.*

His self-imprisonment in his room for so long did not bring about any good. If you send people to prison without a reason, they will protest and clamour in defence of their human rights. Lee lost his right to protest because the guardian of his cell was himself.

His daily life went as usual, most of the time alone, looking for a job and not having enough money. Then he decided to self-publish his book by purchasing a basic package, the most he could afford to pay for at the risk of falling behind on his rent.

Two months later, Lee received the great news: his book was on the market. Few of his friends called to congratulate him or to share with him the great joy. Perhaps the most encouraging support he received was from his mum. Lee's brothers also called, but they were preoccupied with their own problems. Then . . . nothing! No one noticed his book; no one made any review or comment, and no one bought it. A complete silence, more painful than the worst review, was all he could get. Then Lee decided to change strategy and to build his own online community. He invested a lot of time trying to make new friends, joining many groups and participating in discussions in forums, newspapers, and blogs. Still nothing! The whole world seemed to be ignoring him.

Perhaps my approach is wrong, he thought.

Perhaps the title of the book was not shocking enough. Perhaps the superhero did something people didn't like. Perhaps he did not follow all the guidelines necessary for a successful book. But he remembered that for the last two years, he'd been reading many books about success, positive thinking, and overpowering one's fear; they were inspirational and creative books. He'd also read the bibliographies of the most successful people, listened to their talks, followed their advice, behaved like them, and aspired to join them. His room was full of inspirational quotes according to the latest standards promoted by experts. Struggling to find an answer for this failure, his overconfidence began to fade away; all the positive thinking began changing into a nightmare. He had no idea what to do next, feeling himself to be one more loser in a world of winners.

In the big city, Lee was never more lonely or helpless. Perhaps it was time to go back again to the countryside, humiliated and defeated. His mum and his house were still awaiting his forlorn return. So Lee began packing. It was the only thing left to do beyond committing suicide or joining the homeless fraternity.

He learned that a train was leaving the following day, and he decided to go for a last beer in the city. Later, Peter, one of his friends, arrived at the bar, very excited.

"I was looking for you," he said. Then he told Lee the great news: his book was a bestseller. Apparently, Paul was reading the news online and stumbled upon a list of the latest bestsellers by chance.

"Bestseller! What are you talking about?" Lee stared at him to see if he was joking. But his friend looked excited indeed and assuring at the same time. *Bestseller?* he thought. *One hour ago, I was thinking about suicide.*

His friend gave him all the details. A famous writer reviewed the book, and many others followed. In a few hours, Lee's name was relatively well known, and it was not surprising at all to see his name in the news the following day.

Lee became an overnight celebrity. Many TV shows began inviting him, and everyone was curious to know the secret of his success. Of course, his *skills* and *sacrifice* became the new theory of success for aspiring celebrities. His modesty was highly appreciated, as was his *expertise.* When asked about the secret for this unbelievable success, Lee did not know what to say. The truth was that he had no idea. Lee's hesitation was interpreted as a way to hide a great secret, and people became even more curious. However, the most curious of them all was Lee himself.

It was not much later that movie producers contacted him. In exchange for a conspicuous offer, Lee gave his permission for the creation of the movie *Race to Pluto.* All the headlines around the world were about him, his book, and the movie about to be made after it.

Lee was no longer alone. He now had many friends and everyone sought his advice. A huge number of letters and an even bigger number of emails were being sent to him every day. Many people, impressed by his achievements, wanted to know him, and most important of all, there were many girls.

No person on this planet could desire more from life: fame, money (lots and lots), a house, friends, respect, security, and a society that loved him. The only missing thing was a family. Lee was nonetheless confident that that would come soon.

"One thing at a time," he said to himself. "For the moment, just some relaxation. I guess I deserve it."

But life was not as it looked.

Lee had his own theories on politics and always imagined politics to be a dirty game, but he never suspected just how dirty.

One night Lee wanted to relax in his new flat on the top floor of a tall building. He'd always wanted to have a big terrace with a good view and many plants, a peaceful place far from problems and worries. In the distant to the west, he could see the sunset and a few clouds hiding the sea.

"What a lovely place!" Lee exclaimed, not for the first time.

The city centre was far away on the opposite side, and the huge urban sprawl would not disturb him too much with its noise or lights. He had chosen this particular place because it had few lights facing the terrace. That's right; he wanted to enjoy the sky. Finally, nobody could take away from him the right to dream . . .

"Where can we put it, sir?" said one of the two guys bringing a huge box containing a powerful telescope.

"Leave it here," Lee said. "Open it. Let's see what it amounts to."

One by one, the pieces forming the telescope came out of the box, and the two men got busy setting it up.

"Shall I bring some coffee, sir?"

A tall middle-aged woman, his housekeeper, came from inside the flat. Mrs Roberts had five children and lived alone. Her husband had died a few years back. Since then, she had had a few temporary jobs, struggling to maintain her house and to raise the kids. Someone introduced her to Lee, and she was excited and happy to get this job. The second housekeeper, another woman with a similar story, lived with her husband and three children.

Both of them, Mrs Roberts and Mrs Woods, had to do the shopping, cleaning, cooking, and other related tasks. However, their main duty was to stay out of his way and to make as little noise as possible. Lee was already a celebrity, and as such, he had to leave his imagination free in preparation for writing the next great book.

"Not now; when the gentlemen have finished."

Watching the sunset, lost in his thoughts, Lee was trying to make sense of what was happening. Something didn't feel right. That change in his life was so unbelievable and so quick . . . Although everything appeared a normal reward for his hard work, there appeared to be an extra factor that did not tally. What was the meaning of all this?

The two guys left soon, after placing the telescope in the preferred place.

Forget it for now, Lee thought, unable to find an explanation as to what seemed a bit off. *Perhaps I should have a look at those letters. Let's see . . .*

A basket containing many letters was sitting next to his bench. Bringing it in front of him, Lee began scanning the return addresses. It was the easiest way to sort them into categories.

"Charity." He put an envelope to one side. "Charity again."

"Girls." He put an envelope on the other side.

"Girls, charity, business, advertising, friends . . ." And so on.

From time to time, he had to stop and open a letter that looked more interesting. Mrs Roberts brought the coffee and put it on a small garden table.

"Do you need anything else?" she asked.

"No, thanks. That's all."

She said good night and disappeared behind the door.

He continued with the letters, stopping from time to time to savour his coffee. It was a peaceful evening and an amazing sunset. The stars would be appearing soon.

Among the huge pile of letters, two of them looked very strange, so he set them apart for closer perusal.

A certain Mr L with master's degrees in physics and astronomy was informing him that the big bang theory might be wrong, according to his latest research, and was enquiring if Lee would be interested in using his theory in his next book.

This looks interesting, he thought. *What if I call him tonight? Someone has to explain the stars to me.*

On the phone, he sounded very excited and promised to arrive in about an hour. That sorted out, he had a look at the other letter. Mr S, a gardener, wanted to look after Lee's terrace, but he also promised to offer him some shocking information about a matter that couldn't be discussed in letters.

"Perhaps I need a gardener," he said, but he was in fact more curious about the promised information. The gardener lived in the same big city. Once Lee got him on the phone, he promised to arrive in about an hour and a half.

"That's fine. Whenever you can," Lee said.

Finishing the coffee and putting the letters aside, Lee remained comfortable on the terrace, lost in his thoughts and watching the slow setting of the sun.

For the first time in his life, Lee felt secure and in control of his destiny. This is the most important thing when one is a celebrity. All the humiliating experiences in the past felt like an ephemeral dream, a bad dream that he wanted to consign to oblivion. Now he was able to do everything he wanted with his life, buy everything he wanted and travel around the world, visiting all the places he'd dreamed about since he was a child. Most important of all, he didn't have a boss to tell him what to do and how and when to do it.

"Isn't this a good reason to celebrate? Isn't this what all people want: freedom, security, and respect?"

Life can be incredibly unpredictable, similar to playing the lottery. There are winners and losers, with more losers than winners. Losers are not as important, and most people don't care about them. Lee was one of the winners, and that was a great thing. He had the right to feel special and great, lucky and unique. As a result, he deserved people's full attention and admiration.

Too many crappy bestsellers

The first to arrive was Mr L, a tall and slender gentleman in his middle twenties. He joined Lee on the terrace. It was already dark, and most of the stars were visible in the clear sky. Impressed by the professional telescope, Mark started talking about his favourite subject: astronomy. After some time, they felt entirely at ease with one another. The skies above invited their curious exploration. Mark was familiar with every constellation and enthused about the wonders of the night sky.

Time passed quickly, and the second guest soon arrived. Presenting himself as Stefan, an emigrant from the East, he joined them but proved rather taciturn. Talking from time to time and only when asked a question, he used short and precise answers and refused to be drawn out further. After the initial excitement about the telescope, Lee and Mark realised that they were in fact ignoring their companion. Therefore, they decided to devote some time to making his acquaintance properly.

"I am a bestselling author, as you might know," Lee informed them. "So far, I have sold more than fifteen million copies, and the sales keep rising." He was pleased to expound on matters relating to his book.

"Have you read it?"

"Not yet," said Mark, embarrassed, "but it looks interesting."

Stefan appeared to have a completely different opinion. "Do you want to know the truth about your book?" said Stefan, breaking the silence.

"Of course," Lee said, expecting some sort of mild criticism.

"You are going to get upset," he continued.

Suspecting an element of teasing, Lee looked at him, trying to find a sign that this was a joke. However, he looked entirely serious.

"Tell me what you're implying."

"Bad news, my friend . . ."

Mark looked rather unsettled as he waited to hear more.

"Tell me anyway," Lee responded.

"Your bestseller is rather disappointing. It doesn't make any sense, and . . ." Stefan's voice trailed off.

"Continue," Lee said, trying to look braver than he felt.

"It is very similar to most of the bestsellers on the market. The bad guys are punished and the good guy, your superhero, defeats them, and in the end, he falls in love with the most beautiful woman. The same ridiculous subject all over again!"

Lee felt insulted; he had not expected a guest to prove so churlish. Obviously, his book might not be the best on the market, but neither was it the worst. How would this gentleman explain the spectacular sales and media attention the volume had received in such a short time?

"Of course, this is just an opinion."

Trying to save the situation, Lee looked at Mark for help. He didn't appear to be very troubled. In fact, he looked somewhat relieved, as if something might have confirmed his untold opinion.

"You know something? He might be right," Mark said with hesitation, recalling the multitude of mediocre bestsellers recently published, all appearing to have the same subject.

"What is your entire book about?" continued Stefan coldly. "An alien ship is sighted on Pluto, and of course all the aliens are dead so they cannot disturb your ridiculous superhero. Then the world powers start a desperate race to this distant world in order to put their hands on the alien technology and to control the world. This wouldn't be that bad, but why must the good guys always win in books and movies? Why does the government of your country suddenly become the good guy destined to save the world?"

That was hard to listen to, not because it was wrong but because it appeared to be right. All the positive thoughts Lee had about himself started to break apart. He was never so humiliated, not even during the worst period of his life, when he was so close to committing suicide. The most humiliating thing was that the person saying all of this was a person with no apparent education, a person who didn't even have a CV, as he'd confessed in his letter. After a few minutes of conversation, Lee's fantastic CV became a useless piece of paper with no apparent value. More shockingly, his *great* bestseller turned out to be just another crappy book amongst so many crappy books.

They spent the entire night talking and listening to each other's stories. There was a big reserve of beer in the fridge, and they all had good reasons to be upset about their lives.

In addition to Mark's degrees in physics and astronomy, he'd studied for a PhD in theoretical physics, but his teachers were determined to fail him, and they did eventually. Moreover, he did not manage to find any job related to his qualifications and was consequently forced to work as a cleaner in a restaurant, a survival job due to a lack of anything better. His colleagues didn't treat him very well, and he had no choice but to carry on with that humiliating job.

"There is nowhere else to go," Mark confessed with sadness.

The reason his teachers failed his thesis was because he argued with them while doing the research project. The subject of this quarrel was a theory called big bang, which Mark refused to accept as a scientific explanation for the birth of the universe. He came up with his own theory of the universe, ridiculing and challenging his teachers' well-accepted theories. By doing so, he managed to upset his teachers, powerful and influential people who were ready to defend their theory to the last breath. Since their entire careers and reputations depended on stupid things such as big bang, inflation, superstrings, and parallel worlds, they did not intend to let everything go for the sake of the scientific truth.

Of course, they fought back and thus closed all doors into the scientific world to him, from publishing to teaching and research. Nobody would accept his papers for publishing unless approved and endorsed by his teachers. Moreover, his job prospects looked horrendous without proper references. In other words, by challenging the accepted wisdom of his teachers, Mark managed to end his career forever.

"They have taken my money, told me I was doing great, and then failed me," he confessed with sadness.

"Tell me about your theory," Lee said, and Stefan looked ready to ask the same question.

"Perhaps I should explain to you what this big bang is all about and what is wrong with it. Do you have any knowledge in physics? I want to make sure you understand what I am talking about."

Assuring him that their level of physics was above the survival level, Mark began talking with great emphasis.

"This weird theory claims that around thirteen point eight billion years ago, a big explosion created everything that came to exist later in this universe. Everything was created from nothing, but the strangest thing is this huge explosion happening only once in the lifetime of the universe. Let me put it simply: to be true, a theory must be true all the time, not just once. I am not suggesting the existence of more big bangs. This would be even more ridiculous. I simply cannot accept that all the matter in the universe is the product of one event only. If matter is only four per cent of the universe, when it comes to doing the maths, the whole story of the big bang becomes even more absurd.

"Then there is also a singularity, a point of infinite gravity and temperature from which everything was created. How can a point of infinite temperature exist when, according to them, temperature is movement? Why did this tiny dot moving like a lunatic around the universe begin moving in the first place?"

Lee and Stefan were listening with amusement as Mark continued.

"Then comes the inflation. This lunatic dot began to *inflate* for no apparent reason. I would rather say that something else has inflated, but this would be too upsetting for some people in high positions . . ."

Mark was clearly upset, but seeing the others laughing, he started laughing too.

"It must be very funny to study physics, isn't it?" said Lee entertained.

"Perhaps the bank accounts of those supporting this theory have inflated," suggested Stefan jokingly.

Mark continued by saying that the two main points in support of the big bang theory, the background radiation and the red shift of the light, were just the right evidence used in the wrong context.

"What if the speed of light is not constant? What if the light travelling across the universe is influenced by what we call dark matter and dark energy, and if so, through an unknown mechanism, either increases or decreases its wavelength? If this is true, then we don't even need a big bang. We can get rid of this useless inflation . . ."

He took a break and then continued. "For the sake of argument, imagine that neither dark matter nor dark energy existed. How to explain the strange behaviour of gravity on large scales? If gravity can be modified at very large scales, perhaps all the parameters and physical constants can also be modified at different scales. Consequently, the speed of light and its wavelength can be equally modified . . ."

Minutes later, this new theory became clear:

There was never a big bang, and there was no need for a lunatic dot running across the universe. It was instead a period without light and gravity, a period of darkness lasting for hundreds of billions of years. Then something somehow created gravity, and light was created due to gravity. This was the big bang; a kind of chain reaction taking control of the existing matter . . .

"I can imagine the big bang as an event of spreading light across the universe, not as an event of spreading matter. Matter itself will never reach such a huge speed." Mark was visibly excited.

"What about the background radiation?" Lee asked.

"It is not proving to be the result of creating matter in a violent event as scientists say today. It might also have been the result of existing matter colliding with each other. What's more, we still have no idea what dark matter and dark energy are. What if there is some link between them and this background radiation?"

After a short break, Mark continued:

"People who try to unite the four forces of the universe might never succeed. They were probably never united. Perhaps we should instead try to find out if there is any link between light and gravity. If we can prove that both gravity and light did not exist before the event we call big bang and try to figure out the behaviour of existing matter and energy in their absence, well, a horrifying new world comes to light . . ."

When Mark finished sharing his theory, he and Lee looked at Stefan. It was his time to tell his story.

Stefan came to this country about ten years ago, and since then, he'd lived alone. He's had many different jobs, but the job he liked the most was gardening. At that moment, he worked from time to time for various people who had little gardens and terraces of flowers and plants. His pay was not high enough to allow him to rent a flat or a room. As a result, he lived in a forest outside the big city, in a place well hidden from people's eyes. He managed to make a small portion of the forest impenetrable—hiding well the entrance to the secret dwelling so nobody had any idea of its existence.

His life was simple and without stress, although the loneliness could sometimes be overwhelming. A few tents set up close to each other contained all his belongings and a huge collection of books on almost every subject, gathered from the people he worked for when they wanted to discard them. Luckily for him, when someone happened to die, the people who inherited the houses usually didn't care about the books.

Stefan called his collection of books "The National Library" and was pleased to invite his new friends for a visit into the forest.

"There's something of extreme importance you might wish to see," Stefan said to Lee.

Since Mark also appeared to be excited about this trip, they decided to go there the following day.

Stefan continued to talk about himself. For a person with no apparent education, he was surprisingly clever and knowledgeable. In fact, he seemed to know almost everything. Imagine his days without a job being spent in the forest reading books.

He was upset at his government and politicians in general, considering most of them useless. "Politicians are supposed to protect us," Stefan said with anger, "but instead they protect the big corporations and the rich people."

"Following the political events in my country," he continued, "I don't know if I should laugh or cry or simply pretend that I no longer have a country. Everything looks so disappointing and ridiculously comical.

And my beloved government, the worst thing that could possibly exist on this planet, appears to live in a parallel world with no connection to real life. Hiding their dirty secrets behind highly emotional words full of inspirational, patriotic, and heroic intentions but empty of content, they continue mocking and robbing us in the name of *democracy . . .*"

The discussion continued, moving from corruption to the meaning of democracy. They all agreed that there was something wrong with it but were not allowed to discuss such sensible subjects, since *antidemocratic* was clearly a negative word and hence they might get into trouble if someone happened to listen to their conversation.

There was a big difference between criticising democracy and being antidemocratic, but since people were so ridiculously paranoid, perhaps the best thing to do was to avoid this subject, they concluded. Criticising democracy is not the same as antidemocratic, and antidemocratic is not the same as anarchism, dictatorship, chaos, fascism, communism, or any other authoritarian political system provided by the media as the only alternatives to democracy.

Later, Lee showed the two guests his enormous flat. Of particular interest was his library, which contained a few thousands books on almost every subject.

However, soon they began quarrelling about the contents of the library.

What is this ridiculous positive psychology? Why so many books about the same subjects: how to become a superhero, how to become rich, how to be a great leader, how to write a great CV, how to be successful, and so on? Why did people keep ignoring reality? Why was everyone so obsessed about everything related to success?

Isn't this huge amount of positive thinking literature the result of our increasing insecurity? Isn't this obsession with a perfect CV the result of increasing inequality? Perhaps people are desperately trying to convince themselves that they are still worth something . . .

Behaving like a winner feels great, even if one is a loser, doesn't it?

What is wrong with the world? Over the past few years, there has been a huge amount of books about vampires. Even the most respected publishers have fallen to the temptation of publishing the same junk. There's no more quality. There's just the shock culture . . .

Lee realised not only that everything about himself was wrong, but also that he had no idea of being wrong until the two gentlemen opened his eyes. Something needed to be done, and the first step was his library.

Until the next morning, they had great fun burning books. Everything that didn't make sense—everything about monsters, vampires, leaders, and superheroes; everything about success, fantastic CVs, time management, and career planning; every useless book with a big shocking title and a lot of advertising and references—faced the same destination: the fireplace. Watching the books burning, they felt great, they felt happy, and they felt free.

Three-quarters of the books vanished soon, and with them all the stupidity and obsessions of this world. Lee began to wonder why it took him so long to realise that he was heading to the wrong destination. Perhaps all the advertising and brainwashing of modern society were too convincing, or perhaps he was just easy prey in this jungle of experts.

The long and eventful night was about to end, as was Lee's journey into the darkness. His first act of rebellion, an impossible task just one day before, made him feel completely different. He didn't feel stronger or more confident—in fact, he felt more vulnerable and helpless—but at least more suspicious about this world of experts and superheroes built on lies.

The forest of secrets

The next morning was to arrive soon. After breakfast, the three friends prepared themselves for the planned journey into the forest, having Stefan as their guide.

It was a wonderful morning, with no wind and no clouds in the sky. Lee took his car and Stefan sat in front with him because he had to show the way. Lee had crossed the huge city via his car many times during the last few months, but this time was different. It was like going into the unknown without a map and a destination. This time he felt somehow strange, a stranger to himself. The day before, he was a different person, more confident about himself and more proud about his achievements. That day, he had no confidence at all and no idea what to do next. Perhaps the best thing to do was to accept life as it was, full of surprises and disappointments.

One hour later, the city remained behind—and with it the endless noise and rushing people and cars. Much more relaxed, they continued the journey north. A forest appeared in their sight on the right side of the road. Following a complicated path into it, they finally stopped at a place indicated by Stefan. There were many cars around and people having barbecues, playing sports, listening to music, or simply relaxing. The children, like all children, were busy playing, singing, and making a lot of noise.

They continued the journey on foot through a maze of paths into the forest. Finally, they found themselves behind the bushes, crossing a sector of the forest into which not many people dared to venture. There was not a real path, and from time to time, Stefan had to remove different obstacles in the way. At certain points, the journey became increasingly difficult, but nobody had any reasons to complain. Stefan was very happy for his guests, Lee was equally happy to forget his sense of worthlessness, but the most excited of all was Mark. One could see from his face that he desperately needed an escape, and this adventure into the unknown appeared to be just the right thing.

Soon the path with overgrown bushes ended and they were able to see a tent well hidden behind some trees. There were many other tents around, as Stefan assured them, but they were still invisible. From the outside, the tent seemed quite small, but once inside, one realised that it was much bigger than it actually looked. Everything inside the tent looked organised and clean. This gentleman had had done a lot of work there over the years. Lee was curious to know if the tent was also used during the wintertime, when the weather was much colder and unfriendly. Stefan said that there was another tent that was better equipped for the wintertime. Sometimes he had to stay in the forest for weeks during the winter, but there was nothing to complain about, he assured them. He always had a good reserve of food, and there was no need to go to town every day. In fact, he spent most of his time reading, and his collection of books was huge, just as he'd told his friends.

They decided to spend the rest of the day exploring Stefan's property. After a short rest, they went to visit all the other tents and facilities. His shower was nothing more than a plastic canister installed in a tree and facing the sun. There was also a fridge, a place surrounded by stones and mud, where the sun had very little access. The National Library_was very impressive, with somewhere around twelve thousand books. All those books being well hidden in the forest without anybody knowing about their existence was the biggest surprise that Lee and Mark ever had.

The water supply was not very far. A small spring had been enlarged and blocked in order to maintain all its reserve. A few metres down from the spring, a small pond was well protected and contained enough fish to feed a whole family during the year.

"Would you fancy some fish?" Stefan asked, clearly proud of his property. Seeing his friends' enthusiasm, he went to the kitchen, a which contained cutlery, pots, and everything needed for a civilised cooking environment, and brought some equipment for the preparation of fish. Mark took on the responsibility of cooking since he claimed to have more expertise in this field. While Mark was busy with the cooking, Stefan brought a plastic bag containing a collection of documents that he wanted to show to Lee. They sat together to examine them.

There was no chair around, but the place contained many large rocks and a few fallen trees that could be used instead. One by one, Stefan showed peculiar sheets of paper containing various lists of people with no connection to each other. Each person on the list had a number from one to sixty, inserted in circles of four different colours. Some sheets of paper contained only numbers, lots of them, and the same circles of four different colours. From time to time, those circles were separated by a comma in an apparently chaotic way.

"Do you see anything strange?" he asked.

"Everything looks strange to me," Lee said, puzzled.

"Look at those commas. Each of them appears to follow a pattern, increasing the number of circles by one. Look here . . . One plus two plus three plus four. See? Put those circles on top of each other and they form a pyramid."

Mark also became curious. "Let me see," he said, coming closer.

Stefan opened another folder with the same circles but this time organised in a pyramidal structure.

"I designed this myself after carefully analysing all those pages."

"What is the meaning of all this?" Lee asked.

"This is a game, a very stupid game. They are playing with peoples' destinies."

"Who?" asked Mark and Lee at once, equally curious.

"I have no idea, but I guess they must be very powerful to be able to do this."

Every pyramid contained 120 circles, with numbers and colours in a random order. Stefan explained that there were 240 different circles containing numbers from one to sixty and four colours. Those circles were perhaps selected in a random order and the game was played by unknown rules, but the outcome must be the same: a winner. The winner had to be the piece at the top of the pyramid. Then the person on the list corresponding to the winning piece was destined to become a winner in real life.

"Are you sure about this?"

Stefan was clearly expecting this question, for he took out another set of pages from his bag. This time, those pages contained information about the "winners", which he managed to gather through his investigations. All those people were complete failures in life before the "great opportunity" was given to them. One gentleman managed to make his restaurant the most successful in his town in just a few months. Another one became a leader in a big company. Some girls became supermodels, and a guy managed to create a very successful blog. While Stefan was busy with his explanation, Lee's mind was invaded by dark thoughts about himself.

So was that the explanation of his success too? Was his life just a game in the hands of people who wanted to have fun? Perhaps they were having great fun on his behalf since his life completely changed. That explained how a sudden change of his fortune created his extraordinary success. What was success, in the end, and who were those people who were playing with his life?

The day before, Lee had felt great about himself. Suspecting that his great talent was similar to a castle built on sand, and wanting confirmation of his misery, he asked with hesitation, "Are you suggesting that my success is nothing more than the result of a stupid game?"

"Exactly."

"Then am I nothing more than a lucky bastard?"

"Please don't say that," said Stefan, looking embarrassed. "You are now in a position that gives you a chance to change things."

"Perhaps I should tell everybody that I am just a failure . . . Perhaps I should return to my miserable life . . ."

"No. Definitely no," Stefan said with conviction. "That will change nothing. Now that you are in a position of power and everyone respects you, perhaps you will be able to get people's attention as to what is happening."

Mark had a similar opinion. He also wanted to take revenge against his teachers who ruined his life because of that ridiculous theory. Stefan instead wanted to organise a planetary rebellion against politicians. Both of them wanted different things, but Lee just wanted a quiet place to calm down and to forget his misery. He was clearly upset, and both of his friends realised that, so they tried to encourage him.

Mark continued with his fish and put it on the fire, and Stefan brought out a bottle of good wine. In the end, it was his duty not to have his guests upset.

However, Lee's pain was much greater, and a glass of wine was not enough to forget his shame. Lost in his thoughts and completely disconnected from the world around him, he had no more strength to follow the discussion or to hear what his friends were talking about.

"He's fainting!" shouted one of them. Then there was nothing.

When Lee came to, he found himself covered and close to the fire. The two guys were busy studying the documents and were talking quietly.

"Here's some fish for you. You've been sleeping for quite a long time . . ."

Stefan brought the fish and wine while Mark helped Lee rise. Lee was weak and felt the temperature of his body to be at an unusual level. The intensity of emotions and the sense of helplessness, combined with the exhausting events had caused his body to collapse. He felt much better by then, but he had to acknowledge a terrible truth: he was no longer the master of his destiny.

Lee's life was similar to the life of all losers on this planet. His destiny was being played in a secret lottery.

"Tell me about this game," he said to the two gentlemen sitting there. "Who is behind it?"

"No idea," said Stefan with hesitation. "Perhaps we will never know."

"People with money can create good reputations for themselves and nobody will suspect anything," said Mark. "Having enough resources and power, they can turn everybody into a winner overnight."

"How did you manage to discover all of that?"

Lee's question plainly didn't surprise Stefan, and he began explaining how everything happened.

A few years before, he also used to do some removal jobs, working for a certain Mr Greg. One day a businessman had to move house, and they went in Mr Greg's truck to do this job. There were many things to be put in the truck and other things to be thrown in the bin. While going to throw away certain things, he found a folder of documents among other things, and he had a quick look at it in the lift. Realising that it might be of extreme importance, he managed to hide it somewhere and took it home later. The following day, they went on a long journey via the truck and left the businessman's belongings in an isolated villa far away. He'd never seen that businessman again, which was not a surprise. This businessman looked as if he lived a solitary life, with no children or wife. Instead, a mistress and a few housekeepers accompanied him.

Later, Stefan completely forgot about those documents, but doing his job as a gardener for a general, he came across similar documents and decided to investigate. Those documents were in the common bin, and he found them there while throwing away plants from a terrace. He had no idea where those documents came from since at least fifty families used the above-mentioned common bins.

At first, Stefan was not able to make any sense of those strange pyramids and lists of people, and he definitely regarded everything as a curiosity. On further examination, he discovered its suggestive title as the Secret Game of Power written somewhere on a sheet of paper, amongst other meaningless words crossed out by an unknown individual. Of course, Stefan had great fun with it but was still unable to find any meaningful explanation.

Luckily, one day he matched by pure chance a person from one of his strange lists to someone who unexpectedly became the leader of a powerful company. The simple fact of finding that name at the top of a pyramidal game appeared to be more than just a coincidence. Instead, it appeared that there could be a direct link between the game and the destiny of that person.

Since then, the Game of Power, with its mysterious influence and even more mysterious players, became Stefan's main source of amazement, worries, and curiosity; investigating it was soon to become his favourite hobby.

His friends wanted to know more about the businessperson, but Stefan said he couldn't remember his name or address. Regarding the general, he's been unable to discover anything new about him, although Stefan said he spent a lot of time spying on him and the people living around him.

"Well," said Mark, "we are in a great war but have no idea who is the enemy. This looks scary . . ."

"I want to go home," Lee said. "It's been too much for me, and I feel confused. Perhaps we can meet another day to see what to do next."

On the way back, they agreed to meet up the following day at Lee's house. Stefan was going to organise his terrace, and Mark wanted to discuss publishing his ideas in Lee's next book.

When finally at home, alone and helpless, Lee felt no longer able to make sense of what was happening to his life. It seemed as if everything had turned upside down. Perhaps a good night's sleep would put his chaotic mind in order.

Superheroes don't flush the toilet

The next day, they were together for breakfast. Stefan was explaining how he was going to organise the terrace and what kind of plants would be most suited for it. Mark talked about his impossible love and his pain over not having enough courage to confess it to the girl he liked.

"I feel ashamed," he said. "This girl has a difficult life, and I can do nothing to change it."

He then told her story. Lisa, even though had a university degree, worked as a housekeeper for a successful TV presenter. The job of housekeeping included cooking, shopping, washing, ironing and cleaning—especially cleaning. Mr Hook had to look professional all the time and didn't waste his precious time on minor things like being organised or cleaning up after himself. As a result, the house was a mess most of the time, even though Lisa worked desperately to keep it in a good shape. Not to mention that this superhero never had time to flush the toilet . . . or at least looked unable to understand the true purpose of a toilet.

"Why doesn't she leave the job?"

"Because the pay is quite good. She is also afraid to start looking for another job," said Mark thoughtfully.

Lee remembered his experiences in finding a job and how humiliating it could be when one is unlucky enough to be labelled a loser. This girl must be truly scared of this prospect if she voluntarily accepted being treated like that.

Mark explained that there were many other girls working in similar conditions or even worse, and to prove it, he might organise a meeting with Lisa and some of her friends.

"That would be interesting." The prospect of meeting new girls and listening to their stories attracted their curiosity.

After breakfast, Mark had to leave because of his job.

"Another day of hell," he confessed. Going to work was like going to the guillotine since there was very little chance that his work might be appreciated. As a great leader, his boss had nothing else to do but to make his life unbearable, which he probably never included in his CV. Of course, Mr Johnson, realising Mark's potential and intellectual superiority, had decided to humiliate him on a daily basis about minuscule things. If anything went wrong or anything didn't work as expected, it was the cleaner's fault, as he stressed every day with malice.

Mark clearly needed some encouragement, which he received in abundance from his friends.

During the following days, Stefan finished the terrace, endowing it with many different plants and flowers. Using his imagination and passion, he created a little paradise, a place of relax and escape from this frenetic life.

Mark continued with his terrifying work, and Lee didn't see him for a few days.

Lee's life continued a bit differently from before, with fewer interviews and appointments with important people. To be honest, he lost the enthusiasm to behave like a celebrity. He finally admitted that most celebrities were nothing more than lucky curs without any real talent. Given the right opportunity, everyone could be a celebrity since the main quality of a celebrity was to create scandals.

Regarding leaders and superheroes, the situation was a bit different. Not all celebrities were leaders and superheroes since one could be a celebrity without being selfish. However, in the case of leaders, the level of selfishness increased exponentially. Of course, not all leaders were selfish, and this miracle only happened when a good guy managed to make his way to the top. Normally, superheroes were supposed to be less selfish since their job was to fight the bad guys. Flushing a toilet was definitely not on their agenda, but even that could be understandable. As one never saw them flushing toilets in the movies, one believed it was because superheroes were busy saving the world.

There were two extra necessary qualities for leaders and superheroes. Firstly, leaders and superheroes had to be good-looking because at the end of a movie they had to fall in love. Secondly, they also had to be extremely confident regarding their plans for saving the world. This explains why so many overconfident people were able to create economic crises and nobody had the courage to blame them. Sadly, psychopaths also showed a high degree of confidence, and it would be extremely unfair to call them either leaders or superheroes.

Lee began to wonder if being a celebrity also changed his options. His level of confidence increased dramatically, as much as the number of new friends, although his supposed talent remained the same. He realised with sadness that there was no such thing as talent. There was just a piece of paper called a CV, which was almost useless by itself, without the right connection or opportunity.

What is this running around like a lunatic for an entire life, without taking a break, just because one wants to write fantastic things in his CV? Why so much suffering, anxiety, disappointment, hate, and betrayal for a ridiculous piece of paper?

Many questions were passing through Lee's head, questions that needed an urgent answer. Despite all the reputation and wealth gathered in the last months, he felt more vulnerable and confused than ever before. What would he do next? What plan for action could he make when he had no idea who the enemy was? If reputation and wealth were the only things needed to make him an important person, was it possible then to lose them as mysteriously as he gained them? This looked very scary indeed.

Perhaps the people who made his success possible were having great fun watching his progress and expecting him to become as arrogant as most of the successful people who had no idea what created their success.

What the hell is that **Game of Power** *and what are the rules for playing it? Well, it's a pyramidal game,* Lee thought, *and there was one winner only among so many losers. But this life is the same. Society has a hierarchical structure, and there is one winner only among so many losers.*

Lee had no idea about the rules for this **Game of Power**; they were as mysterious as the people who played it. But life appeared to be similar, a pyramidal game with mysterious rules. All the so-called competition was just an illusion. There were limited places at the top of a pyramid, and to get there, remaining honest and respecting the rules was almost impossible. Many people were ready to play dirty, using all possible tricks imaginable, to get a little advantage over the adversary, and again, there was absolutely no mention about such things within people's CVs.

If it were possible for the human race to remain honest just for the necessary time to write honest CVs, one would be surprised to discover a huge list of completely different skills, such as cheating, lying, betrayal, blackmailing, bullying, lobbying, and so forth.

Yes, this is what is wrong with the modern society: too much focus on looking professional and even more focus on hiding the dirty games.

What if we could create a society without CVs? Would this make us more honest and less arrogant?

Possibly!

However, a society without CVs is almost impossible to find on this planet. How to tell politicians that almost everybody could do the job they did, or even do it better? How to tell financial advisers that they were as useless as fortune tellers? How to tell the experts who created the economic crises that a world without experts will have fewer crises? How to tell all the people sitting at the top of the pyramids in any social structure that they were costing us too much for doing so little?

Stefan is right to dream of a world without politicians, Lee thought. This will end the struggle for power and the endless scandals of corruption and lobbying. Most important of all, this will end the electoral campaigns and the illusion of voting and deciding the future. A world without politicians is not necessarily chaotic or anarchic as we are forced to believe. A world without politicians might be possible . . .

Mark is also right to dream of a world without any kind of academic awards. This will force scientists to collaborate more between each other and to unite their forces for the benefit of us all.

Perhaps it's somehow possible to eliminate this endless race for a perfect CV!

Great winners can't exist if there aren't many more losers around them. The pyramidal structure of the society exists all around us, and the whole purpose of CVs appears useless. It also sounds as if it is a complete waste of time since there is no fair competition, there has never been, and there will never be.

As a winner, if this is what society called him, Lee began to feel guilty for all the losers created against their will, losers who simply had to struggle more in everyday life and endure humiliation because of him.

No one has ever become successful using his talent and skills alone. Great generals have conquered the world through the sacrifice of their soldiers, but very few soldiers who sacrificed themselves were remembered. In this case, those soldiers were simply the losers. Revolutions were created by desperate, hungry, helpless, and vulnerable people who sacrificed themselves for the benefit of their leaders . . .

Yes, this explains everything. One can take almost all people, invent reputations and areas of expertise for them, and make them great. There are many losers around to pay the price. It's similar to playing the lottery. In the end, who cares about the losers?

"Wherever people might say about me," Lee said to himself, "some things are for certain: I am definitely not a superhero, and I know how to flush a toilet . . ."

CHAPTER 2

Why superheroes are always ridiculous

A few days later, the three friends met in town, and three girls joined them soon. After being introduced to each other, they decided to go for a drink and to have some fun. Lisa came with Julia and Sara, two of her friends. Minutes later, they were rambling across the city without a destination. Every place was good as long as they were together. Each of them had personal reasons to be happy with this encounter. Mark wanted to forget his stressful job, but he also wanted to get closer to Lisa. Stefan wanted to escape his loneliness and isolation. Regarding Lee, he felt very happy to meet new people and listen to their stories. And the girls didn't say yet what they wanted. Perhaps they had similar icky lives and similar desires to escape from them.

At a certain point, Stefan wanted to show them something. They followed him without asking about any details.

The girls were curious and wanted to know Lee, asking many questions and making a lot of noise. They talked, they laughed, and they had great fun.

Half an hour later, they finally stopped at a place none of them has ever seen before except Stefan. There were many people queuing in front of what looked like a very busy restaurant.

"This place was on the brink of bankruptcy two years ago," Stefan explained, mostly to the two gentlemen. "Then it suddenly became the most successful restaurant in the area. This happened with the arrival of the new chef, Paul. The funny thing is, this guy had absolutely no idea how to cook. As you can see, the **Game of Power** did a really good job."

"What is the **Game of Power**?" asked one of the girls.

"I'll explain to you later," said Stefan, and then he continued.

"There were many customer complaints when this guy arrived, thus the manager decided to fire him. However, one day some customers who'd never come here before left a substantial tip. That changed everything. Coming from nowhere, more and more customers arrived every day, and our chef began receiving more and more compliments. Of course, in a short time, he managed to learn how to cook and also become a good chef. With the success of the restaurant, he took control of everything and fired the former manager. Now he gives cooking lessons on TV, and . . ."

The girls were astonished and refused to believe it. Lee also found it difficult to believe, in spite of suspecting it to be true.

"How do you know all this?" asked Sara with suspicion.

"I have spoken to the former manager and to other people."

"Why would you do this?" asked Sara, even more incredulously.

"Because I am curious about the **Game of Power** . . ."

"Again this **Game of Power**!" complained Sara.

The three girls became even more curious, but the gentlemen promised to explain in a quiet place what the game was all about.

Stefan continued by saying he was able to find a good review of the restaurant in a famous newspaper, praising the wonderful skills of the chef. This review corresponded to the beginning of this new success story.

It was amazing how a person without talent could become so successful just because an important person placed a good review in the right place.

Out of curiosity, they wanted to go inside, but there was no way to do this since the queue was too long and the friends would have to waste a lot of time waiting. So they walked away disappointed, leaving behind the great master chef, who was probably too busy to waste his precious time on unimportant people like them.

Walking along the streets without any apparent destination, they let themselves be guided instinct while talking to each other. Everyone had a good story to tell, and every story was different from the others.

Julia began talking about her job. She worked for Signora Giorgia, and stressed the first word, saying that Mrs Giorgia would be very upset if someone called her differently. This woman wanted to be called Signora since such a word apparently showed more respect than the word Mrs, and of course, Signora Giorgia was a very important person.

The beginning of this story made everybody curious, and they decided to stop for coffee to listen better. A quiet coffee shop was not very far, just the right place for this kind of story.

There was nobody inside except two girls representing the staff, who were probably bored because they had nothing to do. They welcomed the small group with a smile and prepared one of the tables, the one at the corner with the best protection from the outside world. A small wall hid the table, separating it from the rest of the shop. This private corner looked perfect for telling stories or hiding secrets.

Lee sat next to Julia, seeming the most curious of all to listen to this interesting story. Each of them ordered coffee, cappuccino, or fruit juice and a muffin or some other available cake.

Julia continued with her story.

The famous Signora Giorgia married an engineer and had been having a great life since then. No one knew what job she had before, as no one knew any of her friends previous to her marriage. Of course, she'd had no money at all when she married that good-hearted engineer, and she became a shopaholic. In her fifties, Signora Giorgia seemed unable to do any kind of work at home and needed someone to cook. Julia did this job, but she hated it. It wasn't because of the hard work; it was the impossible character of her boss that made her job unbearable.

Signora Giorgia had the habit of spending a huge amount of money on useless gadgets made of silver. Those gadgets were then put all over the house in such a huge number that there was almost no space for anything else. One could see everywhere little silver animals of different sizes and shapes. The coffee table was so covered with gadgets that one had to keep one's coffee in his hands. In the corridor, there was a cupboard full of silver watches. On the walls were many silver canvases, too many of them, without following any aesthetic rule.

Julia, of course, was not allowed to touch any of the silver gadgets or to arrange them in a better way. Her job only involved cooking, washing dishes, and shopping. This was the easiest part of her job. However, there were some extra activities, such as listening to the words of wisdom and taking advice from the "protecting mother", which is what she called her boss. Listening to Signora Giorgia was not only boring but also upsetting. A person who'd probably never worked before and seemed unable to do anything properly had nothing else to do but to give advice to everyone entering her house. In fact, her house was arranged in such a way that everyone entering it had to feel in a position of inferiority. Therefore, Signora Giorgia did two things at the same time: she made everyone feel inferior and then offered her protection.

This protecting mother and living superhero seemed to have knowledge of everything, although she had no idea what she was talking about. Julia had to listen patiently and agree with everything being said while watching Signora Giorgia smoking like a tractor.

Julia continued by saying what happened a few days before:

"We had some guests, and Signora Giorgia, after showing them her full collection of silver gadgets, something like one hundred and fifty kilograms altogether, wanted to know what her guests might think about it. One of the guests who, at first, did not realise those objects were made of silver, asked why there were so many metal objects in the house. Clearly offended, since those objects were made of silver, not of metal, as Signiora Giorgia always stressed, her response was, 'We like them,' stressing the word 'we' while watching her husband, who probably had nothing to do with those silver gadgets. The engineer said nothing, and everyone concluded that he also liked to waste his money on this kind of objects."

"Then what happened?" asked one of them.

"Then Signora Giorgia decided to get her revenge by asking everyone how much he or she earned. At first, people did not want to answer this question, but she insisted until everyone gave her a detailed list of personal income. Making sure that everyone realised her position of superiority, Signora Giorgia said triumphantly, 'Well, we have that much in the bank,' stressing again 'we' while watching the engineer. He said again nothing and preferred to change the subject . . ."

This incredible lady was definitely a superhero, except that her superpower was to exasperate people.

"Living with this woman must be a real pain for the engineer," said Sara.

"Tell us something about him," Lee asked with curiosity.

"He is such a nice person! Never complains about anything and is never upset."

"While his money is being wasted," said Mark.

"He loves Signora Giorgia and doesn't refuse her anything. She is the monster." Julia stopped as if waiting for their approval on qualifying such a woman as a monster.

"Why do good people always end up in the hands of swindlers?" Stefan wanted to know.

At first, no one could answer the question. After a moment of silence, someone said, "Maybe because this is life."

"Because life is for cheaters, liars, robbers and scoundrels?" tried Stefan.

It turned out that honest people were always the losers.

They finished their drinks in silence. There was little to add when talking about losers. At the bottom of their hearts, they all felt like losers, and it didn't seem to matter how professional or perfect their CVs were.

"Perhaps we should visit the great Signora Giorgia one day," said Stefan, breaking the silence.

This unexpected suggestion started a round of laughter among them.

"How come this sudden desire to meet my boss?" asked Julia, laughing.

"I like to see *important* persons talking to me with superiority," replied Stefan, making everyone laugh.

"And I want to discover any other incredible skills this lady might have."

Mark's reply created more laughs. They felt like losers no more, as long as there were incredible things to laugh about.

All of them tried to imagine what a fantastic CV Signora Giorgia might have. Perhaps she didn't even need a CV because of her incredible luck. However, they were still trying to imagine what her CV might look like, supposing she had to write one.

Of course, leadership skills had to be at the top of her list of fantastic qualities. Then this list might contain good adviser, excellent organiser, successful entrepreneur, and why not good manager? Among her hobbies one might find art collection, meeting new people, helping vulnerable people, and who knows what other unimaginable areas of expertise yet to be invented!

Dissecting the life of Signora Giorgia, our friends found themselves in a position of investigating this so-called success story and what really created it. There was no way to talk about talent or skills as the main causes of this success. Perhaps they should not talk at all about success in this case. Ruining someone's life and abusing someone's generosity should not be called a success story.

If ruining the life of a single person and calling oneself great could be unacceptable, what about ruining a whole country and still calling oneself great?

The discussion soon moved to politics, a despised subject and a source of anger for everybody affected by it.

Everyone had a different point of view, but the group all had a common opinion: politics was a dirty game.

It was getting late. They were still in the coffee shop with very few customers. It seemed that the two girls were preparing for closure. After thanking them for the hospitality, the little group of friends continued their journey across town. The girls looked tired, but they still didn't want to go home, whereas the guys did.

The sun vanished beyond the horizon a while ago, and the multitude of people on the street going in all directions told different stories of different people moving at different paces although living in the same town. Everyone carried on, busy with miserable lives and appearing to be ignoring everyone else.

The small group of friends didn't have any need to hurry or any pressure to deal with urgent tasks, so they continued in a random direction, talking to each other and stopping from time to time to admire a shop vitrine when the girls found something interesting.

Luckily, everyone was free that night, and there was no reason to rush.

How to slap a superhero

Half an hour later, they were still on the street walking randomly and still unsure what to do next. There were people who wanted to talk to Lee, asking advice about how to become successful, journalists who wanted an interview, and paparazzi looking for scandals. After a while, Lee managed to escape, and thus he had to hide his face somehow and make himself unrecognisable.

At a certain point, they heard a great noise coming from inside a bar. They entered to see what was happening.

There was a man making all that noise and calling himself a chess champion. On his table, his trophy was on display for everyone to admire and acknowledge his great achievement. There was also a chessboard and a huge amount of money next to it. The chess champion offered that money to the person who could beat him at chess. His friends tried to calm him down, but he became noisier and more aggressive, challenging everyone to play chess with him.

No one had the courage to challenge him, and that gave more courage to the chess champion, who ordered more drink and continued with his shouting and swearing.

Then something unexpected happened. Stefan, visibly irritated, approached the chess champion and said with a loud voice that was heard by everyone, "I will play with you."

Suddenly, all the noise changed to silence.

"You?" asked the chess champion incredulously.

"But not for money," continued Stefan. "If I win, I want to slap you."

This unexpected request caught the attention of all the people present, making them curious to see what would happen next.

"If you win, you want to slap me!" said the chess champion, laughing uncontrollably and dissecting every single word to be sure that there was no room for misunderstanding.

"I want to slap you too. I will kick your arse and make sure you will never play chess again in your life . . ."

"You want to slap me . . . if you win." The chess champion continued laughing, unable to calm himself.

In the bar, people had already begun dividing themselves into groups supporting either of the chess players. They all ordered a new round of drink so they could concentrate on the game without wasting precious time in the meantime.

Some people even offered to do the job of referee, making sure that the rules of the game were followed.

After calming himself, although still laughing, the chess champion was ready for the game; so was Stefan. One of the people present hid two pieces and each of the two chess players had to choose a colour. Stefan got white, and the game began with his move.

At first, both opponents seemed confident and didn't care to think too much about each move. Soon the table configuration became complicated and the speed of the moving slowed down.

Silence prevailed in the bar. All the people were sitting or standing around the table, curious about the outcome.

The girls wanted to know what was happening, but the guys were unable to give them too many details. Although talking quietly to the girls, people around became irritated, thus Lee and Mark had no other choice but to keep quiet. In fact, neither Lee nor Mark seemed to have a great understanding of chess. Furthermore, what they saw on the chessboard seemed more complicated than anything they had ever imagined. There was no way to figure out who had the advantage.

Minutes passed, and the game moved to a new stage. The two opponents began exchanging pieces aggressively. The chess champion started smiling. He clearly had the advantage, for he had captured more pieces than Stefan had. He took one more piece and prepared to celebrate victory, but soon his face changed. That was a trap. Although having a big advantage of pieces, there was nothing he could do to avoid the inevitable. The game was lost in a few moves.

Stefan claimed his "prize" by slapping the still confused chess champion and then headed towards the door. His friends followed him, while people in the bar, astonished by this event, began to celebrate the unknown winner, leaving the humiliated and defeated chess champion on his own.

Once on the street, his friends congratulated the new champion. Such an astonishing victory had impressed everyone.

"You never said you were so good at chess," said Lee.

"You never asked," said Stefan, smiling.

"Perhaps we should celebrate our hero," Lee suggested and invited them all to spend the rest of the night in his flat.

Celebrating a victory was always a good reason to get people together and to feel happy. Victory was for the winners. Losers were less important.

One hour later, Lee was home, accompanied by his new friends. It was almost midnight, but the weather was good, so they could sit on the terrace amongst the wide variety of plants, beautifully arranged and well maintained. The place was quiet and the night was long, perfect for telling stories.

Life is not about writing CVs

Except for Stefan, everyone had a university degree. However, none of them worked in their chosen fields.

They all had the same problem; their CV's were not professional enough, meaning that none of them were qualified to get better jobs. Nevertheless, Lee was the only one who didn't have to worry about his future.

Sara continuously took many different courses in the hopes that one day she might find some work. She'd just finished a certain course recommended by some experts, but she had no time for a break. There was always an extra course to do in order to "boost" her CV, whatever this means. After the process of boosting finished, again there was the same problem: no time for a break. Then she had to enhance her CV, meaning exactly the same or perhaps slightly different things, and with the same result: no time for a break. Presuming she finally managed to bring to an end this last requirement, she had to start all over again, in an endless race towards seemingly unachievable goals.

There were always plenty of other experts with their own agendas and consequently many things to do, such as overpowering her fear, building confidence, developing leadership skills, and most important of all, thinking positive.

Exhausted by so many required skills and before having any chance to take a break, she realised in horror that new intimidating adjectives with indecipherable meaning continued to be invented in an industrial scale. Those mysterious and priceless skills were, of course, highly recommended by experts as necessary for a successful career.

Of course, that was just half of the story.

She also had to do voluntary work; when translated into the real life, meaning working for free. This kind of activity could be very painful when one was struggling to pay rent or fell behind with other payments. Since the activity of working for free was also recommended by experts who probably had secures jobs and had no idea what it meant, Sara had to comply obediently with everything experts said.

Lee was curious to know how Sara had the courage to challenge the experts' wisdom and found the time for a break.

"It's not about courage," she said without hope. "I have no more courage. I am completely exhausted by all this running without a destination."

He believed her, and so did the others. She looked so tired and sad, although she was just in her middle twenties.

What happened to all the positive thinking and confidence, she was talking about? What about overpowering fear? She looked more scared about her future than many people, despite her practice for controlling fear.

A person with a nearly perfect CV, so scared and unconfident, was the real image of a society that preferred to live in a fantasy world, where success was the result of hard work and talent only.

It was an embarrassing moment, and Lee recalled in his mind the multitude of TV shows where contestants were constantly told to believe in themselves, followed by other encouraging and equally ridiculous messages.

"You should believe more in yourself," Lee remembered a TV presenter telling a guy whose singing performance in front of a hostile audience was not much appreciated.

"Believe in yourself," said another TV presenter to a terrified girl in a similar contest.

"Be more positive . . ."

"Try to be yourself . . ."

And so on.

The message about believing in herself would perhaps make matters worse. She was no more herself. In fact, she was just a robot, expected to run her entire life for a sheet of paper called a CV.

Sara started crying helplessly, revealing herself by removing all the defence barriers; she was just so vulnerable!

Her friends surrounded her, offering their support and comfort, but she continued crying nonetheless.

Despite all this running without a destination, life is not about writing CVs.

The whole purpose of a CV is to make life easier, not more difficult. Finding a job should be the main use of a CV. Once one got a job, that person should stop worrying about being perfect; otherwise, there will be no chance to enjoy life. Unfortunately, it appeared that life was divided into stages, more or less similar to each other and related to CVs:

Stage 1
Childhood: Begin to understand CVs

Stage 2
Education: Start writing CVs

Stage 3
Unemployment: Writing CVs becomes a passion

Stage 4
Work: Bring CVs to perfection

Stage 5
Pension, if lucky enough: teach young people how to write CVs

Stage 6
Game over: now one can die thinking of CVs

Lisa began telling her story, a similar story of a woman always trying to look professional and perfect but hiding a similar vulnerable and insecure person.

She talked about her job and her difficulties with Mr Hook, her boss. Lisa told them a story most of them already knew, but she told it again in order to amuse Sara. When the scene about Mr Hook's inability to flush the toilet came into focus, Sara started smiling again. Lisa had told her many times about that story, but that day, Sara wanted to behave as hearing it for the first time. Thinking of other people's problems was an efficient way to forget one's own.

Lisa talked then about her struggle for a career and the impossible rules she had to follow while doing research.

She was not allowed to take any personal initiative, since in case of success, she might outshine her supervisors. As a result, Lisa had to adhere to precise rules and a strict routine. Every single movement had to be approved by the people in charge of the research project, who, in their case, had to follow the rules imposed by people who funded the research.

They started wondering where the freedom of research was or if it would make more sense to perceive the whole process of doing research as a dictatorial practice.

"If you want to publish in a scientific journal, it's even more challenging and stressful."

"Why?" Stefan was curious to know, but Mark believed he knew the answer already.

"Because there is an endless set of rules you have to follow. I have friends who had to modify entire pages of their manuscripts in order to please their supervisors . . ."

That was incredible and confirmed what Mark had said before. It didn't really matter how good someone was or how good the person's theory was. It was more important to be in good relations with the people in charge, even if one's theory didn't make sense. Scientists could have emotional attachments to a certain theory and were ready to defend it against all evidence. When emotions took over reason, an attack on a theory could change into an attack on the person who was in contradiction with that theory, resulting in insults and gossip instead of scientific debate.

This desperate obsession for a perfect CV was only part of the story. One also had to be good-looking and always in good physical condition. To achieve the latter, the person needed to do a lot of exercise and eat good meals. But it was impossible to do so much exercise and be always connected to the Internet at the same time. As far as a good meal, the situation was even worse. Julia, who lived in student accommodation, told them what students usually ate. They were so incredibly busy that most of the time they had junk ready meals heated in microwaves.

"From time to time, I organize cooking events," said Julia, "which are very successful among students. A free well-prepared meal is a fantastic opportunity to see people together. Those professional students just look so hungry."

They laughed.

Stefan, who still dreamed of organising a planetary rebellion, started explaining what was wrong with the political system and how humans could create a world without politicians without descending into chaos.

"Politicians are the source of most of the troubles on this planet. Just imagine a world without wars, economic crises, and inequality— or without the need for writing CVs."

"What does writing CVs have to do with politicians?" asked Sara, puzzled.

"Career and success are the result of political decisions."

Stefan's answer didn't appear very convincing.

"Hard work and talent are just a small fraction of a success story," he completed.

Mark intervened by mentioning the **Game of Power**, and the guys had to explain to them what that game was all about. The girls listened, astonished and incredulous.

"This isn't possible," said Sara with disbelief.

"Are you suggesting that all celebrities . . . ?" began Lisa, not finishing the question, apparently afraid to reach such a terrifying conclusion by herself.

"Exactly. Most celebrities have no idea what created their success, and even if they know it, it might be more convenient for them to keep quiet and enjoy the benefits."

"What about him?" Lisa asked again, and Sara seemed to be ready to ask the same question.

Everyone looked at Lee, making him feel extremely embarrassed. He had to confess to the girls that there was nothing special about his book. Many books on the market were perhaps much better but would probably never manage to catch people's attention.

His confession created a terrible silence. Everybody looked at everybody else, and for a few moments, they were unable to say anything. Finally, Sara broke the silence.

"So let me put it simply. All my effort is just a waste of time, isn't it?"

"I am afraid it's true," said Mark with hesitation.

"And all this time of desperation and suffering . . . ?" Sara asked. "All this mockery called positive thinking . . ." She looked around, inquisitive. "All the time spent working for free and all the sacrifice to save money in order to maintain myself," she continued, visibly upset. "All of this is in vain, isn't it?"

Nobody knew what to say, but Lee began to feel guilty for being a celebrity and not having the same struggle for survival.

Suddenly, Sara turned all her rage, anger, and disappointment towards him, as if he were the only one responsible for her failures.

Before realising what was happening, she was punching and slapping him and crying in desperation. Lee's chair fell on a side, and he and Sara went down as well. The others had to intervene. Mark and Stefan barely managed to get Sara away from Lee and hold her on a chair while she continued crying and screaming. Lisa and Julia embraced her and held her tightly, offering any possible comforting or encouraging words.

But nothing seemed to work. Soon Sara became pale and fell asleep. It was too much emotional pressure for such a fragile creature.

After laying Sara on a bed, her friends sat around watching her crying in her dreams. It must have been a terrible shock for her to realise that a sheet of paper called CV was the source of all her suffering.

It was just a few hours before dawn. The girls slept next to Sara, while Lee, Mark, and Stefan went to sleep in different rooms.

Everything is about winners and losers

Alone in his room, Lee was unable to fall asleep; there were too many questions that needed urgent answers and those people who needed so much help.

"And me, the 'lucky mutt', what shall I do now?" he asked himself.

Soon he would fall prey to his imagination.

He was able to see a pyramid made of different arrangements of numbers inserted on circles of different colours. The more he thought about the **Game of Power**, the more he convinced himself that this game was not actually that ridiculous. It was just a pyramidal hierarchy like many pyramidal hierarchies in our society. Whether people were willing to accept it or not, it was a painful truth, regardless of their personal opinions or feelings. Any social group appeared to have a pyramidal hierarchic organisation, sharing the power and wealth unevenly among its members. Whether it was business, political party, religious institution, school, army, cultural or scientific organisation, or any kind of organised groups or institutions, all of them had something in common: a hierarchy. There was just the illusion that everyone could make it all the way to the top. The reality, however, was much different.

There were very few places available at the top, and the competition was fierce. And of course, not everyone was willing to respect the rules, and that made the matter worse.

This **Game of Power**, whatever its rules, was just a mirror representation of the real life. The lottery was very similar, and it maintained the same principle: many contributed to the success of few.

It happened to be myself, the lucky sham, but it could have been someone else, he thought. *In this case, the success story remains similar. It only changes name.*

Where is my fault here? What did I do wrong? Nothing. My opportunity came, and I only took advantage of it. It could have been someone else; however, this time it was me.

Poor girl; she must have put a huge effort on her career. Who knows what kind of life she had to endure and how many sacrifices she had to make. Is she right to blame me? Supposing I am the winner of a lottery; what rights have the losers to get upset with me? I agree that every person has his or her own tragedy and each one of the players deserves a better life. All the same, each one of us had the same chance of becoming the winner. When buying the ticket, every player has the same selfish dreams about taking all the money alone and excluding all the others. So every player has the right to enjoy all the money alone, although this is morally unfair. No matter how unfair this might be, those are the rules of the game. The winner takes it all, whoever he might be . . .

Lee realised that life was played by similar rules. Every society had a hierarchical organisation, and it didn't matter how much preaching about equality there was, for there were very few available places at the top. The vast majority of people had to contend themselves with a humble place at the base of the pyramid. It was impossible to have more winners than losers; otherwise, the pyramid would not be able to support itself.

This kind of hierarchy was not common only to humans. The animal world had endless examples of this kind of organisation. There was no surprise to see winners and losers in the animal world too.

Lee went further with his philosophising and was not surprised to see a hierarchical organisation, from the human body to plants, mountains, rivers, stars, planets, and ending with the mighty universe. It was a shocking discovery, and he had to admit to himself that talking about democracy whenever a hierarchical structure was involved made no sense.

Back to this planet, more precisely to his bedroom, Lee was still unable to sleep and unsure about what to do next.

It was nearly time for breakfast. He got up and went to the kitchen to prepare something. Soon the others joined him. Sara felt terribly sorry for what happened the day before and asked for forgiveness. Lee assured her that it was nothing and said that she shouldn't worry, but she insisted on being forgiven. So he gave her a warm hug. By then, they were friends and she was smiling again.

During breakfast, they discussed what everybody was going to do next.

Mark was going to quit his terrible job and instead work on his theory, for which Lee promised to offer support and help to see the light. Lisa would continue with her odious job until something better came along. Similarly, Julia would have to endure listening to the advice and words of wisdom given generously by Signora Giorgia. Sara would end immediately all the voluntary work and the inutile building of confidence courses and take a deserved break. Stefan decided to remain in his forest for a few more days to finish reading some books. Although Lee offered him support on renting a room, he insisted on returning to his forest. After finishing the terrace, Lee paid him pretty well, thence he had no excuses for continuing to live in the forest. Perhaps he had his own reasons for acting that way.

The girls became curious about his life in the forest and why he preferred to live so lonely and far away.

"It's a long story," he said, "about false friends, disappointment, and failures."

"But each of us has those things. Some people are even worse off," said Lisa, trying to encourage him.

"This is not a reason to live alone in the forest," continued Sara. "What if something happens to you? Who is going to help you?"

Stefan had nobody to rely on in a time of need. His mum was too far away, and he hadn't seen her for ages.

"When did you last see your mum?" someone asked him.

"Twelve years ago, since I left my house."

"Do you talk to her on the phone?" enquired Julia.

"Yeah, from time to time. About once a month." He didn't seem pleased to be talking about this subject.

His friends were curious to know why he didn't go back to live there or to see his mum.

"There is nothing to do in that village, and the majority of people have left. There are no more young people living there." Stefan also said that going home to see his mum would cost him too much, more than he could afford.

"There are a lot of cats and dogs living in my village instead of young people. There are too many, and it seems impossible to get rid of them. They are everywhere. In the past, people had to fight against wolves for survival; now it's against cats and dogs."

"Why did people leave that place? Why did you leave?" they asked.

"We went bankrupt when my country joined the free market. We found ourselves like unprotected children in a jungle full of hungry predators. That was the first shock."

"Was there a second one?" asked Mark.

"The second shock was a pyramidal game, a Ponzi scheme."

They asked what had happened. Stefan's story was becoming interesting.

"Someone founded a company called Caritas, which was supposed to help people. They promised a return of eight hundred per cent three months after the money was invested. It was madness. People sold their properties and put everything in this game in the hope of escaping poverty. The whole country became hypnotised by this incredible game since it had the approval and support of politicians and economists. It became a televised event, with the collaboration of many celebrities and artists. The founder went so far as to give emotional speeches on TV, praising the hard work of the poor people who deserved a better life, and he promised that he would never do anything to hurt the poor . . ." Stefan paused.

"Then?"

"The first year, everything was magnificent. People had a lot of money, but they were reluctant to take the money home, so they continued with the game. Meanwhile, more and more people continued to join this unbelievable moneymaking organisation. During the second year, the first months showed no signs of problems. But then, a few months later, the payments to people stopped, claiming some technical problems. One day all the money vanished. The founder was trying to escape abroad. He was arrested, of course, but received just a few years of imprisonment, which he managed to reduce by bribing politicians and lawyers. Now he is free and has a great life abroad."

"And the people? What happened to them?"

"Many lost their properties. Some of them committed suicide. Others left the country. Many people are still going to court these days in order to retrieve their lost properties and money."

"What about politicians?"

"They are still in power and still telling lies." Stefan was visibly upset about politicians. This could be seen on his face.

"All that happened with the complicity and support of the politicians. The pyramidal game created its winners and losers. The winners were having a great life. And the losers? Who cared about them!"

"So is this the reason for your personal battle against all politicians?" asked Mark compassionately.

He didn't answer.

"And what have you lost?" asked one of the girls.

Stefan still didn't answer, preferring to watch thoughtfully out of the window, but his friends suspected he had to be one of the losers . . .

Den of wolves

A dark private room situated in the most isolated place of a huge bank was hosting a new meeting for an exclusive audience. A room projected to be a private theatre for the owners of the building changed its use and became the headquarters of the **Secret Game of Power**.

There were few lights on and little need for them since the focus of the audience was to concentrate on the scene, where two players were ready to start a new game. The two players sat in front of each other at a small table endowed with everything needed for the game. A huge pyramid made of equidistant dots could be seen on the screen, the centre of everybody's attention and which would project every move of the players.

There were many important people amongst the audience, including bankers, businesspeople, journalists, and politicians, but most importantly, Mr President. He was there for the first time, and that day was to be a special day for him; he would decide the fate of the winner.

The master of the game, as the members of that secret organisation called him, was playing God; in other words, he had to decide other people's destinies.

Mr President knew that in order to maintain his power, he had to be in good relations with this powerful organisation. There were other masters organised in a pyramidal structure, and all of them received orders from the top of the pyramid, the triumvirate, composed of a first master, a second master, and a grand master. The grand master, the real ruler of this planet, was never seen around, and nobody knew anything about him except the first master and the second master. The triumvirate made all the important decisions about the **Secret Game of Power** and directly controlled all the members of this organisation.

Apparently, Mr President was the strongest person on the planet, elected democratically by the people of his country. But such a powerful person was in fact the prisoner of his own destiny and felt extremely vulnerable that day, alone in the den of wolves. Those ferocious wolves were extremely powerful. No wonder Mr President had to play by their rules.

Despite all that, his power was not totally under their control. He still enjoyed some privileged activities such as defending democracy. His main concern was talking about the benefits of democracy, promoting it around the world, and defending it at any cost. In his numerous speeches, Mr President had to use emotional words in support of the democratic values, to talk about the injustice made to the poor, to promise them justice, and to talk about the respect for their dignity and a better future for them and their children. On the other side, Mr President also had to protect the huge banks from bankruptcy and had to offer them endless governmental funds from the taxpayers' money, although publicly he had to criticise the irresponsible banks and promise punitive measures against them.

Mr President knew very well the secret machinery behind his election.

The Secret Game of Power (or SGP) had decided in his favour for no apparent reason, and then all the members of this monstrous organisation had to support his election. This was easy to achieve, making things look like a democratic election. The members of the SGP controlled almost everything, from media, finance, education, research, and industry to politics.

Mr President knew that his first public speech would have been impossible without the support of the SGP. He had to sign a secret humiliating treaty in exchange for their support. They knew too much about him, and any false move could lead to his public humiliation and hence the end of his mandate. Just a little secret about his personal life published in the right place would be enough to create an international scandal, enough to turn people against him. He didn't have to be guilty of anything. Mr President was just a human, and like any other human being, he was not proud about many things in his personal life. One little unimportant event could be exaggerated in such a way as to create public outrage. People's outrage could then start a chain reaction, leading to the end of his career before having any chance to prove his innocence. In this fast-moving world, where everybody was so quick to accuse everybody else without even checking the events to see whether guilty or not, there was not enough time to prove someone's innocence. This crazy world wanted quick answers and, most importantly, quick punishments.

The secret was to show just a fraction of the truth, the most shocking and outrageous fraction of the truth, exaggerating it for more effect and hiding the whole picture, or simply ignoring it. This is what made media so powerful: the ability to exaggerate things without bothering to check the facts. As long as there was a scandal on the way, who cared about the truth? The elected leader of his country, Mr President, controlled just a fraction of the power, but those who controlled the media controlled everything.

At that time, instead of looking for solutions for the real problems of the present and future, journalism and media specialised in gossip journalism and seemed to be only interested in scandals and disasters. Another specialisation was to terrorise people with advertising and to brainwash them on a daily basis. Except for some minor problems created by the media, journalism was a wonderful tool for the promotion of democracy.

Around Mr President, some important people from the film industry waved their hands towards him. He answered back with a similar gesture.

"Those people are very powerful," he acknowledged.

They had a great capacity to influence people and to show a wrong image of reality. All the movies about superheroes, where a single person was able to beat an entire town and defeat evildoers without even getting a scratch, was a perfect image of their obsession with superheroes.

Such movies had to be inspirational for the common people, who needed some sense of security and justice. But all those superheroes were just so arrogant and confident! It was unthinkable to see a superhero losing an eye or mutilating his face in the battle. He had to remain good-looking until the end of the movie; otherwise, people watching the movie at home or in the cinema could have reacted violently. The movie producers knew well what people wanted. Since losers were unable to control their own destinies, at least they could control the destinies of their beloved superheroes. This apparent sense of control that losers enjoyed in the imaginary world was of great relief for politicians, who were able to avoid any further concessions in the real world.

The most exciting parts in movies were when superheroes had to deactivate bombs. Mr President recalled from past movies the image of a terrorised audience unable to move or breathe as the superhero, always accompanied by a beautiful girl, looked undecided at the several wires of different colours coming out from the bomb, which was about to detonate. Of course, the superhero was desperately trying to figure out which wire was the right one to cut, while the girl accompanying him appeared extremely terrified and afraid to breathe. While watching such movies, spectators were as terrified as the people in the movie appeared to be. When the superhero cut one of the wires and nothing happened, everybody experienced great relief. However, the truth was that since all of them contained electricity, cutting any of those wires would stop the bomb from exploding.

Mr President began smiling at the image of a terrorised superhero in front of an activated bomb.

Some people from the film industry kept staring at him, and Mr President had a feeling that they were talking about him.

"Those people are as ridiculous as the superheroes they create," he said to himself, struggling to hide his real feelings.

This obsession with superheroes was not only ridiculous but also irritating. Unfortunately, Mr President had no power whatsoever to question what kinds of movies people preferred to watch or how they wasted their time. Therefore, he concluded that stupidity had to be one of the most important features of democracy.

Why do people enjoy a big lie more than an insignificant truth? he asked himself, puzzled. *Why do lies become more successful than the truth, and why is it so easy to delude people? If manipulating people can be so easy, then the battle for democracy is a lost battle. Democracy is supposed to represent the power in the hands of people. People should decide their own future. Perhaps the current political system should be called something different. What would be the best name for it? Let's see. Who has the real power? Neither the president nor the people!*

For the first time, Mr President realised that the word democracy did not describe the current political system. In the future, humanity might be able to invent an appropriate name for it. For the time being, it had to be called democracy—and only because humans are rather generous when naming their political systems.

Mr President acknowledged with sadness that the huge pyramidal structure seen on the screen was responsible for his election. That was more of a game of chance; much more chance was needed than talent and skills. He remembered discussing with some mathematicians the total number of permutations resulting from this game. The number was so incredibly big and scary, much bigger than anything imaginable in this universe, to the extent that an extremely powerful computer would be needed to perform the calculation.

So my election was nothing more than a game, a stupid game, and instead of me, it could have easily been someone else, he thought. *The only thing needed for someone else's election was just a slightly different game . . . just another game.*

While lost in his thoughts, Mr President did not realise that the master had given the signal for the game to start, so when he finally focused his attention towards the screen, the first line at the base of the pyramid was nearly completed. One piece at a time, each of the two players took his turn completing the pyramid line by line, heading towards its summit. After the first lines were completed, the game's speed slowed down. There were more calculations to make and fewer options. From time to time, one of the players lost his turn, leaving the adversary to play a new piece and hence gain the advantage of making more points. However, it didn't really matter how many pieces each of them had played; the amount of points on them was what counted. One player could win the game with fewer pieces on the table, and they both knew that.

As the game progressed and was played closer to the summit of the pyramid, the tension rose in the audience. Everyone tried to predict the winner, eliminating the numbers already played and making different speculations with the numbers still to be played. Since the game was played more slowly closer to the summit, there was enough time for any kind of speculations. Each member of the organisation used pen and paper, sketching rapidly and nervously all possible outcomes relevant to the remaining pieces to be played.

What made the game more interesting was that half of the available pieces would always remain unused, making the whole process of finding the winner a challenging task. The winner was always a surprise, and the lucky person who guessed it would receive a special favour. No money was involved since all the people present were extremely rich. But they were allowed to decide the fate of the winner, which was considered the highest favour. In case no one managed to identify the winner, the honour of deciding his destiny passed into the hands of the master.

That day, Mr President had that special honour, in recognition for his intervention in again saving the banks from bankruptcy. The last economic crisis had hit them harshly, and Mr President was again their saviour.

The last pieces were played, and the atmosphere became flammable. There was a lot of talking, a lot of laughing and shouting, and a lot of noise. The master was unable to maintain the order and calm, but that was not part of his program. He only cared that the rules of the game be respected in order to find a new winner.

Finally, the last play was about to be made. The player took one random piece from the stalks in front of him and put it on the table. Unfortunately, his piece didn't match the required configuration, thus he lost his turn. The other player took one piece and put it down on the last triangle. Luckily, the number on this piece was bigger than the sum of the last two pieces played by the adversary. The game was over. Each of the two players calculated his points nonetheless, although by taking some extra points for placing the last piece, the player who played last lost the game. The number of points for each player was announced, and then each was free to go.

Mr President was invited on the scene. The winner was revealed, and the master also appeared on the scene, sitting in front of Mr President at a small table. Someone brought the winner's CV and started reading loud, accentuating every word and taking small breaks after every line while observing the audience for approval and encouragement.

Curriculum Vitae
Name: CR
Contact details:
Address:
Phone number:
And so on . . .

With the reading of the first skills came the first laughs. Soon the situation became dramatic and suspenseful, with the audience becoming extremely noisy and delirious. There was so much to laugh about as far as that guy, an emigrant who didn't speak the language properly and made a lot of grammatical mistakes. However, he spoke many different languages fluently, as displayed in his CV. He probably moved from country to country looking for a better job, and he had many different professions, apparently not related to each other.

"Among his professions," continued the reader, "we have construction, agriculture, cooking, gardening, hotel porter, journalism, web design, and computer programming."

"This guy can be a proper spy," said someone, causing the surrounding people to laugh loudly.

"Or perhaps an accidental saviour from some disaster," continued someone else.

"There are so many disaster stories in your newspapers," said another person, looking at the person who was supposedly in control of those newspapers. "Why not create a new disaster and a new saviour?"

People kept laughing.

"What kind of disasters would you prefer?" the media mogul decided to ask.

"Flood or something similar," said the same gentleman uncertainly.

"What about an earthquake!"

People kept talking and laughing, and everyone came up with a different suggestion. Mr President also laughed with them, but he was clearly undecided. It was difficult to decide when someone's destiny was in his hands. Most importantly, he would probably never get another chance to make this kind of decisions.

Since the people from the film industry are also present, let's make this story a real movie with a real plot, Mr President thought. Then he announced his decision and received warm applause.

Everyone's effort was then put into creating a fantastic plot, a new success story for the lucky winner. As usual, there were plenty of suggestions, and it seemed difficult to select from among them.

Mr President wanted to know if the winner was single. The person who held his personal file confirmed that he was indeed single.

"That's it!" shouted Mr President, excited. "Is there any celebrity woman divorced recently?"

This unexpected question created much enthusiasm, and Mr President received a new round of applause. Having their approval, Mr President continued with his plot. From the available recently divorced celebrities, he selected one, the person who sounded the most suited for his plan.

"What if we create an attempted rape and have this superhero save her?" The president was very excited about his plan.

"He only has to be in the right place at the right time," said someone from the public.

"This could be easy to achieve," said someone else.

"This loser is still looking for a job. Let's create a job interview for him and make sure Mrs X is also in the same city."

"Let's make his life more miserable by creating a humiliating interview."

"And by refusing to give him the job," added the president.

"Then he will walk onto the street disappointed . . ."

Minutes later, the plot for the attempted rape was approved. The people from logistics came into action with all the small details, and then the completed plan was handed to the people who would to bring it to life. They were then free to go home, all of them happy about the outcome of that night.

Mr President thanked all the people present for such incredible evening, shook the hand of the master, and left. Soon everyone else left, vanishing behind a secret door. Behind them, silence prevailed in the empty room again. There was just the mysterious pyramid on the screen, having so much yet to say.

A terrifying secret

Mr President sat alone in his office. There was so much to do and so little time for all the problems he had to face on a daily basis.

Perhaps a little break will help, he thought. It was nearly time for the news, so he turned on the TV while sitting on a divan. He asked for coffee and continued watching TV, lost in his thoughts as a girl put the coffee on his table. She left, and Mr President, alone with his coffee and his problems, savoured little coffee before putting the cup back on the table.

The news started; the headline was about an attempted rape. It was concerning Mrs X and an unknown man who saved her. He had to fight against six masked gangsters, and through a series of coincidences and strikes of luck, the celebrity was saved and so was he. The criminals managed to escape, but no one cared about them anymore. The focus of the news was then on that unknown man, the saviour, who had so many stories to tell. His incredible life, which was in complete obscurity but amazingly eventful, attracted everyone's attention. He was the new superhero, and Mrs X appeared to be impressed.

Mr President began smiling. *Those gentlemen did a good job,* he thought, recalling from memory the people he'd met in the secret theatre. When the news about the latest superhero ended, Mr President turned off the TV and finished his coffee calmly.

"Now it's time for something more exciting," he said, and he called his secretary.

"I want to see Mr Wilson. Send him to my office, please."

"OK, sir," the secretary said.

Mr Wilson arrived with a computer carried on a mobile table.

"Here is everything, sir, as requested," Mr Wilson said. He then opened a certain file stored in the computer and containing a huge register of names.

"Altogether, there are 4,026,531,840 of them. We selected the best people on this planet to match this number. This is equivalent to 120 multiplied by 2 twenty-five times, or 120 x 2^{25}. So you have twenty-five steps for this game, and this is the game," Mr Wilson continued, opening another file in the computer.

The screen showed a pyramidal structure made of dots at equal distances to one another. Since the pyramid went all the way up on the screen, the only available place for the menu of the game was either on the left or right up-corners. As seen on the screen, there were several circles on both sides of the pyramid and some buttons for the menu.

"I have contacted some of the best programmers for the creation of this game," Mr Wilson continued proud of his work.

"Hope you enjoy it."

The president was visibly excited. He thanked Mr Wilson for everything and dismissed him.

Heading towards the door, Mr Wilson turned around unexpectedly, as he'd forgotten something.

"Here is the calculation, sir," he said, handing a sheet of paper to his interlocutor.

Astonished, Mr President examined the calculation: 240 permutation of 120 = 240 factorial divided by 120 factorial equals $6.08 * 10^{269}$. A number with 270 decimal digits!

He was completely speechless in front of such an incredible result, much bigger than anything imaginable in this universe. After a few minutes of contemplation, Mr President turned his attention to the game itself.

Calling the secretary again, he requested not to be disturbed.

Now the game could start. What a fantastic opportunity!

It was his first time having knowledge about this game, and the president realised that it could be used to sort out more difficult problems such as bringing peace to the world. In order to have peace, there was a need for a united planet and one leader only, but how to organise elections on a planetary scale? There were so many countries hating each other, so many languages, so many different religions and cultures, and too many problems. If people didn't vote for nationalistic reasons, they might use their language, race, culture, or whatever factor had any impact on dividing them. Moreover, electing a planetary president would probably create the biggest troubles that ever existed on this planet.

It appeared that the solution was extremely simple. Instead of organising such terrifying elections, this **Game of Power** could be used, eliminating all the troubles, corruption, inutile spending of money, lobbying, and most importantly, all the pathetic speeches. Not to mention that an electoral campaign at this scale would be a nightmare.

At the end, whoever was lucky enough deserved to be a planetary president. This person didn't really need any special skills; just some basic knowledge of economics, politics, and history was enough.

Mr President was ready for the great experiment and pressed the button labelled "start". The game began.

At an incredible speed, the names from a huge register were selected randomly and entered into the many simultaneous games for the first step. The number 4,026,531,840 was reduced by half when the first step ended, then again by half with the second step, then again by half as a result of the third one, and so on.

The president was amazed by how the numbers were displayed at the end of each step and how the game went to the next round, and to the next one again, repeating the same pattern with half of the numbers in the following step. At a certain point, the number of the games played simultaneously was 64, then 32, then 16, then 8, then 4, then 2, and at the last step, the game stopped. At that point, the president was invited to play the last step against the computer.

One by one, pieces in tandem found their way onto the pyramidal structure, completing it from the base to the top. Closer to the end, the game became more challenging. It had a slower speed, but it continued anyway.

By the last few pieces to play, the game became more intense. The president lost his turn a few times but so did the computer. On the last three dots forming the apex of the upper triangle, the president played, as did the computer. Finally, there was the last piece to play, but unfortunately, the president lost his turn. The computer also lost its turn. When the president played next, he placed the last piece. The game ended.

The computer made the calculation of the points. Consequently, Mr President was declared the winner of the game, with a few points more. However, there was another winner waiting to be revealed. The winning number was connected to the corresponding name in the register, and the winner's identity and location were no longer a secret.

A girl from a poor country was the lucky winner, and if this game were an official game, she had to claim her position as president of the world.

Unfortunately, this poor girl had no idea that such a game even existed and that she was so lucky. Mr President began reading excited her CV and then looked for extra information in her file, but this time there was no reason to laugh. She was just so unlucky in life. The local mafia had killed both of her parents. Four brothers and two sisters, all of them much younger, needed her help and support. This poor girl was in charge of her family of little siblings. Everything, from cooking and cleaning to other domestic chores, was her responsibility. They never had enough money, but they had a little garden and some trees on which to rely as an extra source of food. She had to give up her education in order to support her family. The main source of their income was her sewing work. She created many artisanal products, from carpets to rugs and clothes. Her mum used to teach her how to work with the machinery and many other trade secrets.

At that time, she spent most of the time working, while her brothers had to sell those products in town in order to bring food home. Sometimes they didn't manage to sell anything, meaning there was nothing to eat that night.

The president finished reading. He felt both ashamed and shocked by such a story—ashamed because of the courage and determination this girl showed in order to support her family (compared to his own courage of fighting against the secret organisation that controlled his destiny), and shocked because of her suffering after the loss of her parents.

Perhaps something can be done, the president thought.

They needed so much help. After thinking carefully about the best alternative, Mr President called a secretary and gave her a piece of paper with a plan of action and all the necessary information for completing the mission. After the secretary left the room, Mr President could finally feel satisfied. The poor girl and her little brothers and sisters would suffer no more. A great life was ahead of them . . .

However, regarding his own great life, Mr President felt somehow embarrassed. That day, he'd managed to discover the most terrifying secret: the world would have been much better off without politicians!

CHAPTER 3

Smiling in the face of adversity

"I promise to play for the last time," David said to himself while buying a new lottery ticket. The money he's been saving for a promised good meal had to be wasted again on the lottery in the hope of financial relief that would end all his troubles and suffering. Things such as paying the rent, utility bills, and other expenses with so little available money had changed his life into an everyday struggle for survival.

David was working in construction and had many bad experiences related to his job. Mr Luigi, one of his employers, had a complicated type of personality. He was a charismatic, well-educated, and good-looking leader, always polite and smiling most of the time. The car park of his office always had one of several expensive cars, which he used alternately. It seemed that a different day brought a different car. Due to his charming character, beautiful women always surrounded Mr Luigi, although he was married and had two children.

In charge of the construction firm, Mr Luigi had different jobs in many places. David was working with a few other people on restructuring a four-room flat. Mr Luigi stayed mainly in his office, but he popped over from time to time to see how the work was progressing and to give new instructions. As agreed when the job was taken, David was supposed to be paid every week, more precisely on Friday. However, on Friday Mr Luigi was usually nervous or at least pretended to be. He used to come along to see the work, and before anyone had a chance to ask about pay, he usually found something that didn't work, or if there was nothing wrong, he invented a supposed mistake and then all the workers had to resolve the problem. Meanwhile, Mr Luigi left, apparently very nervous, without telling anything about the pay. The workers were left with the hope that the following Friday would be much better. Sometimes their employer didn't show at all, postponing the payday until the following Friday. Such a day was always expected with great hope but often finished with great disappointment.

After working for about two months for Mr Luigi, David was finally able to understand how things worked. This man kept promising to make job contracts for all the workers, but it never happened. Therefore, without receiving their pay, people had no other option but to leave. Meanwhile, Mr Luigi managed to find other desperate people to hire them under the same conditions and with the same promises. Everything started all over again.

One day David left too, hopeless, without receiving any money.

Then there was the next employer—Mr George—with a similar construction firm and similar personality. Mr George, an extremely arrogant and overconfident man, seemed a little more honest, not too much, though. David was paid very little every week, with the promise to get more when things got better. Mr George took responsibility for a huge construction workload and borrowed a lot of money from the bank in order to be able to do so. He also hired many people, much more than he could organise in an efficient way.

However, instead of using the borrowed money to get the work done, Mr George bought a lavish car and started behaving like a great leader who was always right and treating his workers as the people who were always wrong. During this time, he kept telling everyone how great he was, advertising himself in all possible ways. After a few months of splendour, Mr George went bankrupt and all the workers had to leave without being paid.

David tried his luck again by changing places and bosses many times, with similar consequences. In one place, he had to leave because of a self-proclaimed leader with a peculiar agenda. The work entitled demolition involving a team of people who worked very hard, except for some of them, who spent most of their time watching for the boss to turn up. When seeing the boss coming, they immediately became active and competed for the tools with such vigour that the people who kept working, already tired, had no more strength to keep it up. David usually found himself with nothing to do when the boss came, and after this happened a few times, he had to leave the job. Strangely, the self-proclaimed leader was promoted and received bigger pay.

Finding a new job was a challenging task, and David acknowledged soon that he did not inspire much confidence in the eyes of future employers. Seeing such a fragile man for the first time, employers believed he was unsuited for hard work and treated him accordingly. Coming to the Work Market, a place where people looking for jobs gathered, usually in front of a warehouse or a crossroad, David was constantly ignored by potential employers. He was always considered one of the last options, and it required a high degree of luck or a good-hearted employer to be able to get a job offer.

If by lucky accident someone offered him a job, David was constantly watched. It appeared that employers were afraid he was not doing his job or that they were paying him too much. Consequently, David always ended up working more than the majority of people and never being appreciated for his hard work. Of course, people with big muscles received special treatment and much attention from their employers, who seemed to appreciate their large muscles rather than the amount of work they actually did.

People with big muscles had an easy life at the work market too since they were more likely to be taken for a job. Being muscular was also to their advantage when fighting their way to enter the car of a potential employer who just happened to stop by.

For David, fighting against those people was out of the question. Thus he had to stay constantly alert and be the first to reach the car of a potential employer. In the case of such an event, David only had a few seconds to impress his future employer until the big guys arrived.

Finding a job in such conditions was painful but also funny. From time to time, people who lost their way stopped the car to ask for direction. In a few seconds, the car was completely surrounded by angry men desperately looking for work. The unlucky person who happened to stop the car in the wrong place had to listen, terrified, to all those people talking and shouting at the same time and pushing each other, unable to understand anything. It might well have happened that one of them entered the car and refused to get out, believing that everything was about a new job.

Luckily for David, this kind of terrifying scene worked to his advantage sometimes since women looking to hire someone for a job were absolutely terrified to stop the car in front of the big and scary men. They preferred someone who inspired more confidence.

David finally managed to get a new job, and Mrs Rosa, the strangest boss he'd ever had, was also the most entertaining. Although she regularly paid him and never retained any of his money, other things made the lives of those working for Mrs Rosa unbearable.

She had a crazy neighbour, as crazy as herself, and they had made a tradition of quarrelling on a daily basis. There were many opportunities to argue, though without any valid reason. Just glancing at each other was a good reason for a new round of rhubarb, shouting, swearing, and squabble.

David's work was so hard that he had almost no chance to think about what was happening around him. The best thing he could do was smile and keep on working. He had to renovate a huge house, build new annexes, fashion a swimming pool, and maintain Mrs Rosa's huge garden. There was always so much to do that after twelve hours of work without a break, apart from a short lunch break, he often fell asleep on the bus on his way back home. Once at home, exhausted and extremely hungry, he was too tired to eat anything, and he went to bed for a short rest. Of course, that short rest lasted the whole night because he was unable to wake up due to exhaustion. The next morning always started with strong coffee because he needed the stimulant.

Despite all that, there was the funny side of working for Mrs Rosa. No matter how hard the job, there was fun, lots of fun, enough to start a conversation and to disagree with Mrs Rosa on any issue. The subject didn't matter. Just disagree with her and she would talk alone the whole day, commenting on the subject. The other people working for her knew well what was going to happen when David and Mrs Rosa started a conversation; they would have fun too. All they had to do was listen to the conversation and make short comments or give their *expert* opinions on the matter; nothing could possibly be funnier.

One day David made the mistake of mentioning a great general from the past, babbling about some of his mistakes made during his wars. Mrs Rosa was so outraged by this subject to the degree that she nicknamed him "Mr General" for the rest of the time he worked for her.

The funniest subject to discuss with Mrs Rosa was, of course, politics, and after discovering this great secret, David continued talking only about politics. There was always a new political scandal and elections on the way that were a great source of inspiration. Important was to discover Mrs Rosa's position on a political issue and to take the opposite side accordingly. Then the hassle could last a very long time, of course, with guaranteed fun for everybody.

Sunday was David's day off, a day for recharging. He always felt sleepy on Sundays and went to church unwillingly, with the only hope that Claudia, the girl he loved, would be nicer to him this time. However, she always seemed to become more distant and impossible to reach. David had no idea what to do, for nothing appeared to impress her. One day he bought her some flowers. She accepted them with a lost smile and said thanks without any further comments. Then she turned around and started talking to other girls about how great some other guys were.

Another day, he finally found the courage to invite her for a coffee in the city centre. At first, she said nothing. Later, when more people were around, she started shouting at him, asking him to let her alone. David, humiliated, was astonished and didn't know what to say. He preferred to talk to her in private, but Claudia seemed to enjoy sorting out her problems in public. Later, he found out that Claudia behaved like that because she wanted to impress another guy she fancied. And of course, humiliating someone publicly was a most effective way of impressing admirers.

David tried to forget that humiliation and dedicated all his energy to the only possible relief: his work. One day, surprisingly, Claudia invited him to town. Although very tired from work, he accepted the invitation and promised to join her. But Claudia didn't show up, leaving him alone to wait for her for about three hours. There was no explanation, no message to say sorry, and no apologies. She simply pretended to have forgotten, without feeling the need to give any explanations or to apologize.

Dealing with such a girl, David felt that he had to beg for every single smile or act of kindness and that he had to remain perpetually indebted for such an honour.

Claudia, like all the girls in her group of friends, had a university degree, whereas David had only finished high school. Despite working as a cleaner, like all the other girls, such a profession didn't stop her from behaving with superiority and arrogance. The message sounded clear, and David understood it. Obviously, she was looking for someone with a university degree and a good job.

Since David joined a group of boys and girls from the church, around twenty of them, he earned the nickname "The Poet" due to his passion for writing satirical poems and sending them to everybody as text messages. Sadly, very few people found it necessary to reply since he was not considered a person with great expectations and thus labelled a loser. That would make him feel lonelier and rejected. The girls found his poems funny, but at the end of the day, he didn't have a university degree or a good job. Therefore, there was no need to reply to his messages.

Such social exclusion for no apparent reasons continued to make his life even more unbearable.

During the religious festivals, he spent most of the time alone. Everyone was busy organising parties, but no one seemed to want him around.

One Christmas, after the religious service, he found himself completely alone, with nothing to do. So he decided to celebrate Christmas alone and to forget everything. He got some food from a shop and headed to a park. David put the food on a bench and started unpacking. A lonely dog, as lonely as himself, wanted to join him, and David accepted his request with enthusiasm.

There's enough food for both of us, David thought.

He started eating, sharing every single piece of food with his new friend. Then he opened a bottle of wine and poured a full glass for himself.

"Merry Christmas!" he said to the dog.

His new friend began barking and took control of a piece of sausage, waving his tail merrily.

"What is Claudia doing right now?" he wondered aloud.

He recalled someone mentioning that she was invited to celebrate the Christmas with some friends who organised a big party. Perhaps she was having great fun, and David felt happy for her.

Soon he began thinking of his home, so far away and so strange to him. None of his friends from childhood were his friends anymore.

They were more like strangers. Since he left home and moved abroad, they imagined he had a lot of money and constantly calculated the amount of money he might have accumulated by then. David would have liked to call them and tell them merry Christmas, but he knew how it would end. They would ask him for money. Even his brothers had similar opinions about his personal imaginary wealth.

The year before, when he went home, David felt ignored by everybody because the presents he brought were not worthy enough. He would have had to bring more expensive presents in order to please his friends, things that he could not afford. His childhood friends seemed unable to understand that his life was just too hard.

"What are you doing with your money?" they asked him accusatorily.

"Where is your money?" the same people continued to ask.

He remembered one of his friends calculating the time he spent abroad, adding up his estimated salaries based on the salary his friend imagined him eligible for. Then his friend came up with a virtual total, without subtracting such expenses such rent, utility bills, and bus pass, not saying anything about food or the plane ticket needed to go home. His friend, after contemplating that astronomical amount of money, proposed a large sum to borrow from David. The inability of the latter to lend any money to his friend meant the end of their friendship, and David had to endure some harsh remarks such as "selfish and ungrateful". He was even accused of having a great life abroad and forgetting one's friends.

David had enough of explaining to his friends that there was no money. Although painful, being alone abroad was less painful than confronting his old friends, who seemed more interested in his supposed wealth than enjoying the moment of being together after so long.

Meanwhile, he continued celebrating the Christmas with his new friend.

Two days of freedom was a great thing for him, after which he had to start again with his exhausting work. Two days without seeing Mrs Rosa.

"This is what I call happiness," he said, although celebrating the Christmas alone was difficult.

The following days proceeded normally, with the same stressful and tiring work, and nobody called him to ask how he was doing. Every now and then, fellas asked him to help write messages to girls. David wrote them very passionately, as if he himself were the one in love with the girl addressed. David then forwarded those messages to the people who requested them. Girls were always impressed, but they never knew who wrote them such poetic messages. Since the senders were handsome, nobody inquired about their writing skills. In the end, such confident people must be able to do anything, even write impassioned love letters to girls, they thought.

David was happy to see his poems and poetic skills much appreciated. Sadly for him, no one seemed to enjoy the company of a person with so low expectations.

"They seem to like poetry but not the poet . . ." he said to himself, smiling in the face of adversity.

But his troubles did not end there.

There was another guy called David, but he didn't come very often to join his group. Unfortunately for our David, the other David fell in love with one of the girls from the group. This guy somehow managed to get her phone number and stated sending her ardent messages, signing with his name. She didn't reply, obviously. David had no idea about this. He soon became sick and stayed at home for several days. He also had to leave his job, saying goodbye to Mrs Rosa, his impossible boss.

For a few weeks, David did not manage to meet his group, but when he finally did, it was the most humiliating day of his life. Claudia decided to seek revenge against him, even though she had no reasons for retaliation. The other girl who received the love messages was as upset as Claudia was. She simply could not imagine how a guy without any future prospects had the courage to dream of receiving her love. The other girls preferred to keep laughing. David looked for help from the guys he'd helped so many times, but they simply ignored him. He had no more courage to defend himself, and thus he left in shame.

With little remaining money and no friends left, David decided to change country, town, friends, language, and culture. There would be nobody waiting for him. Moreover, he didn't speak the language of the new country. Nevertheless, there was no turning back. He had to go as far as possible.

Alone aboard a train, he began thinking of the only real friend he had in the country he was about to leave behind, the dog, which was as lonely as himself and who spent that blessed Christmas with him in the park.

Next Christmas I will be alone, David thought.

But until then, he had to worry about what to do in the new country, about learning the language and finding a job.

Wow, what a crazy world!

A few years later, David was finally a student and lived in student accommodation. Meanwhile, there was an economic crisis in the country he'd left behind, and most of his friends lost their jobs. None of the girls he knew got married. Although he didn't wish it, David felt revenged.

The good-looking and confident guys were asking for his help again. They had decided by then to study, but they were scared by the need to adventure into the unknown. The hope that he was still their friend made them expect him to do something, anything necessary to help them come to the new country and study. Those good-looking guys got rejected by the girls, who preferred to keep dreaming of better guys. The guys far away had to be much better and perhaps much richer. Some of the girls also contacted him to ask for help. They were much nicer by then, but David did not forget his past humiliations. He didn't know what to do, and he preferred to avoid giving them any answer.

Claudia, after losing her job, simply vanished and nobody knew anything about her.

David was studying business and management, and everything seemed to go pretty well. There was always a lot to do, and he was quite busy most of the time. He also had to work in a hotel as a hotel porter, one of the few places that still offered jobs for students. After so many years of dreaming, he was finally at the university, but he didn't feel as happy as he'd expected to. For starters, there were no job prospects for the future. More and more companies were shut down, and the people had to go home. Students were worried about the last financial crash and its impact on their careers and future. In addition, a boring curriculum worsened matters. Students were supposed to study in groups, and any initiative of any of them to think independently was considered a failure. During any task, no student was allowed to ask tutors anything until all the members of the group had the same question. There had to be a group consensus on everything they did.

Then there was the problem of leadership. Every member of the group was encouraged to become a leader and to comment as often as possible on huge seminars comprising more than a hundred people. As a result, every seminar became a noisy activity, since everyone wanted to talk as much as possible with disfavour about others. David watched it all, amazed by the noise-making people who were supposed to become the next generation of leaders.

Good leaders were supposed to be charismatic and to show confidence, plenty of it, according to the common wisdom. David realised that people who inspired confidence and showed good speaking skills were more likely to impose their personal opinions on the entire group, even if those opinions were wrong. There was simply no time to think and analyse a situation. Quick decisions were highly appreciated, and any delay was considered a weakness by teachers, students, and/or both sides.

David was a shy and quiet person. He found such obsession with quick decisions and making noise quite disturbing. He thought that those decision-making groups, instead of encouraging creativity, did exactly the opposite. There was no way to make a good decision in such a noisy environment.

When they went for training and experience in a real business environment, the situation was even worse. There was no privacy of any kind. All the private offices had vanished. There was just a huge central room which was supposed to be a place for decision-making and creativity. David felt very uncomfortable and unable to contribute to any task. As always, the loudest people were the only people to get their opinions approved. When someone quietly managed to make his voice heard, his opinion was considered lacking in confidence and was hence rejected.

But the most upsetting thing was the constant unfair advantage given to certain people, promoting and rewarding them according to the way they looked or the amount of noise they made. David had good reason to feel marginalised or stigmatised for such simple reasons as being shy and humble.

Perhaps it's time to question the purpose of education and the meaning of democracy, he thought.

After the daily dose of chaos at school, although very tired, David walked home instead of taking a bus. In fact, he never took the bus because buses were as crowded and noisy as his university, and he desperately needed some peace of mind moments alone. Since his accommodation was at walking distance, walking home was to become the best part of his daily routine.

There were many things to see along the way, but nothing tempted him more than a bookshop situated on a quiet street. He always took the longest path, avoiding the crowded streets, and routinely stopped in front of the bookshop to check for the new releases. He might enter the shop and spend half an hour ore more looking into some interesting books.

"There are so many books to read," he said to himself.

Sadly, he could not afford to buy any of them and this is why he spent so much time in the bookshops amongst his beloved books.

David was one of the few students in his class who still enjoyed reading books. All the others seemed to be so incredibly busy. Multitasking was already part of their culture, but David wondered what the heck they were doing. In the discussions they had, those busy students appeared to have no idea what was happening in the world. No wonder, as most of them got news via social networks. They were too incredibly obsessed with the ism of always looking cool, always having the greatest number of admirers, always being the centre of everybody's attention, always having instant gratification for everything they did, and other crazy social rules based on the *wow* culture. Everything had to be amazing, fantastic, the coolest, the greatest, and the craziest.

"*Wow*, what a crazy world!" he exclaimed.

But David really didn't care about the way other people wasted their time. He took full advantage of all the free time available. During the long nights alone at the hotel reception, he had nothing else to do but read books, lots of them.

Reluctant for everything that included *wow*, David continued undisturbed in his simple life until a certain day . . . *Wow*, what a lovely creature!

This girl seemed different. She was polite, modest, and nice, but most important of all, she didn't make a lot of noise. Susan had left her country like many people who tried to escape the financial crush, with the hope that things would be better elsewhere. She'd just moved to the same student accommodation, and they ran into each other by chance. While introducing themselves, both seemed pleased by that encounter. However, David looked reluctant to enquire too much about such lovely girl. He was still a shy person and so she was.

The time passed, and they met up from time to time, exchanging polite "howdies" and comments about their everyday lives. They talked about their problems, their hopes, and their dreams.

"I really like this girl," David said to himself. He had no idea what she thought about him, but as long as she kept smiling, everything seemed to be fine. Unfortunately, there were other guys around, more confident and talkative. Although David almost never got a chance to find her alone, he nonetheless felt relieved when she ran away and then appeared around the following day or a few days later on. It seemed that he preferred to see her alone rather than in the company of such insistent individuals. She always smiled and talked softly, trying to hide her problems and failures.

David understood that she was desperately looking for a job, any kind of job. Susan had to write many CVs and to go to many job interviews, almost on a daily basis. However, there was nothing on the way, no job offers yet. Although realising her suffering, inside David was happy because she was still around. Sometimes they meet by chance on the street, a good opportunity for a little chat and for enjoying her lovely smile alone. Wishing each other a good day, they then went in opposite directions; he went to his school or work, and she resumed her unpleasant job hunting.

That girl seemed to have a difficult life. There were always some guys around looking for her, but Susan locked herself inside her room most of the time. David sympathised with her, yet he felt happy. As long as that girl remained single, there was still hope for him.

He saw her struggling with money, always buying the cheapest food, the cheapest clothes, and never going out. Although his life was also difficult, David was scared to offer her any help in order not to alert the other guys. He didn't want to look like a possible rival in their eyes, a game he would probably lose. Those alpha males looked too confident, too charismatic, and too ambitious. Any false move would cost him dearly.

Sadly, he had to rely again on one of his worst habits: playing the lottery. Knowing that Susan struggled to buy food, he found it painful to buy a lottery ticket, but he hoped the odds, although very low, might change his life.

"This is the last ticket," David promised himself, but he knew he was going to play again the following days, promising the same thing repeatedly.

He received very little money from his work, barely enough to get by. Like all the people who were scared away by what tomorrow would bring, he had no choice but to run a risk and play the lottery. At least creating a very slim chance of winning besides the right to dream of a better future would make him escape into the world of dreams where everything was possible. He felt guilty all the time for wasting money on the lottery, investing money in a Ponzi scheme, especially when he also knew his real chances of winning. He knew for sure that he was being robbed by that hope-creating-hope game. But he was no different to all the desperate people who'd lost hope and found the lottery ticket the only remaining stimulant for their dreams. David knew that taking advantage of people's desperation could make a great business, and that was exactly what the lottery was all about, a legalised robbery at the expenses of the poor. The highly advertised charity activities promoted by the lottery were nothing but a way of hiding a dark secret.

Unfortunately, nothing was stronger than the power of dreaming. The temptation was too big, and the poor people were too desperate to escape a life without an apparent future. As such, a lottery ticket was their right to summon sweet dreams. That's why people will never stop buying lottery tickets. In an ideal society without desperate people, the lottery would make no sense and would go bankrupt. But David did not live in an ideal society, and people around him were utterly desperate.

Theories about success are useless in practice

However hard David was working, it seemed that he would never get over all the present problems. The money was never enough, and the little he had was used just to fill in the gaps. By a quick calculation, the answer was terrifying: he had to work for his entire life, just like this, only to fill in the gaps! There was no room for anything else: no holidays, no family, no friends . . . The nays had it all.

In the meantime, he kept sending his CV to different places in the hopes of securing a better job. There was little chance anyway; he persisted just to cater to his peace of mind.

Looking for a job nowadays is like playing the lottery, he thought, beginning to smile while contemplating his CV in one hand and a lottery ticket in the other.

It appeared to him, however, that winning the lottery, although the chance was pretty slim, was more realistic than finding a good job.

His overconfident generation, which was unable to decide its own future, must have been merely another irony of destiny. David began wondering about the purpose of having a CV, since it appeared to him that chance played a much bigger part in what used to be called success. Of course, he was struggling to find an answer. Busy with his work and studying, he had very little time to answer such mind-boggling questions.

However, one day he received an unexpected invitation for a job interview. It turned out that one of his teachers sent a recommendation to a certain employer who was desperately in need of someone to save his business. A new manager was needed for a nearly bankrupt company specializing in electronic products. Taken by surprise, David didn't know what to say. The references his teacher had provided looked convincing and enthusiastic, and that gave him little opportunity to resist. He was the best person for that place, and he had the duty to save the company from bankruptcy. However, such enthusiastic references looked a bit strange to him. He didn't remember doing anything impressive or out of the ordinary. He didn't even remember doing anything at all that deserved to be mentioned. His colleagues constantly rejected or ignored almost all his suggestions. There was nothing amazing about that and nothing to be proud of.

The interview was a standard professional interview following the criteria imposed by some great experts. After looking carefully at his CV, the interviewer began with a selection of crazy questions, including, "Why the hell are you here?" and "If you were a dinosaur, what would you do?"

There were also some questions about chickens, cats and dogs, and black holes and aliens. David struggled to answer those unexpected questions, totally unrelated to the advertised job. *Since such questions were prepared by experts,* he thought, *they probably had good reasons to per se.*

However, his answers didn't seem to matter. David had a feeling that they would hire him anyway, regardless of his skills or qualifications. The interviewer looked similar to the type of person who was unable to hide his enthusiasm.

What's so great about my CV? David wondered. *There's nothing special about it. I'm just an average person with average skills. What is this sudden inexplicable change of attitude about me?*

David followed the rest of the interview absent-mindedly and feeling perplexed, but that did not affect the outcome. He got the job and was requested to start as soon as possible.

A few days later, after leaving the job at the hotel, David was ready for the new position. When he first entered the office building, he realised that none of the theories he had to learn at school could be applied in practice. There was simply too much noise and no place for privacy and quiet retreat. There was also too much stress. Everyone looked busy, but people just messed around, spying on each other, disturbing each other, or stressing each other out. There was no way to make things work under such conditions. Something must have been wrong with the whole system, likely based on noise making and group thinking.

"What the hell is this brainstorming?" David asked, both entertained and nauseated, and someone began explaining that good ideas crystallised through such process of accidental free generation of ideas developed by the whole group. He seemed, however, unconvinced by such an explanation. It appeared to him that people had emotional attachments to that method because it was part of the common wisdom. People did it not because it was right, but because they wanted to stay with the herd.

Group thinking was nothing more than herd behaviour. The great discoveries and inventions were made by solitary people working on their own and most of the time being ignored by the people around them.

David decided to take the files home in order to study everything while at ease. There was no need for brainstorming or group decision making. All he needed was a quiet place and enough time. The other employers were allowed to contact him via email, and David thought that discussing the problems online would be more productive than reciprocal tension at work within that ridiculously noisy office.

With little knowledge of electronics, he spent days and nights trying to figure out how to make those products competitive. Nevertheless, regardless of what he thought to be the best thing to do, it seemed that things worked out themselves. After a few days in charge of the nearly bankrupt company, they began receiving unexpected orders for their products. Those orders tended to increase day by day, and the company consequently turned profitable after a short time.

One day, a much bigger and famous company in the same field proposed that the two companies join forces in order to attain together a bigger piece of the market. This appeared to work, and David was elected the leader of the two conjoined companies. Then things got more complicated with the international market.

Meanwhile, David had to abandon his studies due to the increasing pressure and high demand at work. He was astonished how things happened so incredibly fast, and he was even more astonished by the further unfolding of events.

However, doing business at such an incredible speed and succeeding so inexplicably convinced David once more that the majority of theories about success were completely useless in practice. Consequently, he imagined himself facing a lion for the first time, armed with plenty of theories about confidence, positive thinking, problem-solving, time management, and winning behaviour. Despite those great theories, he had to acknowledge in a blink of an eye that it was much better to leave all such theories for later and to do the first thing that practice suggested—running away to escape danger.

The incredible success of his company caught the attention of the media. Among other things, by then he had to go for interviews with prestigious press, radio, TV, and Internet to explain the secret behind his success. He had no clue but pretended to be in charge of his destiny and of his business.

Meanwhile, David bought a new house all for himself, the first house he'd ever had. He should have been happy being the leader of a successful firm and having a quiet and peaceful place to live. But he was not. Susan was still on his mind. But what happened to her?

She apparently left, and he had no idea where she was.

All the money he had seemed to be useless. Instead of being happy and leading a successful life, he felt extremely lonely and helpless.

What happened to that girl? he wondered.

Perhaps there was a way to find out. He set up an investigation team to collect all the information required to find her.

Jerks can be very sophisticated

This interview looks different, Susan thought.

She desperately needed a job. She was overburdened with debt and struggling to save money in order to survive. Mr Taylor, her interviewer, was a charismatic and good-looking person, agreeable and overconfident. He appeared to know the answers to all questions.

He is just so polite and nice! Susan thought.

In fact, he was too nice, and his way of behaving started to become irritating. There was a good job advertised for the appointment of a secretary, and Mr Taylor made it clear that the *nicest* person would get it. At first, Susan did not realise what *being nice* meant for him. But when she finally did, she refused, and when she decided to go, the nice and charismatic interviewer became unexpectedly rude. He started swearing and talking arrogantly, the typical arrogance common amongst people who are never questioned for their acts.

Susan left crying, ignoring all the bad words yelled at her. She felt betrayed, abandoned, and forgotten. Alone on the street, Susan walked home trying to hide her emotions. The streets were crowded with people, but all of them were strangers to her and so busy with their own lives to the degree that none of them seemed to care about what was happening around them. She just wanted to wander around without a destination, to forget everything and to calm down.

For a few days, nothing happened. Then, surprisingly, one day Susan received another invitation for a job interview from a company she'd never heard of. Apparently, they needed a new manager for a section of their company that specialised in jewellery. Susan was very happy about the unexpected invitation, and she was looking forward to the interview. Suspecting that many people probably wanted the same position, she prepared herself as best she could.

The interview went the usual way. A nice woman in her middle thirties carefully examined her CV and then began asking questions, a lot of them spanning from her personal life to dinosaurs, aliens, and other strange creatures. Susan maintained her calm when some unexpected crazy question popped up, and she then answered each of them with her usual calm and soft voice. Her interviewer seemed excited and confessed that Susan was the right person for the job. She would get the confirmation in a few days, and if so, Susan would start work soon.

"This is incredible!" Susan exclaimed to herself, struggling to hide her emotions. After so much trouble and suffering, she finally had some good news.

And the good news became assured sooner than expected. By the following week, Susan had taken charge of the new office and immersed herself into work with heart and body alike. Everything went well and everything seemed too good to be true. Her colleagues, mostly women, were polite, so ridiculously polite to the point that Susan, for a moment, thought there was something wrong about that job. She still remembered Mr Taylor, the charismatic and attractive interviewer who turned into a devil. Her colleagues seemed to be similar to him. They were always smiling and always so ready to help with the minor and insignificant things that Susan began to compare them to angels. However, that kind of angel could be very dangerous indeed.

Just a few days later, after a busy and challenging day, while everyone was getting changed and ready to go home, the police entered the office for no apparent reason and began searching everyone's bags. When Susan's turn came, they searched her and found in her bag some very expensive jewellery about which she had no idea. While she was being arrested, her colleagues smiled with malice, as if wanting to say, "We knew you were not an honest person." Susan objected to the detainment, but she had no chance to defend herself; there was just too much evidence against her.

Her humiliation didn't end there. After a few minutes, the media was also present, and some journalists began recording and taking pictures. Susan wondered how the journalists arrived so quickly. It seemed that they knew in advance that she would be arrested and accused of stealing jewellery. Therefore, they started a humiliating interview, making sure that her face, likewise her alleged crime, would be clearly visible. The jewels in question were shown with their overall prices evaluated. Susan was accused of ingratitude and of other crimes. Even more shockingly, her charismatic colleagues turned against her with the fiercest accusations. Susan refused to believe what was happening to her. She had no way to defend herself. Soon she was brought to the nearest prison, waiting for her destiny to be decided.

At the court, she was advised to plead guilty since all the evidence was against her. Nevertheless, she refused to say anything or to answer any questions. There were many journalists and TV presenters around, not to mention the masses that happened to turn up to see her and accuse her of terrible crimes. The case was broadcasted live and hence became soon a national sensation. Susan continued to remain silent and to watch without watching, listen without listening, and hope that everything would finish soon.

"Justice should be done!" shouted people present in the court hall.

"Shame on you!" shouted people again, clearly referring to Susan and staring at her, monitoring every single movement she made.

Under the pressure of the audience, the judge was urged to give the maximum sentence. Susan got two years and was sent to a new prison for her penance.

Just a few days later, not enough to be accustomed to her new life, Susan received an unexpected visitor and was invited to the parlour. She had no idea who it could be, but a few minutes later, the worst of her nightmares came true. It was Mr Taylor, her interviewer, who tried to take advantage of her a few days before. Now he felt happy about her fate, and he was contemplating his revenge.

He began talking, explaining that nobody refused him. He always had what he wanted in life, and he would have her too. After her sentence was finished, nobody would give her a job, as her career had ended forever. She would beg him for forgiveness, and he might give her a job on his conditions. Then he wished her good penance and left without looking back.

That explained everything, and Susan, realising that her misery was in fact much greater than she imagined, began crying helplessly.

That monster created a fake job just to destroy her life. Her colleagues probably knew what was about to happen to her, even before she was hired. All that smiling and politeness were nothing more than a mockery. They hated her from the first moment they met and did fabricate the larceny. Police and the media were notified in advance, and they were probably good friends with Mr Taylor. Perhaps they all conspired to send her to prison.

Susan felt so lonely and helpless. She was ashamed to call anybody of the people who knew her. Their presence would probably make things worse and intensify her suffering. Her parents were far away, and they had no money to come and see her. Apparently, there was nobody who wanted to see her, except the person who ruined her life—Mr Taylor.

Good people must forgive

But Susan was wrong to think she was completely abandoned. A few weeks later, David found her and came to the prison, leaving for later any important tasks related to his work. The encounter was very emotional. In fact, Susan appeared unable to say almost anything, and she kept crying while David was trying to calm her. Both of them were happy to see each other, although they preferred different conditions for their encounter. David promised to come often to see her, and he kept his word.

The next encounter seemed more relaxed, wherein Susan explained everything that had happened to her and how she was convicted. David was perplexed and didn't know what to say, but he was happy that she was innocent and promised to take revenge against Mr Taylor. However, Susan insisted there was no need for revenge because she forgave him. Reluctant to forgive Mr Taylor, David preferred to change the subject and began talking about his job and about all the challenges he had to face constantly. But soon he realised that such dedication to the job had made him forget about Susan; and her troubles and suffering were his fault. He should have acted more promptly to help her, before Susan had the chance to meet Mr Taylor. David confessed that it was his fault and that he felt very sorry for what had happened, but Susan assured him that there was no reason to feel sorry.

However, he realised that it was a bit too late to feel sorry, and thus the only thing he could do then was to make her life easier. He promised to offer her all support possible and to try, if possible, to set her free. He knew, however, that it wasn't that easy. As he would find out later, Mr Taylor was also the owner of the jewellery shop as well as the owner of many other businesses. By then, it was clear that Mr Taylor was wealthy and probably had many powerful and influential friends.

David, of course, was not intimidated. He was determined to liberate Susan, whatever the cost.

So this is how successful people are playing with other people's lives, said David to himself with rage. *Someone makes a huge sacrifice to finish a degree in order to be socially accepted and respected, and someone else takes away everything with a few convincing lies, leaving behind a person with no future. No employer, it appears, will give a job, any kind of job, to a person with a criminal record. It doesn't seem to matter whether guilty or innocent; people are too busy to think for themselves about it. This explains the social stigma against the ex-convicts. But what about someone who fought in a revolution? Fighting against a tyrannical dictator for the freedom of your people and hence imprisoned can bring you the same social stigma . . .*

David recalled his participation in a revolution many years before against his country's dictator, and how he was nearly killed but was saved by an anonymous gentleman who later was to become his best friend. David and Stefan would soon find out that they were students at the same university, David studying literature and Stefan history. However, their studies would end sooner than expected, with new students' shower of protests against the fresh democratic government, which was even more corrupt than the late dictatorial regime.

The revolution was supposed to bring freedom and democracy— most importantly, democracy. There was just trouble instead, too much trouble.

David and his friend Stefan joined the student protests and soon found themselves on the streets again, fighting for democracy against a democratic government. But the student protest was called "Golaniad" by the new government, from the word "golan", meaning hoodlum. In a few days, the legal protest of the students became illegal and antidemocratic according to the new government. The president called the miners to support him, and they came over, plenty of them, armed with crowbars, sledgehammers, and pickaxes. This time, the police stayed neutral. In fact, they had orders not to intervene in the battle between the unarmed students and the miners. Being promised a huge recompense for "defending the democracy", the miners began hunting down the students, beating, torturing, or killing them in the name of democracy. David was lucky to end up in a hospital with minor injuries, while his unlucky friend ended up in prison for apparent acts of vandalism.

Years later, a new government arose, as corrupt as their predecessors. At any rate, this time the government, with the *experts'* help from abroad, destroyed the economic vigour of the country. Fabrics and factories were closed on a national scale. Concomitantly, people were sent back home. This was how the mighty power of the miners ended: in shame and hunger. By then, they were the poorest sector of the country and needed urgent help, too much help from the students they once fiercely beat, mutilated, and killed. But it seemed that either the miners or the students at that moment lived in a parallel universe, preferring to simply ignore the members of the opposite group and their suffering. In fact, there was never a truce between the miners and students, and any kind of alliance between them for a common future sounded impossible. The students were not ready to forget the past, and consequently, the miners had to forget their future.

David was upset for the arrest of his friend many years before in the name of democracy. Then another friend of his was arrested in the name of justice. Both of them would suffer from a social stigma they didn't deserve, for the rest of their lives, whereas the real criminals were having great lives and good social positions. David was perturbed, and he was right to be so. But there was little he could do to make things better. People in power were just too powerful, and they had a great interest in hiding their dirty secrets.

Thinking about politics and politicians was the most upsetting thing for David. He recalled from memory his first democratically elected president and how he was elected. He also remembered how the new political class took advantage of the people's sacrifices in revolution. The real people, who fought and died on the streets or were arrested or injured, didn't get any benefit out of that revolution. When the new government decided to give a certificate of revolutionist to every participant in the revolution, there were new people granted such certificates, coming from nowhere and never happening to roam the streets before. This sort of certificate gave a lot of privilege to its owner; no wonder that most of those people were related to each other and most of them would become later politicians and successful businessmen.

How was that possible? David wondered.

Since those tumultuous events, David lived in many countries and had the chance to compare the different political systems based on democracy, but he didn't seem to be satisfied by any of them. There was no apparent difference between his country and all the others countries claiming to be leading democracies. He concluded with sadness that the only difference was a more professional way of lying to people.

One day, David was surprised to find a letter from his old friend Stefan. More surprisingly, he lived in the same country and even the same city. Stefan had seen him in the news and decided to contact him.

Apparently, David, a successful businessperson, had fallen in love with a girl imprisoned for stealing jewellery. This story caught the attention of the press, and eager to find any new scandals, they made it front-page news, as a shocking story indeed.

The two friends finally met, and they began exchanging their stories. Stefan was sorry to hear about Susan and about what happened to her, whilst David felt shocked by his friend's self-reclusion into the forest. Nevertheless, Stefan assured him there was nothing to worry about. Therein, he had a peaceful life and plenty of time to read all the books he wanted. David was eager to know what happened after his arrest.

After three years in prison, Stefan explained, for the crime of fighting for freedom, he became a pariah and all his friends began to avoid him. No one fancied his company because he was an ex-convict. So he had to leave home, and since then, he lived on his own. Not only didn't he get any recognition for fighting against tyranny, but also his case was never reopened. The person who did the things for which he was accused later became a successful politician. Of course, the latter was interested in keeping things quiet.

A group of teenage aristocrats began smashing everything in their way during the student rioting, just for fun. Stefan intervened, trying to calm them down. When the police arrived, they all accused Stefan of doing it, and he was consequently arrested.

"It's all about aristocracy," David said, "the privileged people who never get questioned. Now it's time to forget and forgive. Have you ever thought about forgiveness?"

"You've never been to prison; that's why you are so generous. Ask your poor girlfriend what forgiveness means. Would she be ready to forgive?"

"I think so. When I suggested taking my revenge against that idiot, she was clearly against it."

"But this doesn't mean I should forgive too."

"So what are you planning to do?" wondered David aloud.

"A planetary rebellion . . ."

"Against whom?"

"Against politicians," Stefan said.

"Against all of them?" Stefan shook his head. "But you've been in a rebellion. What did it change?"

"This time is different. This time we don't replace a corrupt political system with another. Now it's time to send all politicians home."

"And then?"

"Then nothing! This will be the end of our troubles."

David was speechless in the face of such a crazy intention, and for a moment, he remained in silence, looking for the right words to say.

"And how are you planning to do this?" he finally asked. "This will only materialise if they go home peacefully, but this will never happen. They have too many privileges to defend. But supposing such a miracle can happen, with all politicians going home without making trouble, who will rule the world then? Do you have any idea of how many people hate each other and how difficult is to make them do anything useful for the common good? At least now they hate politicians the most and seem united against politicians. Without politicians to hate, they will turn all their rage against themselves."

"Perhaps we need another miracle to make people love each other," said Stefan with hope.

But David had different opinions, and he told his friend to calm down. A planetary rebellion would bring blood and violence, and ultimately many people would die without achieving anything. What's more, a planetary rebellion would have no practical use. It would be impossible to control.

The two friends then decided to forget the rebellion for the moment, opting to concentrate on things that were more realistic. Upon Stefan's request, David agreed to meet Lee and his other friends on a day that suited everybody.

Things never written in CVs

Lee and Sara had begun seeing each other from time to time, and they went to the cinema, to have lunch out, or simply to wander around. They began fancying each other, but neither of them admitted it or showed too much affection for the other. In fact, both of them seemed to be scared to ask for more, and each of them had personal reasons. Lee still remembered all his troubles with other girls in the past, all his failures and rejections. Although in a much better position by then, he still maintained the resentment, as the past painful moments were still hurting him.

Sara, on the other hand, after admitting to the failure of her professional life and career, had no more courage to get involved in anything. She simply wanted to be free and to avoid running for anything that might cause her more pain in case of failure. It was not that she envied Lee for his success or felt jealous about it. If she had any feelings right then about anything, it would be the feeling of complete emotional bankruptcy. It would take time for her to recover from her emotional crisis. But Sara's emotional crisis would end sooner than expected, when she found out that some people had to endure even more suffering. Susan's story and her unjust imprisonment found its way from Stefan to Lee and from Lee to her. Now it was Sara the most revolted and the most willing to help and comfort the poor girl. She urged Lee to make possible a visit to the prison where Susan was incarcerated.

A few days later, David was invited to meet them. Since Mark was busy with his research and the two other girls were busy with their work, neither of them could come. After introducing David to Lee and Sara, Stefan suggested going somewhere for breakfast. Soon they entered a coffee shop and ordered coffee or tea, according to their preferences, and some muffins.

As they sat at a table, David began talking about himself. He definitely had a lot to tell, but Sara was more interested in what Susan was doing, so she managed to monopolise the discussion around Susan. David had to tell her the whole story first-hand, and Sara kept asking many questions about everything that happened. It was still morning, and there was plenty of time until the opening hour of the prison, but there was also a long way to go to get there. To avoid a traffic jam, perhaps it was much better to travel the longer way, which of course would take more time.

Drinking her coffee and questioning the man in front of her, Sara realised that the **Game of Power** got involved once again in deciding someone's destiny. This time, she didn't find such intervention into someone's life too revolting. She finally realised that some people were extremely powerful, and thus were able to play with other people's destinies at will, without being questioned.

"Do you know what the **Game of Power** is?" she asked David unexpectedly.

"Of course I know," he replied. "Stefan has told me."

"And what do you think about it?"

After reflecting for a moment while everyone was waiting for his answer, David finally answered hesitantly. "If Susan weren't in prison, I wouldn't care too much about this game. Perhaps I might be comfortable with my current situation."

"And now?" continued Sara without giving him a break, "what are your feelings right now about it?"

"Disgusted . . ." He stopped without finishing his idea. He knew that nothing could be more revolting than sending an innocent person to prison.

Stefan knew the same thing from his own experience, and he remained silent too. Ruining someone's reputation and turning the person into a social pariah just for fun was not only disgusting—it was more than that. Disgusting was not enough of a word to express such a feeling.

Lee intervened with a completely different question, breaking the terrible silence.

"What about the Caritas? What did he lose then?" Lee asked pointing to Stefan. "He doesn't want to tell us."

"I guess he didn't have too much money back then," David said, then continued only to himself, "When this pyramidal game started, he'd just gotten out of prison."

Looking at his friend, David waited for him to complete the story, but Stefan didn't appear to be in want for any clarifications about his tempestuous past.

"Perhaps he'd lost his trust in politicians," continued David after a spell of silence.

Two hours later, the four of them were at the prison, and Susan was notified about their visit.

They entered the usual visit parlour, and Susan appeared in front of them on the other side of the bars. She was pale and talked softly, almost inaudible, forcing herself to smile but making a great effort to do so. A few scratches were visible on her face and hands, a sign that she had to endure a harsh life.

David grabbed her hands across the bars, shook and kissed them passionately, and then let Sara take possession of Susan's hands. Although Sara tried to comfort her, urging her to be strong, Susan began to weep quietly, hiding her face behind her long blond hair. Sara felt the same need to cry for her own misfortunes and for the suffering of the unfortunate girl in front of her. But she managed to remain calm, hiding her real feelings, and promised to be Susan's friend and to frequently come along to visit her.

When the time was up, two guards took Susan away, and other guards urged her visitors to leave. Susan kept looking back and waving her frail hand before vanishing behind a closed door.

Back on the road, on their way home, Lee, Stefan, David, and Sara kept talking about the outcome of this visit. It was time to concentrate on how to get Susan out of prison. David assured that money was not enough to resolve this issue, and everyone in turn agreed. The intervention of a powerful figure was needed to do this job, perhaps a notable journalist or a big-name politician. But who would be willing to reopen the case of an insignificant person? Guilty or innocent, it didn't make any difference; everyone wanted to earn something or to cherish favour exchanges. This is how life worked, although people were unwilling to admit it. Perhaps if they were able to discover some incriminating facts about Mr Taylor, things might change to their benefit.

Sara wanted to visit Susan again, and David suggested paying her compensation for her efforts since he had enough money and was unable to come very often because of his job. Although Sara didn't have any source of income for the time being, she still refused David's offer. She didn't want to visit the poor girl for money. It didn't matter how hard David tried to insist upon his offer; Sara didn't want to accept.

When David suggested giving her a job at his company, Sara seemed more interested. Since the business had moved into the international market, there was plenty of work to do, and he had to hire new people anyway.

Then David decided to help his old friend too. Stefan would have to leave his forest and move into a proper room in his house. There was no need to pay rent or any other expenses. If Stefan fancied going to the university, David promised to support him financially as gratitude for what Stefan did for him years before, when he saved his life during the revolution.

However, Stefan reluctantly refused this offer. Instead, he wanted to concentrate on investigating the **Game of Power** and the people behind it. This was what he's been doing for the past few years. No wonder he abhorred politicians so much and kept dreaming of a world without them.

Both David and Lee found Stefan's proposal interesting and agreed to support it. Thus they decided to create a job and hire him as a private investigator. Stefan, of course, seemed to be excited that he finally had the opportunity to concentrate on his favourite hobby: creating a world without politicians. His friends then agreed on a salary and congratulated him on his new job.

Later on, Lee remembered something and started smiling. "Now can I see your CV, sir?" he said, breaking the silence.

"Sorry, no CV," replied Stefan, amused.

"What do you mean, you don't have a CV?" asked David, when he realised what his friends were laughing about.

Both David and Lee wanted to have some fun, so they continued teasing their friend for a while.

"You should be ashamed of yourself," said David with a fake seriousness.

"How do you dare not have a CV?" continued Lee with a similar reproaching tone.

Stefan began to feel guilty. It had to be a terrible crime not having a CV.

"Please leave him alone!" intervened Sara.

Stefan was soon accepted for the job without the need of a CV, and his friends congratulated him once more.

Lee invited his friends to his house. The place was quiet, so they could talk in peace and reflect on what to do next. Upon arrival, they accommodated themselves whilst Lee got busy preparing food and drink. David was invited to have a look around, and Stefan was very proud to show him the terrace he'd been carefully maintaining for the last few weeks. Afterwards, they went to the library, completely renewed with new, more serious books, and found themselves fully immersed in the huge loads of books. They thought that it felt quite similar to those long-ago years when they used to go to the same university. But that was a long and sad story, a story that both of them wanted to forget . . .

Sara preferred to sit on a bench on the terrace. She kept thinking of poor Susan and how difficult her life in prison must have been. She also thought about her new job, which would give her the chance to support herself without having to rely on borrowed money from her friends. Now she would be able to pay them back. When Lee offered to support her financially a few weeks before, she refused at first, but then the reality of life had to play its part. Desperately, she accepted the help, but on the condition that she would pay everything back at the first opportunity. The chance of meeting him, and later David, who offered her a job, made her life more bearable. Although luck might be unfair, she had no choice but to take advantage of it, like everyone else!

Sara, at least, got some good reasons to feel safe. Financial security was what everybody wanted. When one didn't have to worry about tomorrow, there was plenty of time to think about happiness.

She continued philosophising for a while, alone on the terrace. Then Lee came to announce that dinner was ready. Sara appeared to be absent, lost in her thoughts and dreams, so he came closer.

"What are you thinking about?" he asked, touching her hair softly with his hand.

She turned around and began smiling. "I find it funny that CVs seems to be so useless, yet people are so obsessed with having them."

"That's because people are not who they really are but who they pretend to be," replied Lee.

"Perhaps things never written in CVs can tell us a lot more about people."

"And I completely agree with you," he said, entertained, taking her hand and inviting her inside the dining room to join the others.

CHAPTER 4

Great artists don't necessarily need great talent

One day the master who was supposed to preside over the next game received the order to create a great artist.

The triumvirate had decided so for obvious reasons, and the master had no right to do otherwise or to question such sublime orders. The master informed a few men sitting around him about the orders received. Soon the news sparked around and the people looked busy trying to match the numbers from a list in front of them, previously prepared for the game, with the word "artist" spotlighted. All they had was a collection of numbers and colours, and that didn't seem to be very helpful. Perhaps the reader, the registrar keeping information on those people, could make a better guess, but he was not allowed to reveal any information or to give his personal opinion until the game was over.

The two players who were selected, according to the rules, from the members of the **Game of Power**, made themselves comfortable at a special table used exclusively for such high-profile activity. They started mixing pieces and then organised the pieces in a few stacks in front of them, with each group of stacks corresponding to the player's colour. Nervous and thrilled, they awaited the start of the game with great expectations. But the master looked busy chattering with some people whilst each player kept mixing pieces and arranging and rearranging them in stacks. In the meantime, members of the jury kept watching over them to make sure that no cheating occurred.

Finally, the master pointed his attention towards the two nominated players, giving the signal to start the game.

The completion of the pyramid went as usual, following the same rules. From the base to the top and line by line, every loop was completed with numbers one at a time, piece by piece, that were randomly chosen and haphazardly placed on the pyramid. The people watching the game kept themselves busy doing calculations and popping speculations, selecting different arrangements and permutations of numbers with each new move. They often started all over again, disappointed or excited. This frantic audience looked like a gigantic supercomputer doing complicated operations at a very high speed. However, there was a big difference between a gigantic supercomputer and this human supercomputer: humans were allowed to express their feelings. No wonder the audience could make biased speculations based on no apparent reasons. If someone fancied a certain number to be the winner, he or she would modify the entire configuration of numbers, creating a new pyramidal configuration according to expectations. When someone's favourite number was lost in the game, the person might scream or sigh in disappointment but would continue anyway, creating a new pyramid with the second favourite number until this number was lost too. Then everything started with a third favourite number. If the person didn't have one, that person might choose one of the numbers that he or she believed was more likely to win the game, and so forth . . .

The pyramid was nearly completed, just the last few pieces to play.

"Fifty-two blue," said the master, following every single move made by the players.

"Forty-nine white," said someone. "Piece rejected."

The rejected piece was put aside, and everyone took note of it. That piece was eliminated from the game and excluded from further calculations or speculations.

One player lost his turn.

"Sixteen red—game goes on," said someone else excitedly.

There were a few more moves until finally it was time to play the last piece.

"Forty-five black, rejected," people said.

In turn, the other player took it into action.

"Twenty-four red!" people shouted. "The game is over."

"Twenty-four red is the winner," the jury announced. "Who has twenty-four red?"

Two people raised their hands, and they were invited to show their configurations to the jury. The master examined them for a few seconds, approved their authenticity, and thus invited the two lucky men to take seats close to him. For the time being, they would receive a different award since the privilege of deciding the fate of the winner for that particular game was reserved for the triumvirate. As was the custom, they would form the jury in the next game, but if they preferred to change this honour into different favours, they had the chance to do it.

After calculating the points, one player was declared winner, and then they were invited to leave the scene.

The great moment for revealing the winner finally arrived. It was time for the reader to do his job. He took a deep breath and looked at the audience, terrified at this solemn moment. A great secret was on the way to being revealed; everyone was waiting for it, and the reader enjoyed keeping the audience in suspense. He took his time, as long as he could but not too long, just a few terrifying minutes, enough to make him a kingmaker.

"The winner is . . ." He paused for a few moments and then added, "Mr Michael Rimmer."

Reading from the winner's CV, people found out that this gentleman was a miner, recently made redundant and currently looking for a job. Of course, his skills and expertise had to be revealed to the audience. There were many grammatical and spelling mistakes in his CV, not to mention the writing style of this uneducated person. He seemed so direct and rough that his entire CV looked akin to a political pamphlet or a poem dedicated to the human lack of imagination. This poor individual appeared to lack any kind of professionalism or talent.

People started laughing and kept laughing loudly during the painful process of revealing the winner's "skills" and "expertise". There was nothing funnier than a rough fella without any artistic inclinations, who would shortly become a renowned artist. However, the real fun would start when people started buying his paintings or admiring them at exhibitions, not to mention this curious personage giving his expert advice or opinion on matters related to fine arts.

Michael was surprised to find an invitation for a job interview among too many rejection letters. The job was not specified, but he didn't mind. Finding a job at that time was a very challenging activity, and therefore any kind of job was good in order to get by.

At the interview, a well-dressed gent who appeared to be the leader of a business he'd never heard of was questioning him. His interviewer sat at a table with two more people, a man and a woman. Each of them examined Michael's CV carefully, passing it around amongst them. They looked very professional, too professional, and Michael began to feel embarrassed because of that situation. He was such a simple guy!

"Do you know how to paint, sir?" asked the lady unexpectedly.

"Never done it in my entire life!" he confessed with honesty.

"Your CV looks impressive," continued the man sitting in the middle, who was supposed to be the leader. "There are a few amazing skills: hard-working, perseverant, innovative, intuitive . . ." He stressed every single word—pausing after each of them.

"This is great," continued the other man. "And what an amazing character! Honesty, punctuality, tidiness, creativity . . ."

The man talking, and likewise his colleagues, seemed excited. They all suggested that Michael had hidden artistic skills, and they were ready to prove it. The leader picked up the phone and called a secretary. Michael was invited to follow her to the art department. They disappeared behind a closed door, and the three interviewers maintained their calm until a second door was heard closing. Then they were free to express their real feelings. The three of them started laughing uncontrollably—so much laughing that one could see the tears shed from their eyes.

Meanwhile, Michael found himself in the famous art department, and was told to begin painting something of his choice. He had everything he needed to finish within half an hour. The secretary made a quick presentation of the available tools and how everything needed to be used. He could start painting then.

After half an hour, the secretary announced that time was up and came to see Michael's accomplishment. A collection of lines, curves, and dots of different dimensions and colours, mixed up and juxtaposed in a chaotic way, formed an indecipherable painting. Michael had paint on his hands, face, neck, and clothes, and he was showing signs of anxiety and frustration. During the last half hour, he'd been struggling to maintain his calm and concentration. His big hands didn't seem adapted to handle such delicate tools for painting. But soon everything was finished, and he truly believed his first painting to be the last.

He reluctantly followed the secretary back to the same office, ready to face a harsh verdict, perhaps a deserved one for his lack of artistic qualities, carrying along the corridors his terrible masterpiece. The same people were awaiting him. Michael was invited to take a seat while the three people took possession of the painting and started examining it thoroughly with keen interest. They seemed to be impressed and kept commenting on it, mentioning different painting styles, different currents, and several far-famed artists that Michael had never heard of.

"This is a combination of impressionism, cubism, and futurism. The features are similar to . . ." the woman continued, and then she gave a few names and historical dates.

"However, there are few mistakes, but we believe you can improve your skills."

"You look very talented and show great imagination."

"This is great. Perhaps we can get it examined it by an expert," suggested one of the two men.

"We'll be contacting you in a few days, sir," concluded the person who appeared to be the leader.

They smiled at him in a friendly way, treating him like a great personality, while Michael listened, astonished and unable to say anything. He was soon free to leave, and once on the street, he began walking in a random direction without caring too much about his destination, trying to calm himself and to make sense of everything that had happened to him during the last hour.

A few days later, he received the positive news about his painting. An art critic gave very good feedback, thus he was invited for another interview.

Of the previous interviewers, only the woman was waiting for him, and she had two new people with her. They introduced themselves, shaking hands, as an art collector and an art adviser.

The former proposed to buy his painting by offering him a payment in advance—as an encouragement for his future work. What was being offered was something equivalent to the money he used to earn in a few months of hard work, before becoming redundant. Whereas the latter offered her services to him free of charge, promising to send him all the material needed as documentation on the subject, to visit him on a regular basis in order to give feedback for his work, and to organise exhibitions of his works in the future. Then Michael received the money and a big box containing painting tools and equipment. He could not have been happier.

The next day, he commenced his artistic life. He opened the big box and unpacked everything, placing each new item in the most suitable place for it. An entire room was filled with painting instrumentation. The only missing things were some imagination and an awful lot of talent.

Michael began sketching randomly chaotic shapes on the canvases, taking regular breaks for inspiration—in fact, too many breaks. He preferred drinking, and his new artistic life was so demanding that he entitled himself to more and more drinking. In less than a week, he discovered the secret of the trade and made it his artistic rule: Painting and swearing—swearing and painting

It didn't matter how he started his work or if he had any idea of what to do next. Everything would move around his rule of thumb: painting and swearing, swearing and painting. Sometimes the rule had to be slightly modified to painting and swearing or swearing and breaking things (or at least throwing them around). But then both his artistic feeling and the golden rule were retrieved. This was the case until the next time his inspiration refused to come around again.

Consequently, his girlfriend was terrified by Michael's artistic habits, but since he managed to sell a new painting every week at a good price and hence provided a secure source of income, she was disposed to endure this suffering. She didn't have a job either, and when Michael announced for the first time his artistic inclinations and talent, she was completely taken by surprise. She could have imagined Michael being anything but an artist. She suspected that such kinds of behaviour were perhaps how great artists lived their lives, with plenty of sacrifice and suffering.

This kind of suffering appeared to be long lasting, becoming a routine. Every morning after breakfast, Valerie left home for shopping and returned in the evening. In fact, she was terrified to stay at home during the daytime. Michael's artistic activity was very demanding, and the terrible noise he made scared her to death. As long as there was enough money to spend, shopping had to be her favourite hobby. Since Michael had been into painting, there seemed no more harmony in their relationship. Everything had changed, and it looked as if they had parallel lives like strangers. They appeared to have fewer and fewer things in common as well as fewer subjects for conversation. Thus Valerie was quite happy to wander around the town the entire day, keeping herself busy with trivial things she classified as high priority just to kill the boredom throughout the day.

On his own account, Michael had to work very hard in order to deliver enough paintings for his first exhibition. His art advisor appeared to be very excited about this exhibition and promised to contact relevant art critics and people from the media industry. The art advisor advocated this to be significant in promoting Michael's works and boosting his artistic career towards higher levels. Some celebrities would also be present, and that excited Michael more than having to go for interviews with journalists, answering all of their boring questions. Most of the journalists appeared to ask the same set of questions in a different order, and therefore Michael wondered whether they were pudding heads or they were just robots programmed using the same software but infected with a different virus. It seemed that journalists were in desperate need of great stories, and since he'd become a potential great story, all he had to do was to provide them with astonishing answers for their dull questions, even at the cost of talking nonsense.

Have a nice CV!

After settling himself in his new home, Stefan wanted to bring all his precious books from the forest. There were too many books to move alone, so he would need the help of his friends. However, since both David and Lee looked quite busy at that particular moment, David with his work and Lee with his involvement in the world of literature, Stefan had to postpone that mission for later.

Meanwhile, he took his investigating job very seriously. Upon Sara's request, he turned his attention to Mr Paul Taylor, the evil businessman with a dubious life. Stefan was surprised to discover that this personage lived in a villa with a huge garden.

Perhaps there is some work for me, he thought.

One day he began wandering around this villa, looking for anything that might be helpful to his investigation. There were many people working there, but he was only interested in seeing who the gardener was. Once he recognised him, Stefan prepared his plan of attack. Day after day, following from a distance, he discovered the gardener's routines. He had breakfast at the same coffee shop in the morning and then stopped for a beer at a bar in the evening.

"Great!" Stefan exclaimed, excited. "How about I invite him for a beer?"

Thus he made sure to let it happen at the gardener's favourite bar at the right time, and Stefan entered when he saw him entering. The gardener ordered a beer and sat at a table facing the television. There was something about sports on TV. Stefan ordered a beer too and sat at a table close to the gardener's table. There were few people around, some of them watching TV, some just sitting at their tables and talking or simply looking out the window, absorbed in their own thoughts.

Stefan introduced himself, and the gardener was pleased to have someone to talk to. They began talking about sports, but minutes later, the conversation changed to their professions.

"I'm a gardener too!" said Stefan.

The gardener seemed excited to meet someone who liked the same things he liked. Thus they started talking about their favourite subject—gardening—and seemed at ease with each other after the second beer.

"Tell me about your work," said Stefan, visibly impressed by his new friend.

Philip, the gardener, happily talked about his great work, how he dealt with everyday problems, the challenges he faced, and most important of all, his great achievements. Stefan pretended to have some problems with his garden, and he asked his new friend for advice. He listened to Paul with great interest and considered himself lucky to have a chance to meet such a helpful friend. Among all the questions about gardening, Stefan occasionally asked subtle questions of interest to him. He talked about his employer—an imaginary employer, not the real one—and began complaining about him, forcing the gardener to talk about his employer and to complain too. When talking about one's boss, there was always something to complain about. The gardener took that opportunity and began giving incriminating details about his boss. Among those crimes, Stefan found out that the evil man had the habit of hosting big parties and destroying his precious plants when getting drunk.

"That is outrageous!" Stefan shouted, revolted.

Then he wanted to know how such a crime happened. The gardener was revolted too, and his anger against his ungrateful employer escalated with the increasing amount of beer consumed. Apart from the gardener's own family, Stefan was the first one to show compassion for the gardener's hard work, so the latter opened his heart, removing all defences. When the discussion came about their salaries, again a good reason for anger, Stefan suggested that Mr Philip deserved almost double for his titanic efforts.

Since both gardeners had odious employers, one real and one imaginary, and since both of them were equally upset, this conversation continued until the bar staff announced the closure time. Almost drunk, the two new friends said goodbye to each other, promising to take revenge against their ingrate employers and to leave them at the first opportunity.

When finally alone, Stefan had good reason to be happy. He had all the information he needed for the completion of his mission.

David listened to this story in amazement. He was still awake, reading a poetry book recently acquired from his favourite bookshop, when Stefan returned home.

"Are you saying that this gardener is ready to leave his job at the first opportunity?"

"Exactly," confirmed Stefan. "Perhaps if we can create a job for him that pays better and is more exciting, Mr Taylor will have to look for a new gardener."

That was good news indeed. Lee and Sara had to be informed immediately.

Next day, in the evening, they all got together: David, Stefan, Sara, Lee, and Julia. Luckily, Julia managed to take an extra day off. Her protecting mother had decided to be generous and to spare her precious words of wisdom for another time. Living around Signora Giorgia for too long seemed to give people the desire to go live in a universe of complete stupidity than have to endure the torture of too much wisdom.

David consulted Lee and everyone present about how to get rid of Philip, the undesirable gardener. Sara suggested focussing on David's many business partners. There had to be one of them desperate enough and in need of a great business opportunity. If such a person also happened to have a garden, then everything was sorted out. This desperate businessman would have to employ the desperate gardener with a good salary in exchange for a better business partnership. They agreed, and Sara offered to find out who might be the best person suitable for their scheme.

But the hardest thing was convincing Stefan of the purpose of a CV. He would definitely need a *great* CV in order to acquire the soon-to-be vacant job. If there was anything he hated most, that was writing CVs, and everyone knew it. How to convince that obstinate lad to accept the facts and to compromise for a bit?

"But I refuse to write this ridiculous CV," he said, determined. Everyone was laughing.

"You don't have to . . . There are plenty of professional CV-writing experts," Sara assured him.

Minutes later, after a lot of fun and encouragement, Stefan finally agreed to break his anti-CV-writing rules and to give the experts the chance to show to the world how great he was and how great his achievements were.

Sara, who perhaps had to write more CVs than all her friends combined, and who just a few weeks before was engaged full time, out of desperation, in the world of CV writing, had the best links to the most relevant and professional experts. She could have written Stefan CV herself, but she found this activity of inventing lies too depressing, so she wrote down an address and handed it to Stefan, wishing him all the best.

Stefan reluctantly opened a door and entered a huge office with plenty of people. There was no private space except for the toilets. Everything was just a huge room with desks perfectly aligned and extremely tidy. There was no room for errors. Everything had its precise place, giving the impression of working with nanotechnology. In the middle was an empty space, with benches and sofas forming a ring. A corner was equipped with a coffee machine, a fridge, cups, and other utensils needed for quick snacks and drinks.

That was the brainstorm region. For people who don't understand such great scientific expressions, that was the pandemonium region. People were supposed to go there to exchange ideas and opinions, ask for advice and help, and above all, make a lot of noise and confusion. That was the spot where all great ideas were generated.

It appeared that the universe had a similar beginning. For some strange reasons, all the primordial molecules of the universe started bullying and hating each other. Such *civilised* behaviour resulted in the Great Pandemonium—called big bang by scientists, that is—an event of great agitation and infinite confusion.

Not surprisingly, creating great new ideas was similar to creating a new universe. It involved a lot of suffering.

Entering that intimidating place for the first time, one was unable to tell what everything was all about, but seeing the well-dressed people, their smiley faces and their confident and optimistic attitudes, one could figure out that they had to be some kind of experts in something.

Someone welcomed him with a smile and invited him to take a seat. Before having the chance to say anything, Stefan was told that his problem was almost sorted out, whatever it was. He was in the hands of the greatest experts on this planet. Well dressed and with a positive attitude, all smiling, with precise professional movements, the person talking to Stefan inspired confidence—in fact, too much confidence, to the point of frustrating and irritating him. He did his best to maintain calm and to show a similar smiley face.

He would have the greatest CV ever written, Stefan was told. As a special customer, he deserved great treatment, and the person talking invited him for coffee.

"Now, tell me the great things about yourself" his host said while preparing coffee.

"I am a gardener," he said.

But before he had the chance to finish what he was going to say, the expert exclaimed, "Great! Absolutely amazing!"

Stefan appeared unable to continue, embarrassed by that sudden interruption. His interlocutor, however, offered help, asking many questions—actually too many of them—and taking notes now and again. Stefan struggled, of course, against the confusing questions, but his interviewer offered plenty of help with ready-made suggestions prepared in advance. Hesitantly, he managed to keep talking, but he was constantly interrupted by exclamations such as Great! Amazing! Fantastic! Astonishing! Wonderful! Unbelievable! Blah, blah, blah. The person talking to him was definitely an expert, and he knew what he was doing, Stefan concluded hopefully, but the bombardment of positive adjectives followed by exhilarant exclamations could be hard to tolerate.

What is so great about being a gardener? he wondered, without finding it necessary to express his real feelings.

The painful interview lasted for about fifteen minutes, and Stefan had moments when he was truly tempted to stand up and slap the expert, at the cost of renouncing forever the privilege of having a CV. Finally the interview ended . . . and likewise his suffering. He was invited to wait for few minutes until his great CV was ready.

Looking around and scanning people's behaviour and speech, Stefan realised their entire energy seemed to be focused on the same thing: writing great CVs. So great that he wondered whether it would be possible to invent something greater than a great CV. Someone left, and instead of wishing him a good day, he heard people shouting, "Have a nice CV, sir!"

What! Stefan thought, astonished and unable to believe what he'd just heard.

"Have a nice CV indeed, all of you," was the reply.

Apparently, writing CVs was not ridiculous enough; they had to invent something even more ridiculous.

Since writing CVs became the new philosophy of life, people were so obsessed with it to the point of becoming absurd. Stefan was scared by the prospect of having to respond with the same fateful remark: "Have a nice CV!" and thus he felt an urge to leave at once without looking back. However, he desperately needed that ridiculous CV. That was how society worked, and he was forced to abide by the rules, even if those rules exasperated him. Encouraging himself with the thought that shortly everything would be over, he waited, terrified, for the fatal moment when he would have to say goodbye.

The moment of terror came soon. The smiley expert handed him a piece of paper, visibly proud of his work, and asked with exquisite exuberance, "What do you think, sir?"

Stefan took the damn CV and stared at it without reading anything, fearing he would be tempted to slap his interlocutor.

"Perfect!" he said, heading immediately to the door, praising their professionalism and expertise, thanking them for the great treatment, and promising to tell everyone how great they were. Such a desperate gesture spared him the need to salute with the fateful "Have a nice CV!" and soon he disappeared through the door without further elaboration.

"Have a nice CV, sir!" Stefan heard from behind him, but he was determined not to answer.

CVs can contain more lies than a political manifesto

"Your CV contains more lies than a political manifesto," asserted Lee, laughing.

Stefan had decided to visit his friend to provide some fantastic news: he finally got a CV!

The two examined it, entertained and dissecting every positive adjective, trying to figure out what the heck it possibly meant. Since the CV-writing syndrome infected society, experts kept themselves busy inventing intimidating adjectives, and the folks struggled to understand them.

"I never knew you had such great qualities," said Lee, who decided to have a little fun at his friend's expense.

"I never knew it either," he replied.

"Just by looking at those adjectives, you would make a great politician."

However, Stefan was determined not to become a politician, whatever his wonderful qualities were.

They laughed. There was nothing funnier than examining a fantastic CV.

"Sara would like to see it too. Do you mind if I send her a copy?"

"No problem," he said, amused.

Perhaps Sara needed to read fantastic things in order to feel less miserable.

In a few days, the gardener left his job for a better position elsewhere, and his place remained vacant. Stefan sent his astonishing CV and waited impatiently. That could be his first job interview ever, where he had the chance to prove his expertise. Nevertheless, there was a catch. There were too many lies in his CV, more than he had told in his entire life, and he had no idea how to deal with the huge amount of lies. He was not used to talking about great things he'd never done in his life. Wondering how the majority of people were able to fake their expertise, he prepared himself as best he could. His friends offered help, of course, most importantly Sara, who went to more job interviews than all of them combined.

She explained to him the main questions to be expected in a job interview, mentioning the question about dinosaurs, which seemed very popular and the most related to the future job. He took note of it and promised not to forget about dinosaurs. Then she talked about professionalism, confidence, and positive attitude—qualities every candidate had to have in order to get a job. However, the most difficult part was explaining the *great* things about himself to the future employer. Perhaps it would have been easier to do what everyone else did in such a situation: lie. Everyone was lying, they told him, and this was what he had to do. But lying was not easy for someone without experience in this field, and for the first time, he felt jealous of politicians. It seemed to come so naturally to them.

One should never underestimate the effect of a "great" CV on a potential employer. Soon Stefan had the confirmation that his CV had made the desired impact. He was consequently invited for an interview at the address he already knew.

Someone invited him inside, informing him that he was being expected. The charismatic Mr Taylor sat on a sofa studying some documents arranged on a table in front of him. The door facing the garden was open, and Stefan could hear some people outside, mostly girls, talking. Mr Taylor seemed like the kind of man who was never alone. He greeted his guest and invited him to take a seat whilst he took all the documents off the table and put them in a bag.

"Would you like anything to drink, sir?" Mr Taylor asked after he was done with his documents.

"Coffee, please."

Stefan definitely needed a strong coffee to be able to maintain his calm. He knew that the person in front of him was not what he seemed to be, and therefore Stefan didn't want to reveal his real feelings or to induce any suspicions.

They moved into the garden. It was a beautiful day, and a table sitting in the shadow of the trees made the perfect place to talk about CVs. A girl brought the coffee and some cookies, placing them on the table. Then she disappeared behind a bush and sat with the other girls.

Following a precise ceremony and with gracious gestures, Mr Taylor served his guest coffee and then served himself.

"So . . . what do you think about my garden?"

"It looks great," Stefan confessed.

At that point, Mr Taylor began his professional speech by introducing himself and giving some details about his work in the financial sector. Stefan was able to find out that Mr Taylor was a financial advisor, and amongst his clients were some of the biggest businesses in town. For such a big town, Mr Taylor must have made plenty of money, Stefan concluded. He also mentioned his private businesses: a few shops, one holiday resort, and a few websites involved in various activities.

Stefan was visibly impressed. Having the privilege to meet such a great person was not something that happened every day.

"Now, tell me something *great* about yourself," said Mr Taylor with emphasis, after being sure that his guest was well aware of the chance given to him.

Stefan was expecting that question but completely forgot the professional answers provided by his friends. All he could remember was the story about dinosaurs.

"If I were a dinosaur . . ." he began, embarrassed and not finishing the sentence.

Mr Taylor, whose next question was probably about dinosaurs, seemed to be rather disappointed that someone had taken his idea. However, he was determined to keep the conversation on his grounds. "Well, what would you do?"

Stefan thought for a moment. What was the craziest thing a dinosaur could do? "I would become a politician," Stefan replied proudly.

"What!"

The girls started laughing from behind the bushes. There were other people around, and they started laughing too.

"I've heard of a horse becoming a politician, but I've never imagined a dinosaur politician!" said Mr Taylor, clearly astonished.

"But they are like dinosaurs," Stefan said, mostly to himself. "Politicians seem to live in a parallel universe with no contact with real life. They are supposed to sort out our problems, but they seem to be better at creating more troubles in comparison with their ability to truly solve problems. Politicians have created more troubles on this planet in ten thousand years of recorded history than the dinosaurs did in two hundred million years! At least there was a huge asteroid heading towards the earth to wipe dinosaurs out, putting an end to an era. I reckon we are not that lucky. Are we?"

Mr Taylor looked impressed by his funny guest. The others joined the conversation. Stefan was the hero of the day, and he was given the job.

Talent is useless without great opportunities

One day Lisa called Sara on the phone, sounding excited. She had a great story to tell and wondered if they could meet somewhere.

"I'm free tonight—with nothing to do," she emphasised. Sara had had a hard day, but she didn't mind meeting her friend.

"Perhaps Julia is free too," Sara said with hope. "Let me call her." Luckily, Julia was also free, so they agreed to meet somewhere in town.

Meanwhile, Lee called Sara, wondering what she was doing. She explained to him about the sudden decision to go out. Of course, he was invited to join them if he fancied. Or why not invite everyone else, perhaps? Lee took responsibility to phone the other guys to see if they were available for a night out. Whatever they were doing, it was time to take a break.

They met on a promenade, and everybody was happy to see one another. But secretly, each of them was happier to see a particular person. Mark was more interested in seeing Lisa, while Lee decided to pop over just to see Sara. Julia and Stefan felt comfortable together, although neither of them wanted to admit it. David preferred to see Susan, but there was nothing he could do about it.

There were a few empty benches, and they chose the one that made them feel more comfortable.

Then it was time for everyone to confess his or her latest sins.

Since Lisa had had the idea of organizing that night out, she had the privilege of starting first.

"Now, Lisa, tell us your story."

Lisa's great story began with fine-tuning her voice. She was invited two days before to accompany Mr Hook, her boss, to an art gallery. There were other people coming along with them, and she was happy with that. Once there, she was surprised by the presence of so many people: plenty of journalists, art critics, and people from high society, plus other celebrities. Mr Hook was invited specially to promote the work of a new celebrity: Mr Michael Rimmer. Apparently, this new great talent was discovered by chance by a famous art critic, and since then, his brush had created a few masterpieces sold at a high price. Lisa became curious, looking forward to her first encounter with the *great* artist.

Mr Hook, an expert in many fields, was also a famous expert in fine art. That was a great opportunity to show his expertise. Furthermore, especially for the great event, he had prepared an impressive as well as touching speech. As always, he looked great, confident, and intimidating. Every single act seemed to be calculated with infinite precision. Every single word appeared the greatest word ever said. Every single person present was supposed to admire and envy his awe-inspiring talent.

He entered the exhibition with gracious moves and a shiny, twinkly face. He walked like a celebrity, talked like a celebrity, and smiled like a celebrity. Moreover, he seemed to ignore everybody . . . like a celebrity.

People greeted him and gathered around him to hear his *divine* voice. Mr Hook, however, was too professional to stop for insignificant things such as talking to his admirers. He had decided to be professional until the end and to show everybody how a professional person should be. This illustrious artist in the media industry was heading towards another noted artist present in this exquisite society—the painter. Both artists greeted each other with pompous adjectives and finely chosen compliments. Then they made the tour around the exhibition, stopping in front of every painting, followed by other art critics, journalists, and the rest of the attendees.

Lisa felt overwhelmed and lost in front of so much ceremony. But she fell soon into obscurity and felt completely ignored by the great personalities present. She was neither an artist nor a celebrity. As such, there was no place for her. Perhaps if she was able to prove her admiration for arts, she might have been accepted as a human being.

The two great artists continued to be the centre of everybody's attention. As a great art critic, Mr Hook examined every masterpiece and gave his precious verdict, while people around desperately strived to grasp every single word of wisdom.

"This is a combination of futuristic multidimensional super-realistic . . ." Mr Hook said with emphasis—congratulating the great artist for the perfect combination of . . . Then followed a curious combination of words that none of the people present, except for Mr Hook, were able to understand.

Lisa couldn't hear more. People around sounded very excited and impressed by the great masterpiece in front of them. Lisa finally managed to make her way inside the exhibition and headed towards one of the paintings with fewer people around. The great masterpiece displayed was the ugliest thing she'd ever seen in her life. It was impossible to tell what it genuinely represented or what the intention of its creator was. Lisa walked to the next painting with more hope and saw similar horrible shapes. The next one was even uglier than the previous two put together!

She could not believe that such a mess could be called art and that people could make so much fuss over such nonsense. Just because someone who claimed to be an expert called it art, it was not necessarily art.

"I can see in your work a new tendency towards a different approach of expressing beauty . . ." Lisa heard Mr Hook saying, and she began smiling. Fortunately, nobody saw her committing such sacrilege.

Completely disappointed, Lisa decided to stay out of the way, leaving the artists to continue with their mockery. She'd truly had enough and felt frankly happy for being ignored. But her moments of terror and exasperation had not finished yet.

After admiring the *masterpieces*, Mr Hook was ready for his impressive speech. Lisa forced herself not to listen, but she caught, against her will, a huge amount of pompous positive adjectives, too many of them. People were touched; plenty of applause followed.

"Someone who is able to create such amazing masterpieces can master any form of arts." Mr Hook was interrupted again by a spate of ardent applause.

"Do you like poetry, sir?" he asked, turning around and gazing at the newly created celebrity painter.

"Never read it in my life," he confessed with honesty.

"Fantastic! I want to prove to the world that you are a poet too." Mr Hook received extra applause.

"I was able to see your poetic skills in your works. Every single one of your paintings sounds like a great poem. Now, I want you to take a pen and write the first poem of your life."

The people, in delirium, invited the great artist to write the requested poem.

"He is an artist, and he can do it," people said with confidence and hope.

"Silence, please!" said Mr Hook with authority. "He is trying to concentrate."

Minutes passed, and people waited in silence to see the miracle. The creation of a great poem was not an easy task. Fortunately, the person trying to do it was an artist. People waited impatiently for the great moment when their expectations will come to life. Nothing was moving, nothing was changing, and Lisa was afraid to breathe. Half an hour later, the painter gave up, defeated. Mr Hook, of course, saved the reputation of the great artist by saying that masterpieces are ideally born within the ambiance of complete silence and isolation. Artists cannot cope with distractions. Artists should be left to live in their own world . . .

"And then?" asked Sara curiously.

"Then we left the great artist *in his own world*," said Lisa, entertained.

"And this means . . . ?" asked Julia, trying to find out what happened next.

"Everyone went home, but the artistic reputation of Mr Rimmer is not affected."

"How come?"

"He was invited as a special guest to Mr Hook's TV night show. Until the beginning of the show, everyone forgot the incident. There was no mention about it whatsoever. Thus Mr Rimmer was presented as an influential artist with superhuman talent and an inspiring life."

The group of friends began discussing the amazing power and influence over people that the media had. If they decided to make someone a superhuman, they were able do it, since it was easy to ignore the bad things and inflate the good things.

All the newspapers seemed to follow the same philosophy. Every article had a big shocking title that told everything about a story. Then a lot of nonsense followed. Perhaps it would be more practical to read only the titles to save a lot of time. The other media organisations, such as radio, television, and online platforms, were somewhat organised on the same principles. People should be shocked in order to capture their attention. Keeping their attention for longer was more difficult but not impossible. That was the reason why great experts such as Mr Hook would always uphold an occupation.

Fifty shades of crap

"Well, this story is astonishing," said Mark, ready to show his compassion for Lisa.

"I guess your passion for artistic exhibitions has ended for good," said Julia, laughing.

Lisa, nonetheless, was not laughing. She seemed still terrified and distressed by that incredible artistic event and definitely needed some encouragement after such a nauseating experience.

"Come on, Lisa, it's not the end of the world. This is how life works, and you have to admit it. Good people never make it to the top."

Sara hugged her friend and felt much better.

"Perhaps you'd like to hear something even more astonishing," enquired David.

"As long as you don't start with the shocking bit first," replied Lee, mocking the journalistic shock culture.

"Only if you promise to include a good deal of suspense," said Sara, finishing Lee's idea.

"Yeah, this story has a lot of suspense, enough to keep you on tenterhooks," David assured them. He began his story . . .

Once upon a time, there was a woman with a broken life and no future prospects. She was struggling to find a job and the money was never enough, so she had to rely on money provided by the local authorities along with help from friends. Out of desperation, she decided to write a book, which publishers completely ignored. One day an editor brought her manuscript home to have a look, and one of his nephews happened to like it. The manuscript was thus published and became an international sensation in less than a year. Then more books followed—all of them bestsellers. Mrs Floyd soon became one of the richest females in the world, just by writing stories about witches and wizards. People craved her books ferociously, and many movies were produced after them, further increasing her wealth. She became an international authority on matters related to writing books, and everyone sought her opinion. Her talent remained incontestable until a few weeks ago . . .

To prove to herself and to the world her great gift, Mrs Floyd decided to publish a new book under a different name. Although the new work was well displayed in the bookshops and well advertised, she did not manage to sell more than five hundred copies during the period of anonymity. A book put on display in bookshops can have a positive impact on sales. When one had enough money, he or she could finance the creation of a great book cover and publish with a great publisher. Despite all that, she did not manage to sell up to her expectations. No one noticed her book, and no one stated that it was great.

To end her misery and humiliation, a journalist decided to reveal the real author. Consequently, she sold an astonishing amount of books on the first day. Imagine! Her publisher had to print her book at the maximum capacity due to the astronomical increase in sales.

Of course, plenty of publishers and journalists, embarrassed by such an event, had to invent a credible story in order to save their public images and reputations. Since Mrs Floyd also had a reputation to defend, plenty of embarrassed experts had to use their influence for modifying the entire story. Soon, the less than 500 copies sold before the revelation became a bunch of thousand. In the end, it became *more* than 8,500. All of the people involved seemed to be busy proving that they knew in advance how great the book really was.

The book was well displayed in bookshops and highly publicised in the biggest newspapers. Plenty of reviews written by the biggest experts praised the great talent of the author. What's more, the reprints of the book contained a huge amount of touching and pathetic reviews written by impressed and faithful readers.

Her book eventually became a bestseller.

David took a deep breath. Everyone was watching Lee.

"I know what you're going to say, but please don't say it," he said, embarrassed.

"It's not your fault," Sara assured him.

"What is your honest opinion about this book?" asked Julia.

"Nothing special about it. Just average," said David.

"Is it worth reading?"

Julia looked at David, expecting his answer.

"If you ignore the nonsense written on its covers, and the fantastic reviews, you might have a pleasant read. It isn't that bad, but neither is it that great."

"Where is the suspense in this story?" enquired Lisa after David had finished.

Stefan started smiling. He knew already the answer. David had brought to his attention another similar success story a few days before, and they had discussed it.

"Suspense is to be found in newspapers. This story is just a fraction of what is really happening," replied Stefan.

"What do you mean?" asked Lisa, watching him.

"People seem unable to think for themselves, as this story shows."

"True," agreed Lee. "If a story is a great one, why does it need a big name to support it?"

"Are you hinting about the *Fifty Shades* syndrome?" asked Sara hesitantly.

"Yes," replied Lee.

"What is this syndrome all about?" asked Julia. No one answered, and she continued: "I want to know, please."

"Someone wrote a crappy book having the fateful title *Fifty Shades* . . . of something. Unfortunately for us, this book happened to become an international bestseller. Astonished by its success, during the following months, people published desperately thousands of crappy books with the suggestive title *Fifty Shades* . . . of anything. It's just utter madness."

Lee stopped talking. His explanation seemed to be clear enough.

"If you go to any bookshop, there are plenty of useless books starting with this disgraceful name. People's obsession for success has no limit."

David was right. The sad thing was to see such successful publishers publishing such nonsense. Was there anybody who still believed in quality and thus gave it precedence over money?

"If you put all those painful books together in a collection, how would you name them?" asked Julia curiously.

"*Fifty Shades of Crap!*" replied Lee and David at once. They all laughed.

At first, there was a syndrome of superheroes, followed by a syndrome of witches and wizards, then the madness about vampires and monsters. Subsequently, people became obsessed with *fifty shades* of anything. Then humanity had a glorious return to superheroes. The multitude of movies made recently expressed clearly people's obsession with superheroes. There was no room for anything else . . .

Lee had plenty of reasons to feel guilty. "I promise solemnly not to write any more books about superheroes."

The girls giggled, entertained.

The herd culture managed to corrupt him too. The temptation was too big, and he therefore had no idea of being wrong. Fortunately, Lee managed to wake up in time. His next book would make no mention whatsoever of superheroes, vampires, or any other ridiculous characters dictated by the herd.

CV or not CV; this is the answer

Sara wanted to know how Stefan found his new job, his boss, and his spying mission.

The work was going well, he assured her, and his boss seemed quite happy about it. So far, he was unable to discover anything useful that might have been beneficial to their inquiry. Poor Susan! She would have to endure more suffering.

Sara felt sad at the thought of unlucky Susan.

"Let's go for a drink," someone suggested.

Good idea. They needed some refreshments.

While everyone was busy talking, David was working silently on his new poem:

> CV or not CV; forget the question!
> What is this madness?
> What is your crime?
> Why are you running like a lunatic?
> Why are you busy
> And have no time?
> You are pathetic, like all the losers
> Who fight and struggle
> For greatness. Please!
> Wake up and stop now this crazy running—
> Your life is wasted
> Writing CVs.
> This is ridiculous.
> No, it's not. Everyone does it.
> This is the poem of a wasted life.
> So is this what you call life?
> Writing CVs?
> Running the whole life like a lunatic
> And never taking a break,
> Always saying, "I am busy."
> Ignoring your friends
> And ignoring your family—
> If you are lucky enough to have friends,
> And if you are lucky enough to have a family—

Feeling guilty for not doing enough,
Not for your friends,
Not for your family.
For a piece of paper instead!
A ridiculous piece of paper!
And then you die;
You die alone.
You die with your piece of paper,
Regretting that there was not enough time
To write a better piece of paper
But if you had another chance
To start all over again,
Would you love your friends, family, and life?
Or would you
Want to be great
And have a piece of paper,
And this piece of paper would tell everyone
How great you are
And all the great things you did
During the short fraction of time
You call life . . .
Too short and not enough
To do even greater things
And to write them on a piece of paper
And to die
Alone
With your piece of paper—
With your ridiculous and useless piece of paper—
And then you realise
That you wasted your time
Writing CVs
When there was no need for so much suffering
And there was no question . . .
CV or not CV; this is the answer.

"Wondering if the horse politician had a CV," said Stefan unexpectedly.

They were sitting outside at a table, not far from a mobile bar that was still open. There were many people sitting at various tables, on some benches, or simply on the ground.

"A horse politician?"

The girls tittered, amused by such an unexpected story.

"There was an emperor who wanted to show how useless the politicians were. So he made his horse a politician and granted him great honours."

Unable to believe it, the girls kept laughing.

"And what did the horse do?" asked Julia curiously.

"Exactly the same thing politicians do today: nothing!" said Lee, feeling happy with his reply.

"It's a pity that they had no CVs during that time," said Sara, starting a new round of giggles. "Just imagine what great qualities the poor horse had."

"With references from the emperor," emphasised Lisa.

They continued laughing, making fun of the unlucky horse that was made politician against his will. It seemed that even horses felt offended if called politicians.

Lee had an idea.

At another table was a woman with a dog. He borrowed a sheet of paper and a pen from a man sitting nearby, and moments later, he was sitting at her table. After introducing himself, he asked her with a solemn voice, "Does he have a CV?"

"Who?"

"Your dog. Does he have a CV?"

The woman burst into laughter upon hearing such an unexpected question.

"What is he doing?" asked one of the girls.

No one had any idea yet.

People around recognised Lee and hence came closer to see what was happening. Lee took the sheet of paper and wrote the headline: CV.

"What is the name of the dog?" he asked.

"Kheops. His name is Kheops," said the woman, continuing to laugh.

Lee wrote the name down and was ready to ask a new question.

"Is he a pharaoh?" someone intervened.

"What a great name for a dog!" someone said, laughing. "Kheops, ha ha ha!"

"No, he is not a pharaoh, unfortunately," confirmed the woman, entertained but looking disappointed.

"What is his profession?" asked Lee again.

"What?" The woman kept laughing, astonished by such unexpected questions.

Lee assertively repeated the question. "What is the dog's profession?"

"Of course. He's a dog," suggested someone in a vehement outcry.

A few teenagers took out their phones and started recording.

"Dog is not a profession," replied Lee. "He must be an expert in something."

People agreed. Everyone had to be an expert in something, even the dogs.

"Secret agent?" tried someone in glee.

"Lawyer, perhaps."

"What about a financial advisor?"

Financial advisor seemed to be the perfect profession for such a cute dog, so he wrote it down.

People ordered more drinks. Lee was the new superhero, and there was something to celebrate.

Soon people began an arduous debate about the dog's qualifications, main strengths and weaknesses, work experience, and anything related to his personal profile and hobbies. Many positive adjectives were being suggested, and therefore the atmosphere became so darn inflammatory that one could hardly hear Lee talking. There was just too much noise and fuss around him.

The great CV was finally completed, and Lee handed it to the owner of the dog, receiving plenty of applause and an ovation from the merry audience. He then managed to escape the crowd, leaving the poor dog surrounded by his new admirers.

Joining his friends, Lee was received with warm compliments. They never believed he would do that.

After this moment of excitement was over, David invited them all to visit his house and to spend the rest of the night together.

On TV, the news was about Lee and about a dog able to predict the market fluctuations by the movement of his tail! In such a short period, his great achievement became international news. The major newspapers published the written CV in big bold fonts on the first page. He was again at the focus of the media attention—this time ridiculing both superheroes and experts. He finally had his revenge.

The aliens must be antidemocratic!

Lee opened the door and welcomed his friend. "Tell me what happened."

Mark didn't answer. He looked terribly sad and completely changed. Lee was surprised to see his friend in such a bad status and tried to figure out what possibly went wrong. They were both free that day and had decided to meet to discuss Mark's progress concerning his manuscript. On the phone, Mark seemed rather excited about his latest findings and wanted to share them with his friend.

"Are you going to tell me?" asked Lee again.

Mark began mumbling something undecipherable. He was clearly upset.

"Look, if you don't tell me, I don't know how to help you," Lee tried again.

Mark finally decided to talk. He was queuing in a shop to buy something. There were many people around, and the queue was going very slowly. Appearing from the middle of nowhere, one of his former colleagues at the university—who happened to be a very successful person—decided to be nasty and to have some fun. Accompanied by a few girls, this man had good motivation to display his greatness. So he drew close against Mark, making sure that as many people as possible could hear, and asked with malice, "Are you still working as a cleaner?"

Embarrassed and shocked, Mark tried to avoid the answer by changing the subject. But his old colleague didn't want to give up.

"So how is the cleaning going?"

Mark answered, frustrated that he did no more cleaning jobs, but his friend pretended not to hear his answer.

"Is this what you are doing the whole day, cleaning?"

The girls began laughing and the nasty man clearly felt great. None of the girls protested for treating an old friend like that. Making fun of someone was a good opportunity to show the world one's inferiority. They were impressed. Girls usually liked guys who could impress them. People around had fun too, and all of them looked with amusement at Mark, who preferred to remain in silence, ashamed.

"Are you free this week? I have some *cleaning* to do," asked the teaser again, stressing the world cleaning, making sure people around could hear him well.

The nasty "friend" eventually left.

Lee wondered if this successful personage was in good relation with Mark's former teachers. Of course he was, asserted Mark; otherwise, he had no chance to reach greatness alone, by himself. This former colleague was a great admirer and supporter of all those strange theories that made no sense.

Lee felt sorry for his friend's public humiliation and tried to raise his morale. Perhaps keeping him busy was the quickest and the best way to make him forget his misery.

"Tell me about your progress," Lee asked, changing subject.

Mark started talking, but Lee didn't seem to follow. He was almost lost in his thoughts.

He wondered why humans were such nasty creatures and why appearances were the only thing that counted in life. No wonder humans preferred a fake version of themselves to show to the world. Reputation was therefore nothing more than appearances. People fought desperately for their reputations, but they were actually fighting to maintain a set of lies.

A CV was a document that *proved* a person's reputation. But what about CVs that showed the real version of that person? Lee had seen many people with perfect CVs who were just nasty, filthy, irresponsible, careless, and impossible in real life.

Perhaps that nasty gentleman was not the one to blame. Society was too obsessed with appearances. Society allowed such unscrupulous people to make it to the top. Most celebrities had dirty secrets: cheating, lying, stealing, bullying, and so on. They made it to the top by taking advantage of the nice people, and the nice people would always be the losers. And then the same nice people, bullied, intimidated, cheated, underappreciated, and taken advantage of, would later become admirers of the celebrities who played all those dirty games on them. Alas!

Not surprisingly, most celebrities treated their employees badly. Apparently, humiliating someone was the easiest way to prove that person's inferiority.

If people with superpowers, superheroes, really did exist, they would not use their superpowers to save the world, as insistently displayed in the movies. Instead, superheroes would use their superpowers for bullying people, beating, torturing, and killing them, raping, robbing, and making a life of hell to their admirers. Superheroes would then subdue and enslave people who desperately needed so much help . . .

"Can you repeat that again, please?" asked Lee, finally deciding to participate in the conversation.

Mark was saying that the decimal system was wrong. The decimal base was too small for our current needs. With the advance of science, numbers became bigger and bigger, and they had become difficult to handle. Moreover, the decimal base was difficult for calculations. The number ten had too few divisors; besides, it was not practical. The number ten created too much confusion and too many difficulties, Mark concluded.

"What would be the alternative?" Lee wanted to know.

"The number sixty," replied Mark, excited. He'd been thinking for a long time about modifying the entire physics book and changing all the physical constants in favour of the base sixty.

"Why the number sixty, in particular?" asked Lee.

"Because it is a practical number; it has a lot of divisors, it's a bigger base, and it allows more permutations. Calculations in base sixty will result in fewer decimals, and the numbers will become much smaller. On top of that, if alien civilisations existed and they were advanced enough, they would definitely use the base sixty."

"I guess your aliens must have sixty fingers," said Lee, amused.

"The number of fingers has nothing to do with the maths. The decimal system is wrong, regardless of the number of fingers we have."

Mark took a deep breath, and Lee waited for him to continue.

"Having ten fingers is just a biological accident, and this does not justify our obsession with the number ten. Whether we like it or not, the decimal system is wrong. The only reason we continue to use it is because we are too lazy to admit it—and hence to make the necessary change."

"And what would be that necessary change?" *The discussion is getting interesting*, he thought.

"Accepting the fact that we are wrong and have been wrong for the last three hundred years. We should get rid of this ridiculous decimal system and use the base sixty instead."

"But this would imply learning sixty new characters. You know how lazy people are and how reluctant they can be when it comes to learning anything novel and useful."

"People use hundreds of thousands of applications on their phones. Every person wastes his or her time memorising thousands or more of those useless apps. Learning sixty new characters is not the end of the world. My idea is very simple. Have a look at this."

Mark looked for a sheet of paper and began sketching while his friend watched in silence. The final draft contained two columns of sixty new characters with their equivalent in the decimal system. The new characters followed a precise pattern. Every single character was somehow similar to the letter L, with equal size, rotated in space in the four available positions. Inside this character was inserted a combination of dots and lines, fifteen of them for each rotation. A line represented five dots, and there were only three lines allowed in each quadrant. Altogether, there were sixty combinations forming the characters for the base sixty. On the right side of the paper, there was a diagram showing the four quadrants of a watch. The first quadrant contained numbers from one to fifteen, the second having numbers from sixteen to thirty, and so on. There was a difference, however, in the fourth quadrant. The character that was supposed to represent the number sixty became zero instead. Problem solved!

After a few minutes, Mark turned the page on the other side and asked Lee to write in base sixty the numbers he told him.

"It's very easy indeed," said Lee after a few successful attempts.

It only took a few damn minutes to learn the new sixty characters. Then came the difficult part: how to make them accepted by the public.

Mark said that regarding mobile phones, we could continue using the decimal system. However, computers and calculators had to be modified to accommodate the new characters. Eventually, we would be forced to use a number system with a bigger base, and the base sixty was the best option. Imagine its impact on mathematics, science, computer engineering, banking, marketing, defence, and so forth. A bigger base had more permutations, and hackers would have more difficulties in cracking codes. Perhaps the base sixty would have the biggest impact on marketing. There were far too many bar codes or matrix codes that were used simultaneously to encode information for a product. All those different codes used simultaneously were very confusing, making use of them impractical. Using the numbers in base 60 would resolve this problem.

"But we are not ready to do it, are we?" concluded Mark, disappointed. "People in charge will not accept such a revolutionary change unless forced or ashamed. People in charge seem to live in a parallel universe, although I don't believe in parallel universes."

"And how are you planning to convince them?" asked Lee.

"By writing a book about aliens! Those aliens go to school to learn physics, sciences, and maths, where they use the number system in base sixty. Those aliens don't have such absurd things such as the big bang theory, string theory, wormholes, and time travel. Those aliens don't have academic prizes, and their scientists collaborate with and respect each other. Those aliens don't believe in witches, wizards, vampires, and don't waste their time on social networks."

Mark's ideas sounded interesting.

"Do they have superheroes?" asked Lee with amusement.

"No, my aliens don't have superheroes."

"Great. Now you are my friend."

They continued laughing.

"What about CVs?" asked Lee.

"Sorry, no CVs. The aliens don't like CVs either. They prefer to spend time with each other instead."

"And the politicians?" asked Lee, somehow undecided.

"It is not my business. I prefer to focus on science."

"But our friend Stefan might be very upset if you don't say anything about the alien politicians."

"He understands better politics. It's he who should write a book about politicians in an alien world."

Aliens had to have politicians too. But whatever their political theatre was, they definitely didn't call it democracy. Who knows what they called it? The aliens knew, of course.

Aliens for sure had no idea what democracy was, but if they had any chance to learn its principles, they might have considered it a kind of public drama, where everyone talked about rights and nobody about responsibilities.

"Those bloody aliens must be antidemocratic!" concluded Lee and Mark jokingly, and continued having fun for a while.

CHAPTER 5

Humble people are supposed to be dumb

One day Lee was at home and wondering what to do next. He had already an idea about the next book he wanted to write, but he hadn't started the writing yet. Since his next book was destined to become a bestseller, why not write something to show how ridiculous modern society was? Mark was right to set his book in the alien world. That way, he would avoid any trouble with *great* scientists who had enough power and authority to make his life unbearable. Perhaps Stefan had to do the same. Instead of a planetary rebellion that would surely end in violence, why not help create a peaceful worldwide movement? There had to be a way to unite people for their common benefit. Openly challenging the politicians was too dangerous. Lee remembered well the multitude of protests around the world in the last few years. What did the protesters achieve? Nothing! Politicians managed to make them look ridiculous. More protests and uprisings didn't seem to be a good solution.

History had shown that the most effective tool against politicians was to make them look ridiculous. The story about the horse politician was a good example of how effective that could be. Similarly, why not create an alien world with ridiculous politicians? No one would get hurt, and everybody would have fun.

Lee was definitely against any kind of social uprising or protests, and he was very clear about it. As a journalist, he was outraged to see so much power concentrated in the hands of so few people. It appeared that the media moguls will always present biased information in favour of a certain political person or organisation. They needed the political support to maintain their empires, and politicians needed the media's support to control the *herd*. Such secret alliance between politicians and journalists proved to be helpful in maintaining the reputation and public image of both social classes involved.

Since politicians and journalists could not do without money, the secret alliance was extended to the financiers, forming the Triple Alliance, the elite who dominated the world in the name of *democracy*.

Lee realised that with sadness. He'd never trusted journalists because they always had interests and privileges to defend.

Despite everything, Lee was still proud of the political system of his country and still believed the president to be a great person. If democracy was the best political system we'd figured out so far, there was still room for improvement.

Does the president know what is happening? he wondered. *Is he aware that so much suffering exists in the world? Does he know that his decisions affect all of us?*

He concluded that it would be great talking to him and telling him about all of that. Lee began thinking about how to reach the president. Which people would he have to contact first in order to make it through? Those people had to be very powerful, and they must have had their own interests. They had to be politicians, journalists, or financiers, and they probably had *great* reputations . . .

"Let's have a look at those letters," Lee said to himself, and he began scanning them. Something interesting had to come out.

And something not only interesting but also surprising came out.

Mr Horton, the leader of one of the biggest media empires in the world, was writing to him, congratulating him for his recent success and spectacular entrance into the world of celebrities. Mr Horton was also informing him about his constant support concerning realising those achievements. He also assured Lee of his further support. However, Lee was informed that he was indebted to Mr Horton, and then it was time to pay his debt. The payment did not involve any money—just a little favour.

Mr Horton had appointed Lee to participate in a TV talk show in two weeks' time. Four other aspiring celebrities would be present, and the subject of discussion was of free choice. All what Lee had to do was to support a certain Mr Fernandez publicly by asking him questions from a list already given to him and show his admiration for this person. Lee also had to pretend to be astonished by the answers given and to convince everyone how great Mr Fernandez was.

Lee examined curiously the list of questions provided. All of them appeared to have a connection with politics. It was clear to him that he had to create the public image of a future politician.

"What are you doing today?" asked Lee with hope.

David had a day off; he wanted to see Susan.

"I'm coming with you." Lee needed someone to talk to.

One hour later, they met, and Lee told David about the strange letter he'd just received. "It appears that I have a debt to pay!" Lee said, worried.

David realised that eventually he would have a debt to cover too. This looked very scary. Those guys, whoever they were, didn't give anything for free. It was all about favours.

But it was the world that made that way. People at the top in any kind of social group exchanged favours amongst them. Such process was referred to as having strong references or reciprocal recommendation.

"Are you going to challenge them and refuse?" asked David, worried.

"Unfortunately not . . ."

Lee knew what was going to happen if he refused. All the major media organisations would start a campaign of demonising him in order to destroy his public image. It was just so easy for them to do it! He would not stand a chance of defending himself. In a short time, he might become the new monster, and people enjoyed reading stories about monsters. People needed to be assured that justice was being done, that someone cared about them. Most importantly, they wanted to feel in control of their destiny.

"I need to see the president," Lee said, determined.

That was perhaps the only option available. Perhaps he could do something about Susan to get her out of prison. Mr President might be the only person who could help him.

David found it a good idea. Then there was the difficult task of how to reach the president.

"We'll talk about this later," they concluded.

For the moment, they just wanted to see Susan.

The two friends were invited in the same room, awaiting impatiently for Susan to come. Minutes later, she sat in front of them, on the other side of the bars. Life in prison had been harsh to her. She was no longer the person David had known a few months ago. Her fragile body had become more robust, and she appeared to be more determined to fight against the tough environment. Perhaps she had to fight a lot against nasty people. David and Lee could see some scratches on her face, neck, and hands. Who knew what she had been involved in?

David gave her a pack, but not before the guards had searched it. She'd requested a few things: cosmetics, books, and a few packs of cigarettes. Susan didn't smoke, but she needed cigarettes to make her life more bearable, so she offered those cigarettes to her colleagues for free.

David took her hands through the bars and held them in his hands. She smiled, and he took his chance to tell her that Lee was determined to see the president. They would do everything possible to set her free.

Mr Taylor left early in the morning, but Stefan was informed to come to his office and organise a terrace. After some successful business deal made recently, Mr Taylor had acquired a new office. He appeared to be very excited about this acquisition, and amidst his excitement, he promised to increase Stefan's salary from the basic rate by 5 per cent. Of course, Stefan had to show his gratitude for such generosity by forcing a smile on his face and by thanking him profusely. Mr Taylor felt great for being in control of other people's destinies.

After examining the empty terrace and consulting with Mr Taylor to survey his taste, Stefan left to make an order for new plants. Three hours later, he came back with a truck full of plants and began carrying them up using one of the two lifts available.

There were plenty of people coming and going, and everyone appeared to be quite busy. The office was still a mess, and a few girls were involved in tidying it up. But the biggest mess was on the terrace. Stefan suspected that he might need the whole day just to finish carrying the plants up, so he began working desperately without wasting too much time on details. A pathway across the office has been left for him, with pieces of cardboard temporarily covering the floor to protect it and make it easier to clean.

The lift was full again with plants, so he was ready to close the doors the moment three men were coming in a hurry, trying to make their way to the higher floors. The other lift was engaged or stuck at the twentieth floor. It didn't move. The three men seemed desperate to go up as soon as possible. Thus Stefan offered them a ride after taking some plants out. They thanked him for his kindness and entered the lift. However, there was not enough space and Stefan took a big pot and held it in his hands. One of the three men did the same thing with a smaller plant. Now they could go up more comfortably.

The man closest to the control panel pressed the button for the twenty-fourth floor. The doors closed and the lift began ascending. The same man turned around and enquired about which floor Stefan was going to.

"On the same floor," he said humbly.

"Great. That's Mr Taylor's office. Are you working for him?"

"Yes, sir," replied Stefan respectfully. "I'm his gardener."

"We're going there too," said the man in the middle, who looked like their leader. "Mr Taylor is a great advisor."

There was a long way to the twenty-fourth floor. The three men appeared to be agitated, and they began looking nervously at some documents. They excused themselves and continued talking to each other; Stefan, from behind the potted plant he was holding in his hands, furtively studied the same documents and listened on the sly to their nervous conversation.

But they wanted to make sure their conversation was safe.

"Do you know what derivatives are?" asked one of the three men. The other two stopped talking, waiting for Stefan's replay.

"I have no idea, sir."

"What about credit default swaps?"

He gave them the same answer. They asked him a few more questions on finance and economics, mentioning confusing and impossible combination of words.

"I am very sorry. I'm just a gardener," replied Stefan, confused.

At that particular moment, they seemed convinced. This dumb man was just a gardener. Their conversation was safe.

Consequently, they continued talking about a great deal they wanted to make, completely ignoring him.

Stefan heard them talking about some high-risk assets they wanted to get rid of as soon as possible. Mr Taylor would facilitate their action and put them in contact with the right client. It turned out that the "right client" was a certain Mrs Graham; Stefan had never heard of her.

Unfortunately, he couldn't hear more. The lift stopped—they were at the twenty-fourth floor—and the doors opened. None of the three men felt the need to hang around to say anything to such an insignificant person. They had no more time to waste.

After empting the lift and carrying the plants on the terrace, Stefan took the journey back in the other lift. There was nobody with him. He felt the need to call David then and ask for some information, but he didn't trust any of the electronic devices installed in the lift. Everything appeared to be kind of a spying machine, and Stefan found it safer texting his friend. David replied with a text message, requesting a few minutes to find out what that deal was all about.

On the ground floor, Stefan took another set of plants and put them in the lift; leaving no space for anybody who might have been in a hurry. The doors closed; he was alone amongst plenty of plants, hiding behind a big plant to use his phone safely.

David was quick at finding the requested information. Mrs Graham, a rich widow with one daughter, was in charge of a successful online firm involved in tourism. She was also highly involved in buying and selling bank products, specialising in the mortgage sector. David took the responsibility to warn her about the risk she might be facing dealing with Mr Taylor and his allies.

It came out that Mr Taylor's allies had been making plenty of money on such dubious deals, leaving all their customers bankrupt.

Although there was still plenty of work to do, Stefan felt more relaxed. That time, Mr Taylor should have been unable to succeed in his devious intentions.

Good people still exist

The assets Mrs Graham intended to buy proved to be very risky indeed. In just a few days, the company selling them went bankrupt. Thanks to David's warning, her business was safe by then, and she was very grateful to him. Therefore, she decided to come personally to thank him.

David was still in his office. Since he took charge of the company, many things changed. One of his most important contributions was the creation of a few private spaces where people could work undisturbed. His little office was almost completely isolated, and his colleagues had to open two doors in order to talk to him. Although stress did not completely vanish, David managed to reduce it significantly. His workers were free to do what they wanted as long as the job was being done. Putting almost no pressure on them had made him extremely popular amongst his colleagues.

Mrs Graham entered the office, and David was notified of her presence. He was ready to receive her. After a few formalities, they began a vivid conversation, and soon they felt completely at ease with one another.

Mrs Graham took the opportunity to express her gratitude to him for the unexpected help. Perhaps she could help him too, Mrs Graham suggested.

I have everything I need . . . he said to himself, *almost everything . . .* The only thing missing was Susan.

They began chatting, touching on their own stories. It turned out that Mr Graham had died a few years before, and since then, Mrs Graham lived alone with her daughter and a handful of housekeepers. Her daughter, Claire, was studying for a degree in finance, and she was supposed to take over her mother's business in a few years' time, when she decided it was time to retire.

Then, it was time for David to talk, so he mentioned the **Game of Power**, how it changed his life, and all the other events that came with that change. He also talked about Susan, her unfortunate imprisonment, and his struggles to get her out.

Mrs Graham listened, astonished. The story about the **Game of Power** seemed so shocking that she refused to believe it to be true. She was well aware that some people had huge quantities of money;

however, spending such lumps of money on having fun with other people's destinies seemed much more incredible than a fantasy movie.

"But nobody forces you to believe," said David. "I hardly believe it myself."

"Let's focus on the fate of that poor girl," said Mrs Graham, changing the subject.

She wanted to know how everything happened, and David gave her all the requested details.

"This Mr Taylor must be such a jerk!" she said with rage.

Perhaps time had come to teach him a good lesson.

"I will take personal care of him," she promised.

David's right to revenge the reputation of that poor girl had become her own personal revenge.

"I don't want revenge, though. I only want to see her free," he said.

"And you will have her free," Mrs Graham promised, stressing every single word.

She finally left, thanking him once again for his help and for the pleasure of talking to him.

David closed the door after his mysterious guest and remained thoughtful. He was still unsure what to believe, and he had no idea what to do next.

Three days later, Mrs Graham invited him for dinner, urging him to come, as they had to discuss something of extreme importance.

"I would be very pleased if you would invite your friends too," she said. "Also, don't forget to bring all the evidence you have related to the **Game of Power**."

David promised to come, and he thanked Mrs Graham for her kind invitation.

David and Stefan came together in David's car and joined Lee, Sara, and Julia. Unfortunately, neither Mark nor Lisa was able to join them. The two cars continued their journey until they arrived at the address given to David.

Mrs Graham and her daughter, Claire, were waiting for them. There was also a certain Mr Anderson, and he was introduced to her guests as a rich entrepreneur who was looking forward to hearing the incredible story about the **Game of Power**. He had become incredibly intrigued and curious when Mrs Graham mentioned it to him.

The guests were invited inside. A large and cosy room had some divans arranged in a semicircle around an oval coffee table. Each of them took a seat in a random order and participated in the general discussion. The adjacent room had a long table adorned with everything needed for a marvellous dinner. Two housekeepers were busy with the final preparations.

Dinner was ready soon, and they were invited to have a seat at the table. There were more chairs than there were people, and the dinner was arranged and served from only one side of the table.

As they sat down, it turned out that the plates and cutleries were arranged for one extra seat.

"We have a special guest," said Mrs Graham with a smile when her guests began wondering about the need for an extra portion. "Before we do anything else," she continued, "let's open this champagne. We have something to celebrate."

While Mr Anderson was grabbing the bottle of champagne to open it, Mrs Graham asked one of her housekeepers to welcome the special guest in.

"It's Susan!" shouted Sara, completely taken by surprise. She ran towards her.

None of Mrs Graham's guests were expecting to see Susan, and they looked very surprised indeed.

Sara took possession of the poor girl, hugging and kissing her. The others joined too, and Susan became the centre of everyone's attention. David appeared to be the most excited of all. He hugged Susan with passion, and in his delirium, he hugged Mrs Graham too, mumbling plenty of thankful words.

"It's him you have to thank," she said, smiling and pointing towards Mr Anderson.

Thus Mr Anderson received a huge amount of thanks and compliments, and he became the "kingmaker" of this happy society.

David, however, wanted to know how much he owed him . . . and how did he do it!

"It's not important how I did it," said Mr Anderson. "Everyone has his own little secrets."

Everyone has his own connections, thought Lee. *But it doesn't matter. She is free now.*

Everyone was standing around Susan, and she struggled to answer all the questions thrown at her. There was a big fuss caused by the jolly people around her.

Mrs Graham was equally struggling to convince her guests to sit down. Dinner was ready, but nobody appeared interested.

Finally, they began to calm down. Susan appeared to be tired and needed to sit down. One by one, everyone took a seat, and Mr Anderson began pouring champagne into the glasses provided.

"To the little princess!" he said, pointing towards Susan.

She smiled happily.

"To Susan," replied the others, emptying their glasses of champagne. Then they started eating.

David asked again how much he owed to Mr Anderson for his help, but Mr Anderson insisted on saying that there was no debt amongst them. Should he need any help in the future, he would ask for it, so David assured Mr Anderson that he was ready at any time to return his favour.

After the initial excitement around Susan, the discussion changed course.

Mr Anderson began asking plenty of questions related to the **Game of Power**. He wanted to know everything they knew and dissected every response with great care, making suggestions and asking even more questions. Susan, Claire, and Mrs Graham followed the discussion with astonishment, and they came up with their own questions. The dinner table soon became a truly political debate, and all of them appeared to be politicians destined to solve a great problem.

Meanwhile, Lee took the opportunity to mention the dilemma he was facing. Mr Anderson's suggestion was not to challenge Mr Horton, unless he wanted to support the consequences of Mr Horton's revenge. The others seemed to have a similar opinion.

The damned TV show would probably produce an undeserving politician out of so many undeserving ones. With one "dummy" extra or minus, nothing would change. If Mr Horton really wanted to have fun creating a new superstar politician, he had a mountain of resources for doing it.

Therefore, Lee was advised not to take any risk against such an influential person. Life was full of compromises they had to make in order to defend themselves against people who were more powerful than they were.

Mr Anderson continued by saying that although his wealth was quite significant, he also occasionally had to go to a halfway house kind of deal with certain unscrupulous people. To survive the fierce competition and to escape it and hence remain an honourable person was almost impossible.

As one rose higher to the top of a pyramid, it became more difficult to maintain position, unless the person was lucky enough to be a member of the elite.

"I can help you see the president, if this is what you want, but I'm not sure how much help it would be," assured Mr Anderson.

Lee confirmed that he was determined to talk to the president.

"But keep it in mind that even the president has interests, privileges, and a reputation to defend," Mr Anderson continued.

Assuring him that he wanted to take this risk, Lee thanked Mr Anderson for his kindness and support.

Two hours later, the guests left, and Susan went with them. She promised, of course, to keep in touch with Claire and wholeheartedly thanked Mrs Graham and Mr Anderson again for their generous help.

Susan will live with Sara in the flat she'd rented after taking her job. For the moment, Susan would enjoy some free time. Mr Anderson promised to give her a job when she felt ready.

The rise and fall of the Cabbage Empire

Susan announced excitedly that the Cabbage Empire had just collapsed.

"What? The Cabbage Empire! What kind of empire is that?" asked Sara, perplexed.

Susan and Sara alike started laughing.

They were alone. Sara had just returned from work and was both hungry and tired. Fortunately, dinner was ready, something that Susan had prepared.

As they sat at the dinner table, Susan continued, excited about her unusual story, while Sara attacked the delicious food in front of her.

"It's a financial and political empire created by Mr Cabbage."

"And who the hell is this Mr Cabbage?" Sara was becoming increasingly curious.

Susan didn't answer at once, preferring to keep her friend in suspense.

"He has a different name, of course, but people call him Mr Cabbage because in the language of his country, to be cabbage means to have no idea whatsoever of what happens around him . . ."

Apparently, Mr Cabbage, a shepherd without education, started doing small business on the streets. He then became involved in some speculations and was lucky enough to make a respectful amount of money. Consequently, he began investing in the housing market, and through a series of fortunate events, his wealth increased even further. Soon, a great opportunity propelled him into the sphere of billionaires. Close to a big city, the capital of his country, a military campus was going to be dismantled, and Mr Cabbage managed to corrupt some officials and thus took possession of the field. In a short time, the price of the land increased so much that Mr Cabbage became the richest mogul in the country.

Then came the funny thing: Mr Cabbage decided to become a politician!

Taking advantage of the divided political parties, fighting amongst them for power, as none of them had a strong leader or a clear agenda, Mr Cabbage would become an expert in politics. In fact, he managed to create troubles everywhere. As such, he had to move from party to party and from doctrine to doctrine.

Having a great talent for offending everyone and saying incredible things that made the whole country laugh, he became the special guest of most of the TV reality shows and the most desirable celebrity. What's more, the TV presenters began a fierce competition amongst them for the most desired special guest, desperately trying to engage more audience.

It appeared that not only the TV shows benefited from Mr Cabbage's great talent of exasperating intellectuals with his incredible replies, but also politicians did. While Mr Cabbage was involved in never-ending scandals, the other politicians remained in obscurity, free to run their own businesses.

When Mr Cabbage announced his intention to become president, no one appeared strong enough to challenge him. His popularity was greater than ever due to his involvement in charity and other awe-inspiring activities.

Unfortunately, due to a recent financial crash, the famous and powerful Cabbage Empire began to fall apart.

From the richest person in the country, Mr Cabbage moved fifteen or twenty places down and therefore became more vulnerable. For politicians, this was the opportunity to take their revenge. The case related to the obscure deal on the military field was reopened. Consequently, the once-invincible superhero would have to spend years behind bars. He still had plenty of resources to make his life easier, and his sentence would probably end much sooner than expected. However, he would never become an influential politician again.

Perhaps Mr Cabbage had finally realised that talking nonsense and talking so much could be very costly indeed.

Sara opened the door. It was Lisa, struggling with a big valise. Some other bags could be seen on the stairs beside a bunch of boxes; it looked as if she'd brought the whole caboodle.

"What happened?"

Lisa appeared exhausted and completely changed. "Help me, please," she said in despair.

Sara called Susan to give a hand, and they carried all the bags and boxes inside.

"I left the damn job," said Lisa sadly.

They could see that.

It turned out that Mr Hook, her *great* employer and living superhero, had decided to study a new and exasperating kind of life philosophy. This philosophy involved making plenty of *inspirational* noise, and to Lisa's terror, he had decided to practice it as often as possible.

Mr Hook made the habit to come unexpectedly and shout "Be happy!" although there was no reason to be happy. Or he tried to sing his special songs—with plenty of positive adjectives and words of hope for a better world. Nevertheless, nothing was more exasperating than hearing this comical personage repeating constantly with a pathetic voice, "I am *great* . . . I am *wonderful* . . . I am *amazing* . . . I am *unbelievable* . . . I am *astonishing* . . ." and many similar combinations of fantastic adjectives.

At first, Lisa tried to adapt to this change or to ignore it, but neither alternative was possible. After a few days of inspirational terror, feeling completely exasperated, Lisa finally decided to leave.

Despite this, both Sara and Susan were happy to have a new flatmate, and Lisa was equally happy to have such warm support.

Instant celebrities can be very noisy

Lee was sad to know that Lisa had to leave her job because of her insufferable employer. "Those nasty celebrities!" he exclaimed.

What was so great about being a celebrity? Why did people strive so desperately to become one of them?

He was invited to participate in a TV show he didn't want to go to. Meanwhile, the common people competed desperately to take part in those TV shows to be seen by the world. Lee began smiling, thinking that such TV shows had about ten times more applicants than the top universities of the world. The competition for stardom was so ferocious that one had to be extremely lucky just to have the opportunity to say hello to a bored audience.

Finishing a top university was not necessarily a guarantee to become a celebrity. It usually required a long time in addition to plenty of hard work and perseverance. Patience didn't appear to be appreciated much.

Conversely, a TV show could create instant celebrities. Therefore, the attraction was much greater and the struggle fiercer.

In a world where instant gratification was to become the only philosophy of life, what was the point of spending a few years at a university, even if it was a world-leading university?

Sadly, nobody appeared to realise that instant gratification meant instant talent, which was either shallowness or incredible luck. Being able to match one's average talent to the opportunity given—and to become an instant celebrity—was not something that everyone could do.

In an intense world, there had to be superficial friends, superficial thinkers, superficial talent, superficial economies, and superficial leaders. There was no wonder that our future looked equally superficial.

Lee would have preferred to give his place in the TV show to an unknown desperate person who struggled to find his or her way to the public. Such a thing was not possible though. The *expert* touch was needed to make someone a celebrity, and Lee felt ashamed to call himself an expert. Unfortunately, too many people out there felt ashamed for not being called experts.

Although Lee confirmed his participation in the reality show, he felt extremely reluctant and was ready to change his mind at any time.

There were a few hours left, however, until the evening, but he was still undecided. Sara knew that he didn't want to go and kept phoning him from time to time to encourage him. She wanted to make sure he would not change his mind.

Perhaps I should go, he thought. But he soon realised in terror that Mr Hook was a TV presenter at the same channel. That would have been the worst of his dreams, and in desperation, Lee phoned Lisa to enquire about Mr Hook's public appearances. She was not sure about it. Since Lisa had left her awful job, she didn't bother to check the timetable. Perhaps by phoning the people in charge of the show, she might be able to find out.

Lisa phoned back few minutes later. Good news! The distasteful TV presenter was off that evening.

Lee gained a little more courage.

Time passed, and he became more and more agitated. Then it was time to go. The life-changing moment, not for him but for someone else instead, was to come soon.

As Lee walked into the television station, someone guided him to the right department. A few aestheticians then took possession of him, and Lee went through a short period of quick transformation of his looks. Minutes later, he met the requested standards and looked as close to perfect as he could get. Then Lee was invited to await the beginning of the show. There were four other people present, two men and two women, waiting impatiently, with extreme confidence, for such a life-changing event. He introduced himself and shook hands with them one by one. Each of the invitees then gave a short presentation of himself or herself.

One of the two women was a singer, and the other one was a miraculous healer. Lee began smiling; he felt the need for some miraculous healing that night. The men introduced themselves as a successful performer and a financier. The latter, an anonymous personage and would-be politician, was Mr Fernandez.

This is good to know, Lee thought.

Mr Fernandez proved to be less scary than Lee had imagined. He was polite and talked with extreme confidence, using great pompous words. It appeared that he had the right skills for becoming a politician, with the exception of politeness, of course.

Then the fortunate invitees began talking about Lee's bestseller, congratulating him for the great book, and Lee found himself in the centre of their attention. He smiled, trying to appear as friendly as possible, and thanked them for their appreciation. However, he was determined not to talk too much that night.

Fortunately, those people appeared to be infected with a rather unusual syndrome. Once they started talking, it was almost impossible to stop them, thus Lee didn't have to answer all the questions.

Later on, a member of the staff urged them to get ready; the show was about to start. They were given the order of entrance; Lee was the last of the five participants. One by one, they were announced, and the public received them with a storm of applause.

"And now for the special guest, Mr Lee Norris, author of *Race to Pluto*, the latest bestseller."

They were invited to take a seat on the sofas provided. Lee managed somehow to occupy a place farther away from Mr Fernandez, making sure that the conversation with him would be more difficult. He knew that his friends were watching and wanted to make that show less painful.

The TV presenter, a charming woman, welcomed them. When the show began, there was fierce competition for stardom amongst the guests, each of them trying to monopolise the microphone. Lee was lucky that night. He had little chance to talk and little chance to promote the aspiring politician.

One hour later, the embarrassing TV show was finished, and Lee was happy to leave. His friends were waiting for him to celebrate the end of his painful public appearance. Sara and the other girls promised to cook something special, and he was looking forward to enjoying it.

Friendly wolves are dangerous

After being confronted by Mrs Graham for trying to bankrupt her, and pressured by Mr Anderson, Mr Taylor was forced to facilitate Susan's liberation in order to avoid a public scandal or going to court.

Humiliated, Mr Taylor decided to take his revenge. Wondering what Mr Anderson's advantage for liberating Susan was, he set up an investigation team with the mission of secretly keeping an eye on her.

A few days later, the investigators had all the information needed. Astonished, Mr Taylor listened to their report.

"She lives in a flat with two other girls, financially supported by a certain David M—leader of a struggling company that turned into a very successful one since he became in charge. One of the girls living in the same flat happens to work for the same company. Not surprisingly, your new gardener is also a friend of them . . ."

"My gardener!" shouted Mr Taylor, outraged. "This is not possible . . ." He hoped that his interlocutor was somehow wrong.

"We believe this guy is spying on you," said the other investigator.

"Spying on me!" shouted Mr Taylor, unable to believe it. Then he continued more calmly, convinced that they were wrong. "This gardener is not able to do that. He is such a moron!"

"No, he is not. He just pretends to be," replied one of the investigators in conviction.

"This gardener is sly as a fox," continued the other.

If that was true, Mr Taylor thought, *then it explains many things.* He remembered the sudden decision of the last gardener to leave and the unexpected job request from the new one.

"How did he know I was looking for a new gardener? Why was his CV the only one I received at that time?"

But there was something that didn't seem to match. What was then the connection between Mr Anderson, Mrs Graham, and that girl?

Mr Anderson and Mrs Graham, it turned out, had been long-time friends . . . But what about the girl?

Mr Taylor told the two investigators about his concerns and asked them if they knew anything about that.

They didn't know. Nonetheless, one of the two investigators remembered that Mrs Graham mentioned something about a favour made to her by Mr David, a favour she had to return.

Mr Taylor wondered if that favour had anything to do with spying on him. Had this gardener provided the right information to his friend David and the latter consequently sent this info to Mrs Graham? If true, then the mystery was solved. Reaching this conclusion, Mr Taylor announced his decision.

"One more task, gentlemen. I want you to dig into this Mr David's company, or whatever his damn name is, to find out how to get rid of him and his secretary. Regarding the gardener, I'll take care of that myself."

At that point, Mr Taylor gave each of them a conspicuous handful of money and shook their hands, pleased with their accomplishment. "One more of this each when the job is done," he said gratefully.

The two men thanked him and left, hiding the money deep in their pockets.

By then, it was time to deal with the gardener. Mr Taylor called a person in charge of his security and gave him some instructions.

Stefan left his work at the usual 5 p.m. and began walking slowly on the crowded and busy streets towards the train station. There was no hurry. He stopped from time to time in front of a shop, examining the things exposed in the vitrines, or sat on a bench and watched amazed to the people hurrying up and down the streets in all directions. Along his way, there was a park on the right side of the street, and Stefan took that opportunity to go across it and enjoy a moment of calm while watching from a small hill a section of the huge city.

Unfortunately, he did not notice the three people coming from behind with clubs, but when he did, it was too late to run away.

Stefan remained unconscious for two days. When he woke up, a nurse asked him how he felt and who should be contacted. He hoped to feel better but wondered what had happened. An ambulance had brought him to the hospital, she said. He was found in a park, bleeding and severely injured.

His friends were informed about what happened, and they came to see him. Stefan was to remain one more week in the hospital. However, it would take a rather long time for a complete recovery.

Mr Taylor was informed that one of his enemies had been punished, and he contemplated his revenge with a misanthropic smile. That day, he had to finish the job somehow.

"When the two gentlemen arrive, bring them here!" he yelled at his secretary. She nodded her head approvingly.

Later on, the two men were escorted to Mr Taylor's office, who received them with a warm, friendly attitude.

After a few minutes of formalities, Mr Taylor changed subject and began explaining to them the reason they had been invited. Apparently, two of their current employers managed to upset a very powerful and influential person. Of course, he didn't find it necessary to mention the name of the powerful individual in question. Mr Taylor then assured his interlocutors that the mysterious high-profile gentleman had enough power to destroy their business in the blink of an eye, but he wanted to be generous and so proposed them a deal.

The two honourable men would be offered a fantastic business opportunity, with one condition: as soon as possible, they had to sack, without notification or explanations, the two evil employees, namely Mr David M (the manager of the company) and a certain Miss Sara R.

Listening to Mr Taylor, the two men remained bewildered by such an unusual request. They began protesting regarding the sack, not too convinced, though. Soon their greed and selfishness proved to be more powerful than their feelings, and they both jumped without remorse into the great opportunity ahead of them.

The next day, David and Sara found themselves jobless. Nobody gave them any explanation or any reason for that sudden decision . . . Indeed, the door was closed against them, and they were invited to leave.

Imagine a world without politicians

The great day finally arrived: Lee was given the chance to meet the president. Mr Anderson had made this encounter possible, but Lee had no idea how the secret machinery at the top of the pyramid really functioned.

Mr Anderson perhaps had a heck of connections amongst the elite, and who knew what kind of favours he had to return?

Lee, however, worried less about Mr Anderson's connections and more about his encounter with the great president. He was given ten minutes only for this appointment; it appeared that Mr President was a very busy person.

Ten minutes should have been fine for informing the president about the **Game of Power** and hence convincing him to do something about it. Perhaps the president could have taken his side against this monstrous organisation. At any rate, what if he didn't believe this story? What if Lee was unable to convince the president to consider his concerns? What if he consequently failed to obtain the president's support? Those were good reasons to worry.

Lee made the final preparations and carefully reviewed the main points of his short speech, along with the questions he intended to address in front of the great leader.

The meeting was late in the afternoon, but Lee left home early in the morning. He had to be ready in advance for such a high-profile encounter. Moreover, he had to take the train and travel for a few hours, enough time to clarify and refine his ideas. There was no reason to worry yet.

"Mr Lee Norris," called someone, and Lee was invited inside.

That was not a life-changing reality show; this was a real-life life-changing show.

Mr President received him with a smile and shook his hand warmly. "How can I help?" he said in a friendly tone, inviting Lee to talk.

Lee began thanking for the privilege granted and then used the next minutes for talking about the **Game of Power** and its obscure activities. He then took out a folder including the evidence, passing the high-profile portfolio to the middleman in the presence of the president.

Mr President examined it for a few minutes without saying anything.

The two men watched each other furtively for a few painful moments, during which Lee was afraid to breathe or to say anything. Finally, the president decided to talk.

"What do you want me to do about it?"

Lee was expecting a different question. He was hoping that the president would be impressed by the discovery of such a terrible secret and that he would be interested to know how he and his friends managed to do it.

"I don't know," he replied, embarrassed. "Anything that you can do would be of great help."

The president lost his smile, and his voice became icy. "Sorry, there is nothing I can do."

Lee, astonished, was invited to leave without further explanations. The president took the folder and put it in a cabinet under the desk, then locked it in a hurry, as if scared of something.

"This discussion never happened, *understand*?" said the president, stressing the last word and making sure that his request was pretty darn clear.

Lee, already close to the door, was ready to open it; turning around, he could feel the president's hostility.

"Yes, sir."

He never imagined that an encounter with the great leader of his country could be so disastrous. Disappointed and shocked, Lee left the room, thanking Mr President again for his time. The president didn't answer. He had more important things to think about.

Sara and her friends waited impatiently for any news from Lee. They all wanted to know about the outcome of this important meeting, but Lee seemed to be unreachable.

"He should have called two hours ago," said Lisa.

"But why doesn't he answer?"

Sara phoned him again. The phone rang, but Lee didn't answer.

Susan began worrying that something must have happened. Perhaps the encounter didn't end as expected so he didn't want to talk. In vain, they sent him a few messages telling him that they were worried, urging him to reply . . . There was no word from him.

Initially, Lee was so excited about that meeting with the president. If it ended badly, he was perhaps upset or ashamed of this failure. He had to be disappointed too. Lee put so much hope in Mr President and used to highly respect and admire him. Who knew what he was thinking of right then?

Supposing Lee had caught the train, the journey would last a few hours. He was probably to arrive just after midnight.

"I'm going to wait for him," said Sara, determined.

Lisa and Susan wanted to accompany her, of course. There was enough time to have dinner and to take a shower.

That night was supposed to be for celebrating the great help, protection, and support Mr President rendered on his people. Instead, the same night had to be a night of anger and disappointment. Alas!

Meanwhile, Mark phoned Lisa to enquire about Lee. He was wondering why he didn't answer the phone. Minutes later, David and Stefan were informed about the girls' intention to wait for Lee at the train station. Apart from Stefan, who was still recovering from his injuries and had to stay in bed, the two other men, namely David and

Mark, decided to join Sara and her friends at the train station. They could not leave the girls alone in the night.

Before midnight, Mark arrived at the train station, and minutes later, David arrived too. All together, the girls arrived a few minutes later and joined them. Checking the timetable for the train that was supposed to arrive from the capital, they all sat on a big bench on the corresponding platform, waiting for Lee. If Lee was to come with the train they expected, he had to arrive in about twenty minutes. There should have been no delay.

If their assumption was right and Lee's meeting with the president had had no real outcome or even worsened the matter, the future appeared to be very scary indeed. It appeared that they were in big trouble, and there was a slim chance that they could defend themselves. Perhaps it was wise to wait for Lee first and hear what he had to say before seeing red or getting panicky.

The conversation became increasingly loud and agitated, but the platform was almost empty. Still, there was no reason to worry. In fact, there were just a few homeless people wandering around, who were probably too hungry, sleepy, or exhausted by the everyday struggle for survival to bother worrying about pathetic things such as politics.

Finally, the train arrived. Doors opened, and people began descending onto the platform, hurrying towards the direction of the exit.

Lee didn't appear in a hurry. He had no reason for doing so. There was nobody he wanted to talk to, and that day he had good reasons for being sad; the person he trusted the most had betrayed his expectations.

His friends came towards him, and Lee was surprised to see them. They were worried about him, and Lee felt terribly sorry for not replying to them.

Lee didn't have to explain anything; his pitiful face betrayed his feelings. His friends were able to imagine what had happened. Sara gave him a hug and said some comforting words. His friends gathered around him and offered their support too.

It turned out that Mr Anderson was right. The president had privileges to defend, and he did not intend to bother about insignificant people. Their cause might have been noble, but they were on their own, powerless, fighting against an invisible as well as extremely powerful foe.

On their way to the exit, the group of homeless people said hello to them. They stopped for a moment, and Lee gave them some money.

It would be great to listen to their stories, he thought.

Those unfortunate people, ignored by society, were stigmatised for being *losers* by a different kind of losers who were more arrogant and proud of their own miserable lives.

Those homeless people were also ignored and stigmatised by the *winners*, who preferred to direct their "good causes" to more glamorous activities that involved great fanfare, live TV broadcasting, and great emotional speeches to inspire a pathetic audience.

Lee realised that his friends, without any secure income or job prospect on the way, might have had a similar fate without his support, and he felt honoured for such a privilege.

When David left home to go to the train station, Stefan began suspecting that the outcome of Lee's encounter with the president had to be disastrous. Later on, when his low expectations were confirmed, he felt entitled more than ever to create his ideal world of harmony and peace.

Imagine a world without politicians, and without all the troubles they create, he said to himself.

There had to be a way to get rid of all politicians.

Sadly, this ideal world without politicians only existed in his imagination.

The best alternative to democracy

There were a few hours left until the next morning, and Lee invited his friends to come to his house. They would have breakfast together and discuss what to do next. It would be perfect if Julia could join them for breakfast. Thus Lisa phoned her, and she promised to pop over.

It appeared that this happy society was in big trouble.

Stefan was still recovering from his injuries, and he had to stay in bed for a few more days.

David and Sara, after being unfairly sacked, found themselves with nothing to do and with no income. At least David had some savings to rely on. Unfortunately, Sara had barely managed to pay her debt and then had to start all over again.

Regarding Susan, she did not get any compensation through the deal between Mr Anderson, Mrs Graham, and Mr Taylor, but she was more than happy to be free—surrounded by genuine friends.

On the other hand, Lisa too, after leaving her exasperating job, with no source of income, had to depend on Lee's generous support.

Mark, with a similar story, had finally accepted Lee's invitation to live in his flat; he was going to move there that afternoon.

As long as Julia managed to maintain good relations with her super-wise employer and was able to avoid desperation, she could continue working without fearing for her future.

Finally, Lee decided to get a job in journalism. It had to be much easier by then, as he was a celebrity. In fact, he had already had some offers, but they didn't look very tempting, so he didn't bother to reply. Meanwhile, he wanted to continue his research for the next book he intended to start writing soon.

Julia finally arrived, bringing a bagful of fresh croissants and muffins, which Lee had asked her to buy from a coffee shop. The tantalizing odour of the hot goodies invited everyone to get ready for breakfast. Sara and Lee prepared some coffee and tea suited to everyone's taste and put it on the table. Breakfast was ready.

While the others were busy with their breakfasts, Susan kept thinking of a story her mother had told her years before. She still remembered it because the story was so unusual and happened to be very upsetting for the political class.

After minutes of silence, Susan decided to join the general conversation and to share her incredible story.

"I believe there might be a solution to the political equation," said Susan unexpectedly.

"And what might this solution be?" They were eager to know.

Susan began telling her story.

There was a city troubled by political divisions and fierce competition for leadership amongst its inhabitants. Everyone wanted to be a leader . . . Gradually, things started getting worse and worse. There was no way to agree on anything and no way to make peace. But one day, someone came up with an idea. Instead of fighting desperately for power, continuing with this never-ending political nightmare, he suggested the election of their leader in a novel way.

Innovatively, each of the candidates who was believed to be good enough for becoming their leader had to be aligned with the other nominees at the base of a hill. Someone at the top of the hill was going to throw a pumpkin down the hill, towards the candidates. The lucky person hit by the pumpkin had to be their leader!

"And if the pumpkin hit nobody, who was going to be the leader?" asked Sara, amazed by this incredible idea.

"Well, we might then elect the pumpkin instead," suggested Susan, "and spare all the money allocated for the leader's salary."

Everyone laughed. Electing the president with a pumpkin was a good opportunity to save plenty of money and spare all the pathetic speeches the electorate had to endure during elections.

"Just wondering, what would be the name of this political system?" asked Lee.

"What about pumpkin-*ocracy*?"

Susan's suggestion sounded great, and they kept gagging and having fun.

The amazing thing about such an innovative political system was that it offered so many advantages. The pumpkin could not be corrupted, brainwashed, influenced, intimidated, bullied, lobbied, or sent to prison for its political decisions. What's more, there was little chance of seeing a pumpkin following the herd or voting for its politicians just because they were good-looking. Just imagine how much money could be saved this way if compared with the traditional presidential elections. The money might be used to create jobs instead. The multinational corporations and financial institutions would have a hard time surviving without the political support. And most importantly, without political scandals, the majority of journalists would be out of a job.

"This is the greatest political idea I've ever heard of," said Lee, astonished.

Their friend Stefan would be delighted to know that there was finally a solution to the enormous challenge of electing a new president.

Susan had made a point, and they were having a great morning. She was the new superhero.

David began smiling. He'd just remembered something funny, and his friends were curious about it. So he told them about Mrs Rosa and how incredibly funny it was discussing politics with her. She was just so talented at changing politics into entertainment!

"Wondering what her reaction would have been after listening to Susan's story," David said.

Time to burn all CVs

By then, it was time to concentrate on more serious things. Eventually, they would have to face a reality that didn't look very promising.

Unfortunately, none of them had secure incomes, except Lee and Julia, but they had to rely mostly on Lee.

However, Lee's income couldn't last forever. If Mr Horton decided to take revenge against him for his low performance on the infamous TV show, everyone's future was at stake.

Lee suggested that it was better to be paranoid and to prepare for defence than to ignore reality in the way psychopaths did, bearing the risk of finding themselves unprepared, though. Since the best defence was attack, they had to figure out how to attack such a powerful enemy. Fighting against politicians, multinational corporations, and media empires at the same time was almost impossible. This disgraceful alliance controlled almost everything on the planet.

Perhaps they could find a way to unite people on a planetary scale without the use of violence. Politicians should not be given any reason to intervene, using the police or the army against people.

The success of the social networks was a good example for organising an online revolution. However, there was a problem with the social networks; everything concentrated on the individual. Everyone was just too busy updating their profiles or doing cool things to impress the others. Otherwise, people enjoyed spending their time bullying or being nasty to each other, to kill boredom or to have a feeling they were doing something.

Forming united groups appeared to be a mission to tackle. Convincing people to collaborate was even more difficult. It was a clever move to offer people so many video games and so many opportunities to waste their time. That way, they didn't have time to think about politics or about what was happening around them.

"We have to offer people something they desperately need in exchange for their collaboration," asserted Lee.

His friends listened, amazed, whist Lee shared his ideas.

"Now, the question is, *what do people need*?" asked Lee stressing the last words.

"Jobs," spontaneously suggested Lisa, remembering her exasperating experience a few days before.

"Jobs, perfect. What else?" Lee was waiting for more suggestions.

"Financial security," tried Susan.

"Social justice!" shouted Mark emotionally.

"Equity! Equality."

"Exactly. Equality. You are all right. Inequality is the biggest problem in the world today. The question is, how to fight it?"

Lee's reply set everyone on fire. Plenty of suggestions were made, but no consensus was reached.

Inequality was not just a reason for envy and jealousy. It was also a reason for anxiety and despair. Both social classes, the privileged top performers forming the elite and all the rest (namely losers), seemed to live in parallel worlds—in segregation and having absolutely no idea of what was happening on the other side. Those parallel worlds were supported by two different economies moving at different speeds. Moreover, there was an increasing hostility among the members of the two parallel worlds, resulting in lack of dialogue and pitiful state of empathy.

It appeared that Lee decided to leave—for later—any philosophical issues about aliens, preferring to concentrate on the social issues of this troubled world which was tangled with more urgent problems.

"What is the most relevant thing symbolising inequality?" he wondered aloud.

"Income."

"Social status."

"Privileges."

The suggestions his friends made were good, but they did not represent the whole truth. There was, however, something else much more *unequal* than inequality itself.

Lee vanished into his room for a while, returning with a sheet of paper in his hand: his CV. His friends watched him inquisitively; they had no clue about his intention.

"What do you want to do with that?"

"You will see," replied Lee firmly.

He took a lighter and set fire to the CV he held. Everyone looked stunned as they watched the infamous CV being burnt to ashes.

"Great!" yelled his friends, astounded.

"There is no more inequality between us," said Lee zealously, proud of his action.

But Sara was not convinced. "This might be a great thing; however, it changes nothing. What about billions of other CVs present in this world?" she continued.

"We have to convince people to burn them," suggested Lisa.

That seemed to be a good idea.

If people agreed to write no more CVs, it was a good opportunity to save many trees on this troubled planet. The biggest benefit was to spare the time of billions of desperate people who wasted their entire lives for a damn ridiculous piece of paper.

Understandingly, Mr Anderson was reluctant to the idea of an online revolution. Creating a website, as Lee suggested, where jobless, hopeless, and disappointed people could join to fight inequality might have ended up being an epic failure, as many "attempted revolutions" had miscarried before. Of course, it was great to offer everyone the minimal survival income in order to reduce anxiety and despair. It was equally great that people had a sense of some protection and consequently, at least, the adequate minimum of control over their futures.

In order to raise such a huge income, their start-up had to expand fabulously fast. Fortunately, there were plenty of venture capitalists ready to go plunging by investing money in the hottest start-ups. This priceless help had to turn things to their advantage.

But they didn't have to forget who their competitors were. The multinational corporations were ready to fight to the death and make use of all their resources and influence to maintain their privileges. In addition, those huge corporations could use their money to buy their competitors. It turned out that it was much easier buying their competitors than investing in innovation and competing fairly. Those huge corporations already had the monopoly status with the lion's share as for a considerable fraction of the market.

Since they maintained such privileged status to accommodate their own interests only, they had no intention whatsoever to let everything go in the name of fairness, transparency, or other stupid things.

"Just look around at how many promising start-ups have been recently bought, incorporated into the bigger companies, or simply eliminated from the market," said Mr Anderson. "They have decided not to take any chances, should those hot start-ups become incredibly successful and consequently pose any threat to them," he continued.

Despite all of that, Mr Anderson promised to support their initiative with a conspicuous amount of money. He also gave his word to convince some of his friends and business partners to get involved too. However, this support was conditional. If their initiative was to become successful, they had to promise not to get involved in politics. Moreover, they had to avoid becoming the next generation of arrogant, superficial, and nasty superstars, or to give journalists any opportunity to create front-page scandals.

Mr Anderson could foresee the danger of fighting against politicians, journalists, and financiers simultaneously, and he therefore wanted to leave an escaping route in case of any troubles.

"One thing a time," he said.

In order to save money, Sara, Susan and Lisa moved into Lee's flat. The two housekeepers had to be released from their duties, but Lee promised to give them a job at the office within a couple of days.

Meanwhile, Stefan had recovered and felt much better, although some scars were still rather visible on his skin. Mr Taylor had informed him that he'd been fired for unjustifiable absence from work. Thanking him for his kindness, Stefan sent his greetings, for the last time, to his former employer.

Soon Stefan began using the free time by organising regular visits to his beloved forest, accompanied by any of his friends who wanted to go with him. The girls were visibly excited by such a new experience, and those trips proved to be useful in forgetting their everyday problems. But those merry trips ended sooner than expected . . .

Lee had finally decided to write a new book and to start a revolution in the alien world, leaving Sara in charge of the terrestrial one. Organising two revolutions in two different worlds at the same time required money—and plenty of it.

But there was also some good news. The movie based on Lee's book was to be released soon. If things turned out well, some additional income was on its way, quite handy for hard times.

Nevertheless, Lee had his little secret. An online revolution did not necessarily have to start on the Internet.

With the money available from his savings, from Mr Anderson's and Mrs Graham's contribution, and from a few more people recommended by Mr Anderson, Lee and his friends had rented a huge office in a strategic and easily accessible place, from a company which went bankrupt not long time before. There were plenty of rooms, enough for each of them to have his or her own office, plus a few extra rooms, used for additional services.

In the meantime, Julia joined them too, and together with Sara, Susan, Lisa, David, Mark, Stefan, and Lee—in fact, all of them—they formed the recruitment team. There was no need for managers, directors, financiers, or any other highly paid jobs. A couple of computer scientists and web designers had been hired to create and maintain a website and promote their activities online. Those people worked in adjacent offices, separated from the main offices by an extra corridor.

A central hall containing plenty of benches, chairs, and tables was used to accommodate people waiting to take their turn for the job interview. There were many of them waiting anxiously with the hope of getting a blessed job. The two housekeepers offered the interviewees drinks, snacks, and cookies. People were invited one at a time for the interview, in one of the offices available.

A website called Galanthus (meaning snowdrop) was launched a few days before, and at the same time, a good deal of part-time jobs were advertised. People responded by sending their CVs, plenty of them, taking their chances, hoping that some good-hearted employer might invite them for an interview. However, those desperate people didn't know that all of them had been invited, and they considered themselves lucky for the privilege of being there.

Sara opened the door of her office and recognised among the people present one of the homeless gentlemen she saw in the train station about three weeks before. She invited him inside and offered him a seat.

Mr Tom Evans introduced himself and then Sara began searching in a folder for the corresponding CV. After a quick examination of his CV, she put it to the side and invited her interlocutor to talk about himself. It turned out that this individual was a doctor, had had his own private clinic, and was involved in research before becoming redundant.

"Why did you end up on the streets, sir?"

Such an unexpected question had a massive impact on the homeless person, such that he became pale and began trembling. He had the feeling that his cause was lost without hope.

"Please . . . I need this job," he replied in despair.

Sara assured him not to worry. "We don't judge people according to their social statuses," she said in a friendly tone.

With more courage, the homeless gentleman began telling his story.

As the owner of a private clinic, he used to have a great deal of patients, and some powerful drug companies began pressuring him to accept their new drugs. When Mr Evans refused to accept some drugs on the basis that they were insufficiently tested and had poor credence, he began having troubles. In a short time, he lost his licence to practice medicine. Subsequently, he lost his private clinic too. Jobless, he lost his family and friends as well, and consequently, he became homeless, without any future prospects.

Sara felt sad about this story and watched her conversational partner with compassion, while Mr Evans waited in silence his fate to be decided.

"The job is yours, Mr Evans," Sara informed him.

He thanked her with a bright face and began asking questions related to the job: whats and how-tos, when to start, and how much the salary was.

"The payment is basic. We want to give a chance to everyone," said Sara.

He could start immediately through active participation in the website maintenance, in discussions, and making suggestions, besides taking part in activities relevant to the company's promotional campaign and initiative.

There was no fixed schedule. He had a flexible timetable, about two to three hours per day. He could work more if he wanted, but the company couldn't afford to pay more for the moment.

From time to time, he had to come to the office to say hello, have a chat with someone, and then take a few leaflets to distribute in public.

"Just to make it clear, sir, this is not a charity," said Sara. "We need your support as much as you need ours. The success of the company and the future of your job depends on how actively involved people are."

At that critical moment, Mr Evans appeared to fully understand what everything was all about and felt overwhelmed by the situation. Nevertheless, he happily signed his blessed job contract and was ready to leave.

"One more question, Mr Evans."

He turned around while Sara continued.

"Why did your friends from the train station not come along with you?"

"Because they have lost hope," he replied.

"Could you do me a favour, please? I would like you to kindly bring them here."

"Yes, madam," he replied, thanking her once more for her kindness while leaving.

Sara's friends were equally busy interviewing people with similar or completely different stories, but every one of the applicants felt equally desperate to acquire a blessed job.

CHAPTER 6

No superheroes needed

Every day was a hard day, with plenty of work to do, and everyone was exhausted. Unfortunately, it wasn't finished there. Lee and his friends had to work at night too, in rota. There were too many desperate people joining them, and they had to give people something to do.

David and Stefan moved into Lee's flat after David sold his house in order to provide more money for the entire operation. It was a huge gamble they all were taking, a desperate race towards an invisible target. Those desperate and insignificant people, eight of them, lived under the same roof by then, and they had decided to fight together against the most powerful people in the world.

Lee was delighted to know that the movie made after his book was to be released that week. Superheroes or not, it didn't matter anymore. If people liked it and the movie proved to be successful, Lee's celebrity status could attract further attention and thus sponsorship for their risky initiative.

A people's corporation, without leaders and highly paid almost useless experts, where the profit was evenly shared amongst its members, could also attract powerful enemies. Sensing the danger all of them were facing, Stefan finally had to agree to give up his dream of creating a world without politicians. But he was nonetheless allowed to create this utopic free world on a distant planet somewhere in the alien world, far from troubles and political reprisals. He was, of course, allowed to dream, as long as he didn't share his dreams with the wrong people. It appeared that dreaming could be as dangerous as actually turning dreams into reality.

Instead, they had to take a different approach regarding politicians. What if politicians had to pay some sort of fee for the people to vote? Wasn't such an approach similar to the tribute politicians had to pay anyway to the media in order to get their support?

The huge amount of money wasted on electoral campaigns to enrich journalists and other media representatives could be instead redirected to desperate people struggling with everyday life. However, that was still a long-pursued aim, as they had to be powerful enough to get politicians' attention. Otherwise, their revolutionary initiative would only produce another group of angry people whose voice was destined to become even angrier, especially that politicians and media continued to ignore them.

For then, however, they had to concentrate on survival. Since they desperately needed more and more money, Lee finally agreed to publish a new book as soon as possible.

This time was to be different. Everyone had to participate in writing the book, coming up with suggestions or providing useful feedback. Working mostly at night, after the exhausting work during the day, they kept writing the manuscript until everyone fell asleep.

Lee's flat had been transformed into a night-time publishing company, where its eight inhabitants worked desperately, each of them on a different chapter of the manuscript, followed by interchanging those chapters amongst them for further polishing or exchanging of ideas.

The subject of the book was about a magic spaceship, able to travel across the universe in a blink of an eye and to teleport its passengers to places of incredible beauty and harmony. How this travel was possible wasn't that important and remained an insignificant detail. Humanity always enjoyed dreaming about escaping this crazy world and finding peace and happiness in a better world. If dreaming was the only way to offer humans relief from their suffering, it was perhaps a good idea to give humans some opportunities to dream.

The magic spaceship would offer everyone a ride to any destination in this universe. And of course, those lucky travellers had to come back and tell everyone their incredible stories.

There were no superheroes involved and no need for them.

Fortune tellers and their lies

The movie *Race to Pluto* was finally released, and the outcome seemed to be very promising. There had been a great deal of good reviews—with people queuing in large numbers to see it. As the lucky author of the book, Lee was being pressured by the media to give interviews or to participate in TV reality shows. To date, he'd managed somehow to escape, but the media was getting more and more aggressive insofar as he wouldn't be able to continue ignoring them for long.

People wanted to see him, to admire his great talent and to be inspired by him. Among all the invitations he received since the release of the movie, there was, not surprisingly, a pompous, sophisticated invitation from intimidating and extremely overconfident TV presenter Mr Hook. Lee was invited to participate in his reality show the following evening, and there was a big surprise for him, a surprise that Mr Hook couldn't reveal in advance.

"Now what are you going to do?" asked his friends, amused.

"I don't know yet."

Lisa began to smile. She was the only one of her friends who knew Mr Hook personally, and she was imagining how entertaining an encounter between Lee and Mr Hook would be.

"Perhaps you should go," she said with a chuckle.

Sara was, of course, the next to come up with encouraging words, and soon everyone joined the supporting team. Lee had no choice. The majority had decided, and he had to participate in the damn TV show.

"Democratic actions can be dictatorial for the minority," Lee complained. Everyone laughed.

Nevertheless, that time, he agreed to comply and accept the majority's decision. Lee was also damn curious about meeting the famous TV presenter that Lisa talked so much about.

The TV show was about to start in a few minutes, and everyone was excited. That day had been another long day, with plenty of interviews and a lot of work to do. And then they were at home around the coffee table, still working on the manuscript. Julia and Susan had prepared some cookies for the event. The sight of the two girls coming with two plates full of tempting cookies encouraged the others to put aside the pages of the manuscript they had been working on.

The show began. Mr Hook entered the scene, accompanied by Lee. The audience received them with prolonged warm applause. Mr Hook began talking with great emphasis, using a lot of curious adjectives and incredible metaphors. His speech became a real poem.

Lee was introduced to the audience with the same poetic language, and a new round of hand clapping started. When the applause calmed down, they sat on two sofas arranged around a circular table adorned with flowers beautifully arranged. There were three more sofas forming a semicircle facing the audience. Mr Hook took the middle place and invited Lee to sit next to him to the right.

Sara wondered about the need of the extra seats present there . . .

After enduring a few more poetic minutes, Lee was invited to talk about himself, but he was constantly interrupted with new questions or suggestions made in abundance by his host. Sometimes Mr Hook would give incredible exclamations to express his admiration and amazement, and then he would suddenly change tone, continuing with a few more poetic expressions. Such conversation continued for a while, with sudden changes between poetic expressions and exclamations, until everything finally became kind of a mixture between poetry and exclamations.

Lee felt completely lost and unable to contribute to the conversation that seemed to be more of a monologue, with Mr Hook the only person talking. Fortunately, Lee's salvation was on the way.

A new guest was announced, Mrs Potato, having the professional name Mama Sunlight, and it turned out that she was a famous fortune teller.

Lee's friends were watching in terror how he became increasingly irritated by this unexpected encounter. They were well aware that Lee couldn't stand fortune tellers, miraculous healers, or any kind of wizards and witches.

"Something's going to happen," said Sara, worried.

"He'll probably lose his temper," said David.

"I hope Lee won't be tempted to slap anybody," Susan finished.

The fortune teller sat next to Mr Hook, and Lee's friends felt a small sense of relief. Nevertheless, they believed that there were troubles on the way. David left the room and returned soon with a bottle of wine and some glasses.

"We need some strong support," he said with sarcasm. He put the glasses on the table and began pouring wine into each of them.

"That's enough for me," said one of the girls.

When they each had a glass of wine, they turned their attention back to what was happening on TV.

Mr Hook had just finished his exuberant presentation of Mama Sunlight's great achievements. Then, with a more suggestive voice, as if saying there was still more to come, he invited the great fortune teller to tell Lee what was going to happen to him in the next ten minutes.

"Just looking in his eyes, I can predict amazing things," Mama Sunlight said with extreme confidence. "I can see a big surprise . . ." she continued, moving her hand across the table, trying to grab Lee's hand.

Visibly nauseated, Lee reacted quickly by taking his hands off the table and hiding them behind him. But the intrusive Mama Sunlight didn't want to give up. She stood up, intending to come towards Lee. In the meantime, as Mr Hook watched the scene, he tried to say something funny, but nobody laughed.

In a split second, Lee stood up too and shouted in the microphone, "Stay away from me!"

This unexpected reaction left her speechless. She took a step back, but she was still standing. Mr Hook stood up and tried to take charge of the situation. People were plainly flabbergasted, and they kept watching curiously to see what would happen next.

"Come on! We're amongst friends," Mr Hook said with a friendly voice.

"I'm here to help you," tried Mama Sunlight with a similar assuring voice.

But Lee got even more irritated and turned his rage against Mr Hook. "Why did you invite me here, Mr Hook, to talk to me or to advertise witches?" cried Lee.

Some children in the audience were plainly scared by the overly loud voice, and they started crying.

"She is not a witch, and I can assure you of her good intentions." Mr Hook was gambling everything to save his public image and to calm his interlocutor.

"Witch or not, she is still a liar. And I suppose, her *good intentions* include humiliating me publicly."

"Honourable gentleman, this poor innocent lady was only trying to predict your future," tried the TV host, his attitude humble and his voice as smooth as honey.

"And this implies that I am as much an idiot as everyone else who believes in fortune tellers or any kind of useless experts who make fortunes predicting the future but never getting it right. This also implies that I believe all the swindlers and liars that make their livings taking advantage of desperate people simply in need of some reassurance for their future . . ." Lee was unable to finish his idea.

Mr Hook mumbled something inaudible.

"How much did this *poor innocent lady* pay you to participate in this show?" roared an irritated Lee.

The show was soon interrupted. A new TV presenter appeared on the screen, announcing some technical problems and apologizing for the disruption.

Lee arrived home after midnight. None of his friends was in bed yet. Everyone wanted to know what happened next.

"Applause for our hero!"

Lee entered the lounge victoriously and received plenty of greetings and congratulations from his friends. Lisa was the most excited of all. Her arrogant former employer was finally taught a lesson.

"You must be hungry," said Sara. "Here are some cookies for you."

He took some and began eating while his friends continued to stare at him. They desperately wanted to know what happened next.

"You wouldn't believe it," said Lee, maintaining the suspense.

"Come on, tell us!"

"As the broadcast went off, Mr Hook became very aggressive and started shouting at me for ruining his show. He then pushed me over the sofa whilst the guards were intervening to take me by force to the exit. However, something incredible happened—the public stepped in, supporting me in defiance. Mr Hook and the fortune teller were beaten while the guards were surrounded and immobilised. Consequently, people proclaimed me as their hero and followed me to the exit in delirium."

Lee finished his story, an incredible story indeed.

They japed a lot . . . Democratic actions could sometimes be very useful!

"What about the big surprise, the one that the ridiculous Mrs Sunlight or whatever her name is predicted?" asked Susan.

"She predicted a big surprise, and she had a big surprise," replied Mark assertively.

"At least her prediction came true," said Sara with a chortle.

"But not the way she fancied it," completed David.

The future looks great, thought Lee, grinning hopefully.

It looked as if all the troubles they had before were not enough. The list of their enemies was extended to witches, wizards, and fortune tellers. Fortunately, there were plenty of fortune tellers and experts around, willing to tell them what to do next!

Predictions, the most successful lies

It was a shame that the great fortune teller had no time to predict what would happen the following days. Severely injured, she had to stay in her bed for an unpredictable length of time, leaving humanity deprived of her precious predictions.

Lee was again on the front pages. Some teenagers had recorded the unpredicted event and put it on the Internet. Consequently, his popularity increased dramatically, and the news of a new book to be published soon added more fuel to the fire. What's more, after the incident, the movie sales increased even further.

The future looked quite promising, but Lee knew it wasn't that simple. He couldn't predict the future. Nobody could.

Soon after the incident that made him a superstar, Lee was surprised to receive an email from Mrs Anna Harrison, a famous independent journalist and blogger, congratulating him for succeeding where she had failed. Apparently, Mrs Harrison had the same allergy against the false prophets. She was very pleased to have Lee on her side in the common battle to expose them. Furthermore, Mrs Harrison considered herself revenged by Lee's action. Therefore, she would be much obliged if Lee considered her one of his friends.

Lee wondered what happened to Mrs Harrison and why she considered herself revenged. Showing the email to his friends, he asked if they knew anything about that.

It was just another day with plenty of work to do, and they returned home tired as usual. Julia and Susan got busy preparing dinner. The others worked on the manuscript. The following day was the great day—Lee's manuscript would be submitted to a publisher. His friends were busy scanning the manuscript and making the last suggestions and modifications.

Sara recalled something from memory and began searching the Internet. A few minutes later, she said disappointedly, "They have managed to take it off. The video has vanished."

"What video?" asked Lee. The others were curious too.

"Mrs Harrison was publicly humiliated a few years ago. It was on a TV show on New Year's Eve."

"How come?" they wondered aloud.

It turned out that a financial forecaster was also present on the show, and Mrs Harrison began questioning him for his failed forecasts. Mr Kelvin, of course, didn't want to admit his failures, and the production team came to his rescue by breaking for adverts. But Mrs Harrison didn't want to give up so easily. After the ads finished, she took out a sheet of paper and showed the evidence of the forecasts that Mr Kelvin had made a few years before. Astonished, Mr Kelvin remained speechless, but the TV presenter came to his rescue: "For the sake of the argument, let's just move on!" he said.

Consequently, they changed the subject and began talking about political issues whilst Mr Kelvin was carefully preparing his revenge. Five minutes before midnight, he began a vigorous speech against Mrs Harrison, using incriminating words and plenty of accusations. She protested and asked for the right to defend herself. But the malicious Mr Kelvin replied resolutely, "Sorry, Mrs Harrison, but you had your time. Let's just move on!"

Mrs Harrison was then accused that her attack on Mr Kelvin was just to advertise her website. She protested again by saying that she only repeated what he said years before. Unfortunately, she had no time to finish her idea. The TV host ended the conversation, saying cheerfully, "Happy New Year!"

"She wasn't given the chance to defend herself!" Sara said.

Dinner was ready and Susan invited them to the dining room.

Meanwhile, an intense debate began around Sara's story, with everyone dissecting any part of it. There were too many provocative questions which needed urgent answers.

Why wasn't she given the chance to talk? Why did they change the subject so quickly, with the host's resentful attack against a person who simply reported the facts fortified by evidence? Why did they ignore her evidence? Whose reputation was at stake: the reputation of the failed expert or the reputation of the media industry? Or maybe both.

Lee said that a failed forecast was just yesterday's news and no one was interested in it. It was definitely more exciting reporting late-breaking news than repeating what had been said yesterday. It was damn clear that the media was only interested in maintaining their credibility, not in telling the truth. Unmasking failed forecasters would be of no benefit. Those people who called themselves experts had to make plenty of forecasts, and most of such foretelling didn't materialise at all. It was just a game of hit and miss. In case of a hit, the lucky forecaster would become a superstar and consequently rich. In case of a miss, no one gave a tinker's damn to remember anything about it.

Mark began complaining that not only financial experts but also scientists had become fortune tellers. Apparently, predicting the future was the easiest and quickest way of becoming rich and famous. Not surprisingly, plenty of popular science books using the authority of science and some great scientific titles for their authors had fallen for the same sin.

"But what about politicians?" asked Stefan. Apparently, they formed the biggest social group of fortune tellers. Therefore, politicians had to be on the podium with the highest percentage of failed prophecies. Pressured by either electorate, who wanted quick responses for all the problems, and also squeezed by the necessity to maintain their public images and to appear in control of any situation, the poor political class had become an efficient machine for making predictions and telling lies.

"If the majority of forecasts and predictions are supposed to fail, then why are they so successful?" said Susan.

"Because people want to feel in control of their destinies," suggested Lisa.

"They want to be continuously assured that everything will be fine. That's why people involved in making predictions and forecasts are so popular," said Lee.

"And so rich!" David added.

Luckily, Stefan found an opportunity to display his knowledge in history: "In time of troubles or disasters, the easiest way to become rich is to start predicting the future. History is full of examples . . ."

"That's why fortune tellers will always have jobs," said Julia.

"And great lives," said Stefan.

"At the expenses of those who believe them," confirmed Lee.

"Predictions and forecasts will always be the most successful lies," said David, showing that Stefan was not the only person with a good grasp on history.

David's comment appeared to have closed the discussion. Susan remained thoughtful for a moment, and then she came up with a new question, surprising everyone: "What happens when those predictions fail?"

"The same thing that happened to Mrs Harrison: no one is interested in them," replied Sara.

"No wonder this poor woman was publicly humiliated," added Lee.

"*Let's just move on!*" said Sara with fake seriousness, trying to mimic the TV presenter, imagining for a moment that she was a TV presenter who wanted to shut someone's mouth, while pointing to the deadline for the delivery of the manuscript that was the next morning.

They began laughing. When everyone finished eating, it was time to go back to work.

Reputation factory

As the leader of one of the biggest media empires in the world, Mr Horton followed with scepticism and curiosity the spectacular rise in popularity of many unknown people. Many losers had been presented to him, and in exchange for other favours, he and his army of journalists had to create pathetic stories about those losers to make them noticed and appreciated.

Every loser had a different story of failures, but it appeared that all of them had a similar desire to be noticed and consequently become a celebrity.

Fortunately, creating a celebrity out of nothing was an easy task for Mr Horton. It was similar to creating a new universe. At first, there was a place of high temperature and infinite confusion, followed by noise, plenty of it. Problem solved.

Coming with a shocking or incredible story and placing it on the front pages or in bold headlines was all that was needed to raise temperatures and create confusion. Then followed the noise . . . and the result was a new celebrity!

Of course, this lucky ready-made celebrity also needed a good reputation and an area of expertise.

Since no one was perfect and everyone had plenty of sins to be ashamed of, the reputation factory worked in parallel with the process of creating noise. The experts in reputation had plenty of work to do: cleaning people's dirty pasts and creating new amazing ones.

However, creating a reputation was only the first phase in the process of creating a celebrity. A reputation also had to be maintained and defended. That was fulfilled by a different kind of expert, always ready to give a hand to any celebrity in trouble.

Lastly, there was the easiest task: the *expertise.*

If the person in question happened to be a struggling writer, offering him or her a good editor to innocently make numerous suggestions and hence give a lot of help was indeed a fast way to solve a complicated problem. Eventually, even the worst would-be writer couldn't be that bad at writing as to fail finishing a pain in the neck called a damn book.

In the case of a scientist, it was a bit more complicated. Nevertheless, convincing a top scientific publication to publish the work of an aspiring celebrity might not have been that difficult. Even top scientific publishers were humans, and as such, they too needed money and favours.

Creating the expertise of a politician was definitely much easier; it only required teaching him or her how to make fantastic promises, how to show confidence in the promises made, and how to make a lot of noise and effing nuisance.

Since the job of financial experts involved mostly predicting the future, creating their expertise was quite challenging. Every would-be expert had to make as many predictions as possible in order to maximise the chances of getting it right. If by luck one prediction came true, it had to go on the front pages, while simultaneously getting rid of all the misses . . .

Mr Horton was always in a good relationship with the celebrities he "created". This was because his reputation factory could work in both directions, and that made him so powerful. If he could so easily create a reputation, he could equally easily destroy it.

Celebrities owed him a lot, and in exchange for his protection, they would become his faithful subjects and would refuse nothing to satisfy Mr Horton—their benefactor. His authority was not to be questioned, and his will couldn't be ignored.

But Mr Horton had good reasons to be angry.

The news was worrying. After the scandalous TV show went viral, Mr Norris's popularity was greater than ever. Consequently, his second book about a magic spaceship was expected to become even more successful than the first one. People seemed to be desperately interested in this book and looked impatiently forward to acquiring it.

This was not good. That loser was given a chance to stand out of the crowd and to have a decent life, but he forgot to say thanks. What's more, he also forgot who the boss was, and that was outrageous.

There was a limit that losers couldn't cross; it didn't matter how popular they were. Surpassing this limit meant war!

"What the hell is this Galanthus initiative all about? No worries. We will find out soon enough."

Mr Horton was waiting for the head of the secret police to arrive. They had been spying on the ingrate Mr Norris and his initiative since they began suspecting that something was not right.

Mr Lucas finally arrived and entered the office carrying a bag in his hand. Mr Horton welcomed his guest, shaking his hand and tapping him on his shoulder in a friendly manner. "Tell me the good news," he said.

"I'm afraid there is no good news," replied Mr Lucas hesitantly.

"Tell me the bad news, then."

"This website already has more than ten million subscribers just three weeks after its launch."

"I know that," said Mr Horton, worried. "Tell me what I don't know."

"They give a basic job to everyone who joins them. People are desperate and join in by the thousands." Mr Lucas paused.

"But they need money to pay people," suggested Mr Horton.

He was hoping that those pains in the arse would get into trouble soon.

"Mr Norris is gambling everything on this move. He not only has a good income from the book sales, but plenty of venture capitalists continue to join as well. This appears to be the hottest start-up ever."

"However, what is his intention? He is paying his users to do what?"

"Nothing for the moment—or at least they seem to be involved in advertising, writing product reviews, and chatting online with each other. Nonetheless, he wants to get involved in politics. Once his company is powerful enough, he wants to force politicians to make reforms and to pay a fee to his subscribers in order to vote. There will be no more electoral campaigns, I am afraid!"

"What!" shouted Mr Horton, outraged.

Organising electoral campaigns was his biggest source of income. How would this loser dare challenge his authority? But Mr Horton's horror hadn't finished yet.

"People will refuse to vote unless paid," continued Mr Lucas.

This would be a global corporation without leaders and without highly paid jobs. Everyone would be ensured the minimum survival income. In case of profit, it would be equally shared. This corporation would also ensure a pension for everyone on this planet and would protect all the poor against the abuses of the rich. There would be no more bailouts for banks and multinational corporations. The politicians would be forced to bail out only the people's corporations and to support their initiatives.

"However, there is some good news," said Mr Lucas, after conveying his devastating news.

"And what would that be?" replied Mr Horton with sarcasm.

"Mr Norris is not the only author of his latest book. There are seven other people living with him in the same flat: three guys and four girls. They did most of the work."

"Are you sure about that?" said Mr Horton with hope.

"Here is the evidence."

Mr Lucas opened his bag, took out a few CDs, and gave them to Mr Horton. "You may find some useful information. Here is everything about their current activities, their phone conversations, and the discussions they had during the past two weeks."

Mr Horton thanked his interlocutor. He had done a good job and was free to leave. But Mr Lucas was still waiting for his reward.

"You can go now. I promise your daughter will have a secure place in a top university, as agreed upon. She will have the confirmation shortly."

Mr Lucas finally left after thanking them again.

Mr Horton was then free to think about what to do next. His army of reputation experts had to be mobilised and moved against that ingrate loser. He picked up a phone and called someone. Minutes later, a secretary arrived and took away the CDs plus a note with instructions. When she was gone, Mr Horton seemed to be more relieved. Anyway, he had plenty of other things to do.

Spaghetti theory

"When Emeritus Professor Dr Ross arrives, send him up immediately," Mr Horton informed his secretary on the phone.

Meanwhile, he was going to kill his boredom by looking through Prof Ross's credentials and achievements.

Working as a science teacher at one of the world-leading universities, Prof Ross had spent most of his career in research around a well-known theory: string theory. He had published plenty of articles about the results of his research in prestigious scientific publications. Unfortunately, none of his articles managed to attract much attention, and if they ever did, they were quickly forgotten. As a result, although working as a researcher at a top university, Prof Ross was still unknown. With a few years to go before his pension, there was little chance that he might come up with a spectacular breakthrough that would ensure his stardom status.

Mr Horton was never able to understand this strange string theory. During his career as a media mogul, he had to promote many strange theories, but none of them appeared stranger than this one.

Strings vibrating in eleven dimensions . . . he recalled from past articles he'd read. *What the heck does it mean?*

Out of curiosity, Mr Horton had watched plenty of documentaries and videos on this topic. He still remembered a famous theoretical physicist and popular science writer talking in one of his videos about "a gigantic string left over from the big bang . . ." Apparently, this gigantic string might be found in the night sky among stars and galaxies.

Mr Horton began grinning.

If this gigantic string really existed, it must be very big indeed in order to be noticed. However, something didn't make any sense. According to string theory, those strings were supposed to be infinitesimally tiny, much smaller than the stuff that made up atoms.

How come there is this gigantic string!

After a few minutes of intense meditation, Mr Horton hit his forehead with the palm of his hand, with the feeling of someone who's just had his long-sought eureka moment.

This gigantic string must be somewhere in another dimension! It must be so; otherwise, we might be able to see it.

He thought for a moment and began smiling. *Or perhaps in a parallel universe . . .* This fantastic conclusion made Mr Horton smile even more.

What is this nonsense all about? Perhaps Prof Ross could explain to me this strange theory.

The academician arrived a few minutes later, accompanied by the secretary, who offered to show him Mr Horton's office.

Mr Horton received his honourable guest with a warm welcome and a vigorous shaking of hands. Then each of them continued for a while with boring formalities, stressing the honour each of them granted to the other in this high-profile meeting.

After a few minutes of banalities, the discussion changed to a more serious topic.

"Prof Ross, could you please explain to me this story about a gigantic string left over from the big bang? I was never able to understand it."

"I don't understand it either," replied Prof Ross frankly.

"But you spent all your life studying string theory," said Mr Horton. "You must understand it better than I do."

"No one understands string theory!" replied Prof Ross, stressing every single word and pausing shortly after pronouncing each of them.

Mr Horton was not expecting such an answer and remained astonished. He then considered a different approach.

"What about your career? What have you done all those years?"

The scientist didn't seem to care that much about defending his reputation. "I wasted my time," he murmured sadly.

Mr Horton could see the man's sadness, suggesting that his cause was lost long ago.

"The reason I called you here, Prof Ross, is that I wanted to offer you an exchange of favours. I intended to promote one of your scientific articles, of your choice, and to welcome you into the world of celebrities."

"In exchange for what?" the professor wanted to know.

"To secure a place at your university for a person recommended to me. Have a look!"

Mr Horton took out a folder and handed it to his interlocutor. As Prof Ross studied it for a few minutes, Mr Horton waited impatiently for his response.

"I think I can do it. However, regarding my scientific articles, unfortunately, there is nothing that deserves any special attention and nothing that deserves a front-page article."

Prof Ross looked vulnerable and defeated after so many years of research on a theory that didn't seem to make any sense. He was convinced by now that everything was in vain. Perhaps he just needed to do something for a living.

Mr Horton, however, was curious to know what was wrong with that theory. He wanted to hear it from someone who dedicated his entire life to studying it.

"It would make more sense if we got rid of the extra dimensions, supersymmetry, and parallel universes along with complicated formulae and theories that explain nothing. It's time to leave behind our pride and to accept with humility that we have no idea what the world is truly made of."

"But after so many years of research, you must have your own opinion about such complicated matters," suggested Mr Horton with hope.

"My idea would not make sense either," said the scientist.

"Tell me anyway."

"It's not my version of the world. A student of mine suggested it to me jokingly. He imagined a ball made of ribbons. Those ribbons are different fields that interact with each other, giving all the proprieties to a fundamental particle. For simplicity, imagine a dish of spaghetti made into a ball. Now, imagine billions of similar spaghetti balls sitting close to each other. What do you see?"

Mr Horton, puzzled and not appearing to have a clue, waited for Prof Ross to continue.

"There is none similar to each other," said the professor, proud of his answer.

"Impressive!" admitted Mr Horton. "And what would this prove?"

"This would prove that even what we call fundamental particles will be very complicated. In this world, one plus one does not necessarily equal two, which makes things even more complicated. But at least we might be able to explain the multitude of fundamental particles and their different properties."

Prof Ross continued talking with passion about this new theory— just another theory that didn't make sense.

A similar feature to all human beings was that they tried desperately to make sense of everything, coming up with fantastic theories that were supposed to explain their romanticised version of reality.

Mr Horton began smiling. Perhaps spaghetti theory was not that crazy. What if the world was very complicated indeed and there was no theory to explain it? What if humans were more humble regarding their capacity to explain everything?

Understandingly, Prof Ross was reluctant to both the publication and the support offered for such a theory. He didn't want to end his career in shame. All the experts that tried to make sense of the universe would turn against him and his spaghetti theory. He will end up as an outcast, and he surely didn't want to lose his friends. Most importantly, he didn't want to be bullied by the scientific community, as usually happened when scientists supporting old theories were challenged by a new one. Prof Ross remembered very well the story of a poor scientist who was so terribly bullied by the other scientists that he ended up hanging himself in despair. Just one year after his death, his theory was proved right, and all of its opponents were ashamed. However, this didn't stop them from claiming that the poor scientist was suffering from depression. Of course, no one was interested in mentioning anything about bullying . . .

Minutes later, both agreed that Prof Ross should try his luck with some scientific predictions. Such an approach could be a glorious end to a long career. Should any of those predictions materialise in the future, Prof Ross would have guaranteed eternal recognition and admiration for his great insights.

Only losers write CVs

Mr Sanders was on his way to Mr Horton's office. As the leader of a multinational corporation based within online services, he was already a billionaire. Habituated to always travelling on either his private jet or in one of his lavish limousines, he did not have many chances to meet common people. However, that day he wanted to make an exception by catching the train. His expensive suit had to be packed and carefully arranged in a valise carried by one of the men that secretly followed him. A cheap suit was used instead, to mask his real identity and avoid attracting too much attention.

At the train station, Mr Sanders bought a standard travel ticket. There was plenty of time left, so he began wandering around the train station, observing in silence and evaluating each person's worth, as he normally did with his business partners.

Those people look so busy, but what are they busy with? he thought.

People ran in all directions carrying heavy bags, completely ignoring each other. They were all busy with their own miserable lives, and nothing appeared to capture their attention.

Out of boredom, Mr Sanders began to imagine how much each of them might be earning and what he or she did for a living. Perhaps many of them were still looking for jobs and dedicated quite a bit of time to their favourite hobby: writing CVs.

"Losers," he muttered to himself, nauseated. "Only losers write CVs."

The train finally arrived. Of course, as a normal passenger, Mr Sanders needed something to read. He looked around to see which was the most popular magazine bought by losers, and he acquired one for himself. It was a magazine about celebrities. He smiled and began walking in the direction of his train, thinking that the losers' only consolation was dreaming of a day when they would be among celebrities.

Mr Sanders entered the train and took a random seat at the window. The train was still empty, but people continued to come in and take seats. A group of five noisy young people in their late twenties, three boys and two girls, took seats close to him and continued talking and laughing. It turned out that they were all students, postgrads. He continued listening in silence while pretending to read the magazine.

Those young people seemed proud of their accomplishments. After a few minutes of listening to their conversation, Mr Sanders could say with confidence that they were studying economics, business, management or finance, or a combination of these subjects. These were the most popular subjects and the most promising at that time. However, there was one little detail missing in this equation of success: jobs.

Out of curiosity, Mr Sanders decided to intervene in their lively conversation. "May I ask you what you are all studying?" he asked politely.

It turned out that his guess was right. They were studying something that would make them rich and famous in the shortest possible time.

He asked for more details, pretending not to understand.

The group of young people took this opportunity and began talking with pride and emphasis about their subjects and how privileged they were to be among the pioneers that would change the world. They talked with confidence about their future careers and the great titles attached to their names that would give them respect, high status, and money. Then they asked him what his profession was.

"I am a history teacher," Mr Sanders replied with a humble attitude. He knew that almost nobody wanted to study history anymore.

They looked disappointed, as if suggesting that history was just for losers, and they were clearly wondering why he decided to study such a useless subject.

"Because I'm not good enough to teach anything else," he replied with humility. *Because history contains plenty of pathetic losers like you,* he thought.

Then Mr Sanders changed the subject. He wanted to know if any of them had a job. None of them had, unfortunately. However, they had something called zero-hours contracts that would give them great opportunities, should there be any need for them somewhere. Meanwhile, they kept themselves busy by taking endless courses about everything, and that was supposed to give them, consequently, new titles, which were fundamental for a great career ahead of them.

Mr Sanders was surprised to find out how obsessed the common people were with having great titles.

We are going back to the Middle Ages! he thought.

It was during that time that the most incredible titles for the ruling class were invented. People with great titles also had the money. Nowadays, the situation had changed dramatically; some people had the titles, and others had the money. There were exceptions, of course, when lucky individuals could have both titles and money at once, but this didn't change the general rule.

Let them have the titles; we'll keep the money, Mr Sanders thought to himself with a smile.

The group of youngsters began smiling too. However, they had no idea that this apparently old fashioned gentleman smiled for a completely different reason.

Mr Sanders made a quick mental calculation. Those people with great expectations must be spending at least twenty years of their lives studying because they were constantly told that they were not good enough and not yet ready to get jobs. When they finally did find jobs, if they managed to, they were already too old and inexperienced to keep them and would probably lose them soon in favour of luckier or more compatible persons. So that was what losers called life: wasting almost twenty years studying for great useless titles and then spending the rest of their lives alone, disappointed and hopeless.

"What about your debt? How are you going to pay it?" he asked.

After so many years of studying, those would-be celebrities would have to pay back the huge debt accumulated during all those years.

They didn't seem to care, however, about their debt. Not right then. There was still plenty of time to do it . . . An overly anticipated dream job would solve that problem.

However, until the dream jobs materialised, they desperately needed any kind of damn jobs that would give them the damn chance to survive, while wasting their time studying for half of their lives with the hopes that somehow in the near future they would be ready to get better damn jobs, if they could find them.

Mr Sanders again made a mental connection to the Middle Ages. Things had not changed too much. Getting into debt to earn a living or bearing debts for great pompous titles was just the same shit.

Damn it! They would have to pay the debt back.

Two hours later, Mr Sanders entered Mr Horton's office and was immediately received by his old friend. They could not discuss on the phone the reason Mr Horton invited his friend to visit him. Mr Horton, however, mentioned some very urgent business that couldn't be delayed.

Seeing his friend in a modest suit was something unusual. "It must be funny walking around unnoticed amongst common people," said Mr Horton with a chuckle.

Very funny indeed. Mr Sanders began talking about the overqualified students he met on the train and how confident and proud of themselves they appeared to be.

"Let them dream!" said Mr Horton with a diabolic cackle.

They both knew that those overconfident and super-qualified people would never make it to the top unless they allowed it. The forbidden class would *always* be forbidden for outsiders . . .

Social status could be achieved differently at different levels.

In the losers' class, a great title might be useful to distinguish between different levels of losers. Alternatively, some people might use the force of their muscles or their physical aspects to reach the same result.

Within the forbidden class, things changed dramatically. There was no more need for big muscles, great titles, or amazing bodies. All that was needed was just money, loads of money, and power.

"But it's even funnier when they look at you with superiority and pity!" said Mr Sanders.

They kept laughing.

"You should have shown them your bank account," suggested Mr Horton.

"To see them have heart attacks? No! I am not that evil. Am I? Let them at least feel *great* and *useful*!"

"And tell everyone about the loser they met today," added Mr Horton, guffawing.

"Those arrogant losers would better mind their own miserable lives before labelling someone a loser," said Mr Sanders sarcastically.

By then, it was time to discuss business. Mr Horton began talking about a certain Lee Norris who had become very successful and popular recently, the latest sensational success story.

"I heard about him," said his friend. "And I saw the movie last week. Was great!"

But Mr Horton was not impressed. He had plenty of reasons to be worried. This ingrate was too popular and very soon would be dangerous too, unless stopped in time. He explained his concerns to his friend and urged him to join forces against the common enemy.

If that website continued to grow at the same vertiginous speed, after a few months, it would be too late to stop him. They had to buy his business, whatever the price was, in order to eliminate him as a competitor—as soon as possible.

Later, the two friends agreed on a plan of action. However, there was still a problem. Supposing they were able to make a deal, then they had to face more than ten million users of that bloody website that were in fact employees with permanent work contracts. How to get rid of all of them at once without creating troubles?

There had to be a way to do away with them.

Two days later, Mr Horton was looking forward to receiving some great news. He was alone in his office and had informed one of his secretaries not to let him be disturbed. But apparently, the good news was not good at all . . .

"What do you mean he doesn't want to sell his firm? I specially instructed you to make him a mouth-watering offer," said Mr Horton with anger, talking on the phone with one of his representatives.

"He doesn't want to consider any offer. He just doesn't want to sell."

The man talking on the phone gave a few more details about the failed negotiations, further exasperating his interlocutor.

Things were getting complicated and out of control. Mr Horton needed to take quick action.

The super world of superstars

A small town in the mountains was the place for an annual conference held by the members of the forbidden class. This was a good opportunity for all of its privileged members to make new friends and establish new connections, exchange ideas and favours, discuss new trends, propose new businesses, and last but certainly not least, to discuss any possible threats to this exquisite society.

All the members of the super elite had the responsibility and duty to support each other in maintaining their privileges and monopoly over the world economy. Thus they were always ready to make a solid common front against any possible foe.

Apart from money to be a member of the super elite, each individual needed to possess two things that symbolised high status: Firstly, owning a private jet was a must. Many people could afford to buy expensive cars. Therefore, an expensive car had lost ground as a symbol for the social status of the crème de la crème.

Secondly, owning a private charity organisation was also an essential prerequisite. This could make its owner very popular amongst losers and should prove useful for its owner in avoiding paying as many taxes.

Everything in the world of plutocrats had to be specially tailored to support their superstar status. Their clothes were fashioned by the best designers in the world, using the most expensive materials. The luxurious decorations of their houses had to be forged and adorned with opulence by superstar painters, and their gardens had to be maintained by superstar gardeners. What's more, superstar chefs created the most incredible dishes possible, using the most expensive ingredients. Not to mention that their superstar cleaners had salaries much higher than those earned by engineers or scientists.

The *super*star Mr Horton sat at a *super* table with some *super* friends, examining a *super* menu, whilst a *super* server of a *super* restaurant took a *super* order and wrote it down with a *super* pen in a *super* notebook. Then she left with a *super* smile and returned *super* fast with some *super* dishes and some *super* drinks served on a *super* tray . . . After a while, she brought a *super* bill and received a *super* payment and a *super* tip, and they began exchanging *super* thanks for this *super*-duper experience. The *super* guests then left, making a *super* exit, and went outdoors to enjoy their *super* lives on such a *super* day.

This was just a normal day in the life of a *super*star.

Mr Horton was engaged in a vivid conversation with Mr Clark, the CEO of a multinational insurance company. Mr Clark complained that since the Galanthus initiative, people didn't want to pay for insurance anymore.

"Just this week, we lost almost fifty thousand customers!"

"But what do they say when leaving?" asked Mr Horton.

"They say that paying the insurance is a waste of their money, getting nothing in return."

That loser is really looking for trouble, said Mr Horton to himself, worried by Lee's latest activities.

He was attacking the insurance companies by then. Later on, he would attack everybody else. All the plutocrats were in danger if his movement succeeded in reaching its goals. It was time to mobilise forces to get rid of those losers and their ridiculous movement.

Mr Horton expressed his concerns to his friend and urged him to join forces in the battle against their common enemy. Mr Clark, of course, accepted with enthusiasm. He'd already lost too much!

A common meeting was held later on, amongst a few members of the super elite, to discuss an urgent matter. Amongst them was Mr Foster, the CEO of one of the biggest Internet companies, who suggested using his spying machine to provide relevant data that might be used to their advantage. Everyone agreed on that. Thus they decided to meet a few days later back at home to analyse the available data and see what could be done.

The conference followed the usual agenda, with plenty of pathetic speeches and inspiring stories. Each speech had to contain highly sensitive words such as *innovation*, *professionalism*, *fairness*, *sustainability*, and most importantly, *transparency*. And like always, the vast majority of listeners where those people who needed the most of such inspiring stories; the losers.

Manufacturing evidence and other dirty games

A media empire as powerful as Mr Horton's empire had plenty of enemies, and he therefore needed a powerful army to defend it. This army was composed of a huge number of experts who specialised in different tasks.

Mr Fox led a team specialised in creating and destroying evidence, depending on the circumstances.

A few days before, Mr Horton handed him a case containing various CDs with Internet data, phone conversations, text messages, and recorded face-to-face conversations. After carefully analysing it, he spoke on the phone a few times with Mr Horton to decide what had to be done. His team had been working non-stop ever since to get the job done as soon as possible. When everything was ready, Mr Fox took the responsibility of handing in to Mr Horton the requested "evidence", which was to be used against some irritating losers.

Driving across the huge town, Mr Fox headed towards one of the residential areas, far away from the city centre. As he moved on, the houses were getting bigger and bigger, and the size of the gardens also increased proportionally. At a certain point, the gardens became so big that each of them could include a bunch of football fields. Every garden had some common features: a swimming pool; a playing field; numerous paths; and plenty of trees, bushes, and flowers. There were also some distinct features relevant to the owner's taste. Nevertheless, there was another common feature in all gardens: a private jet. This was the latest symbol showing the high social status of its owner, and it was a necessary requirement to be accepted by the community of haves. A runway connected all the gardens to each other and was considered a common good.

Mr Fox stopped in front of a big gate, which opened automatically after he identified himself, and then continued driving astonished across the garden of wonders. He parked his car on the side of the huge villa.

Mr Horton was waiting for him, he was told. Mr Fox took a bag from his car and followed one of the housekeepers on a path across the garden. On their way, they left behind a big villa and a swimming pool, where some women were having fun swimming or playing around. Wearing bikinis only, they were beautiful, with perfectly shaped bodies, and were extremely young indeed. Mr Fox continued walking until he vanished behind the trees and bushes. A wooden refuge with a small terrace was completely surrounded by trees and almost isolated from the outside world. All the humans, with their frenetic lives, their hopes and dreams, failures and disappointments, were in a seemingly different world far away.

Sitting at a table with two mysterious men, Mr Horton seemed lost in a few documents he was examining with great interest. He welcomed his guest and invited him to take a seat. The housekeeper was leaving, and his lord instructed him not to be disturbed.

The two men were introduced to Mr Fox as two friends, without mentioning their names, their professions, or the reason they were present. Wearing lavish suits and showing professional attitudes, they looked extremely confident, powerful, and intimidating.

As Mr Fox sat down, they took all the documents away and put them in two folders, and then they made them vanish in a bag each of them had in front of him. A few documents left on the table appeared to be less important, and nobody bothered hiding them. They just put them away on the same table and waited for Mr Fox to open his bag and to show its precious contents.

Embarrassed, Mr Fox would have preferred to talk in private to Mr Horton and thus made signs showing his intention, but his host assured him that everything was fine. With more courage, he opened his bag and began taking out one CD at a time, explaining its content, while the two mysterious and intimidating individuals continued to watch and listen in utter silence.

"This is the evidence for their anarchic intentions. This one contains proof of sexual harassment and exploitation of the girls. And the last one is the evidence that they intended to destabilize the world economy." He put the three CDs on the table in front of Mr Horton and waited anxiously for his reply.

"Perfect!" said Mr Horton, very excited. "Good job."

However, the two nameless individuals wanted to see for themselves the quality of the work done. Guessing their intention, Mr Horton went inside the refuge and returned straight away with a laptop. He then inserted one of the CDs, and with a few clicks, they could listen to a seemingly real conversation. There were some fellas talking about their plan to rebel against governments and to install a new order. They also mentioned a secret hiding place and the need for sacrifice and for challenging the law. Most importantly, they talked a lot about losers and about a secret pyramidal game that would give them the opportunity to rule the world.

Listening to this conversation for the first time, one would have likened it to facing the most ferocious, heartless, and dangerous criminals ever.

Mr Horton and the two mysterious individuals appeared to be happy about the quality of the evidence created.

"Now, could you please remind me what you wanted me to do for you in return for your favour?" asked Mr Horton with generosity.

Mr Fox hesitated to answer. He felt both embarrassed and intimidated by the two men. However, Mr Horton assured him once more of his friends' confidentiality.

"It is the daughter of one of my friends, who is participating in a TV talent contest," said Mr Fox, embarrassed.

"No worries," said Mr Horton in a friendly tone. "Your problem is almost solved." He gave him a sheet of paper. "Please write down the name of the girl, the name of the TV show, and the date of broadcasting."

As Mr Fox was writing on the paper, Mr Horton assured him that his friend's talented daughter would win a deserved first place in the competition. However, he didn't find it necessary to ask about further details concerning the girl's supposed talent or even to enquire about the kind of talent contest in question. She would win anyway. Everything else was just insignificant details.

Soon Mr Fox was free to leave, and he thanked Mr Horton once again for his kindness. Then he said hello to the two men while heading towards the path that would bring him back to the exit. After a few steps, he turned around, apparently to say goodbye again and to wave his hand. But in fact, he was extremely curious to see what they were doing.

The two mysterious men took out their documents again and spread them on the table.

They must have some important business to do, he thought, and he continued walking back.

"Almost done," exclaimed Mr Horton, excited when finally alone.

The most difficult part of his plan was not bankrupting a hot start-up but eliminating a popular hero. He had to come up with a credible story that would create public outrage. And what would create more public outrage than a new story of sexual abuse, physical violence, and anarchic intentions?

Mr Horton had the feeling that the herd would be on his side this time without even realising it. Intoxicated on a daily basis with news focussing only on scandals and disasters, it appeared that the herd had lost any inclination for critical digestion of the news. Nevertheless, making someone a hero today and a traitor tomorrow might not necessarily result in compunction of pathetic behaviour. Both winners and losers were humans; therefore, human feelings such as cruelty against members of the opposite social class could be very rewarding—resulting in raising their own social statuses and increasing their reputations.

Mr Horton desired neither a higher social status nor a better reputation. He was using all his energy, power, and influence, to acquire something completely different, but that was his own secret . . .

CHAPTER 7

The "monsters" have been revealed

One day the girls were allowed to leave earlier than usual. After one month of working without a break fifteen hours per day, seven days per week, each of them was completely exhausted and wouldn't mind a much-deserved break.

Lee had decided to be generous and thus allowed Julia to prepare a special dinner that night. Everyone deserved it, and everyone was looking forward it.

The prospect of their hard work was anticipated to be good. The company had attracted more than fifteen million customers, and their numbers kept increasing dramatically. Also, the number of venture capitalists joining them seemed to follow a similar pattern. If things continued the same way, they would have to go global very soon. However, the company was still extremely vulnerable and might have got into trouble at any moment. Their survival depended on the willingness of venture capitalists to join and provide the necessary finances.

In order to avoid running out of money, Lee and his friends had decided to employ people at a slower pace, putting many of them on the waiting list with the promise to give them a job as soon as possible. But those people on the waiting list could become full members and thus get involved in all activities in order to promote and support the company.

For the time being, they were not yet in a position of negotiating with politicians to gain their support. It appeared that politicians would continue to ignore them until they had enough power to be noticed. Nevertheless, some politicians followed, with interest and curiosity, the unfolding of events, undecided what to do next.

Sara, followed by Lisa, Julia, and Susan headed excitedly towards the exit of the office. The guys would have to remain a bit longer to finish the entire job for that day. The dinner should be ready by the time they arrived home.

The four girls took one car, leaving the other one for the guys, and drove across the huge city. The streets were busy like always. Sara followed the usual path from office to home, but at a certain point, she turned right and continued in that direction until reaching a supermarket. She parked the car amongst many other cars. They had to do the shopping.

When they got home, they brought all the items to the kitchen and then went to change their clothes. Julia then took charge of the kitchen environment and assigned the girls to various tasks. The menu was quite complicated, but Julia had enough cooking experience to make it look easier. There were four different dishes, from starters to deserts, and Julia took the most difficult task—preparing deserts—while closely watching her friends, making sure they knew what they were doing so that everything went well.

Two hours later, dinner was ready, with the pots and cutleries arranged on the table, besides other stuff such as napkins, drinks, and glasses. There was also a beautiful bouquet of flowers in a vase placed in the middle of the dinner table. The guys should arrive at any moment. The chosen menu would surely please them. Julia preferred to keep it secret until they arrived.

For the starters, there were roasted vegetables, marinated olives, smoked cheese, sausages, and salad. The first course was pasta with mushrooms, peppers, onion, chicken, tomato sauce, fresh basil, and chillies. The main course consisted of rice, roast beef, and a sauce made of different stir-fried vegetables. A special cake, beautifully decorated, plus various muffins and a fruit salad would be the delicacies to end this special dinner. Of course, there was plenty to drink as well.

The girls were waiting excitedly for the guys to arrive. Meanwhile, they took advantage of the free time available to prepare themselves, working on their make-up and helping each other when needed.

Sometime later, there was still no sign of the four guys. Running out of patience, Julia tried to reach on the phone any of them but nobody answered. She had a good reason to be upset since her delicious food was getting cold.

Hungry and tired, the four girls sat on a sofa in the TV lounge, watching indifferently a boring TV show. Two hours later, they were still waiting for their friends to arrive. It was not their habit to come home so late when they knew that dinner was about ready. At least they should have phoned to let them know that they were coming in later. But they'd agreed to get home on time that night—

"Perhaps we should call them again," suggested Sara. She picked up her phone and tried to reach Lee. The phone rang, but no one answered. She tried again with the same result.

"Let's try calling somebody else," said Lisa.

They called David, then Stefan, then Mark; nobody answered his bloody phone. Something must have happened. Suspecting that they would have to wait awhile until the guys showed up, Susan went to the kitchen to make some coffee. The other girls followed her out of boredom, not knowing what else to do.

"Make it strong, please," said Sara.

She had a bad feeling, but she did her best to remain calm. There was no need to alarm her company and no reason to panic. Not yet.

"I am so hungry!" complained Lisa.

Everyone was starving.

"Let's have the coffee first," said Julia.

"If they don't come in half an hour, we might start eating," suggested Sara.

"But at least can we have a muffin with the coffee?" tried Lisa again.

No one answered, although the other girls were as hungry as she was.

"Please!" she continued with the same complaining voice.

It was almost midnight, and they'd only had a light sandwich for lunch in the hopes of having a great dinner later. Ironically, there was plenty of food on the dinner table, and the temptation was greater than ever.

Julia decided to be generous. "All right! Only the muffins, though."

When the coffee was ready, everyone poured some milk into mugs with one or more sugar cubes. Lisa, however, went for the muffins first, making sure they would not change their minds. Now they could go back to the TV lounge. Sitting on a sofa was far more comfortable than sitting on a kitchen chair.

The girls sat randomly on the sofa and began eating the delicious muffins. Julia received plenty of compliments. They were delicious indeed and were gone in a blink of an eye. While drinking the coffee, all of them tried to imagine what might have possibly happened. They hoped that nothing had happened and that everything would be fine. As they finished the coffee, they fell asleep one by one on the sofa.

Sara was the first to wake up.

She'd slept very agitatedly, and her worries did not vanish during her dreams. It was still dark, mostly because of the clouds. The sun should be rising soon; however, it would be difficult to notice it until much later.

"What's the time?" she wondered aloud.

It was half past five. Her friends were still asleep. Sara went to the terrace and slowly closed the door behind her. She then sat on a bench surrounded by plants of different sizes and shapes, which were beautifully arranged and maintained. Perhaps it would be a good idea to call Lee again.

The phone rang.

"Police Department of Criminalistics," answered an unfamiliar male voice. "This is Major Green speaking. Who's there?"

Sara was surprised by the reply, expecting to have Lee on the phone instead of the police. She introduced herself and then asked to talk to Mr Lee Norris.

"This is not possible," said Major Green with a fake friendly voice. "He is not in condition to talk," he continued, whilst Sara could hear the noise made when someone consulted some sheets of paper in a hurry.

"You must be strong, Miss Sara . . ."

"Oh my God!" she exclaimed. Sara remembered from all the movies she'd seen that when someone asked you to be strong, something terrible must have happened.

"What happened!" she asked desperately.

It turned out that Mr Norris was dead, with three other chaps who were with him. Major Green gave their names and continued with further details. Apparently, they had opened fire against the police, and the police had to defend themselves.

Sara lost grip of the phone, and it fell on the pavement. The major was probably still talking, but nobody was listening to him. She started to wail in despair.

Hearing her sobbing, the other girls woke up and joined her on the terrace. Sara was pale, her body was trembling, and her voice was unrecognisable.

"They're dead . . . all of them," lamented Sara in despair.

When the weeping girls finally managed to calm themselves down and accept the utterly horrendous news, they had to acknowledge that there was nothing they could do to change anything. They had lost their battle against the elite, who preferred to fight back in a cowardly way. By then, there was nothing left but to admit defeat and to resume life, or what was left of it, pretending that nothing had happened . . . if they really had the strength to pretend that such a terrible thing never happened.

"This story must be on the news," suggested one of them.

Lee was pretty well known, and this story could not go unnoticed. However, the news itself sounded more terrifying than anything they had ever imagined.

The headline read, THE MONSTERS HAVE BEEN REVEALED! The four guys were presented as ferocious monsters planning to turn the world into anarchy. Apparently, police suspected something and wanted to stop them for a regular check, but then the monsters opened fire, thus the police fought with heroism and managed to shoot the monsters down before they had a chance to manifest their evildoing selves to the public.

"They didn't have any guns!" roared Sara in anger. "Liars!"

"They're all lying!" cried the other girls.

Evidence of their supposed anarchic behaviour was promised to be revealed soon. Meanwhile, plenty of comments were being made by various TV stations about the secret monsters living amongst us, praising the hard work of the police in uncovering them.

The girls couldn't watch anymore, so they turned the TV off.

A humiliating compromise

One hour later, someone knocked at the door.

"It's the police. Please open the door!" shouted an unknown voice with authority.

They opened the door, and two men in uniform and another one wearing a suit entered one by one, introducing themselves as the people in charge of the "monster case". Before saying anything else, one of them showed a search warrant.

The men in uniform began investigating everywhere. It appeared that they knew everything about this house, and they followed their pursuit with high precision. The dinner was still on the table untouched, and they took notice of that. The person in a suit, who identified himself as the inspector, invited the girls to sit down. They had to talk, he firmly said.

"We are very sorry for your loss," the inspector began compassionately. After a brief touching speech, populated with some pathetic encouraging words that were used by him as a psychological tool to calm the hopeless girls, he suddenly changed both tone of voice and body language.

By then, the inspector appeared more serious and less emotional. He began talking about the terrible crime against humanity of which the four monsters were being accused. The girls protested against the harsh words, but the inspector appeared prepared for all contingencies. He touched on all the evidence they had so far, enough to send the four of them behind bars for years to come. However, he wanted to be generous and said he would offer them a deal in exchange for their collaboration.

The girls were astonished and refused to believe it. Lisa and Susan, however, couldn't maintain their calm any longer and began crying and shouting despairingly. They wanted to know why the guys had to die and who was behind this atrocity. At first, the inspector tried to avoid answering by changing the subject; however, the poor girls continued with their desperate accusations for a while.

The inspector lost soon his temper and suddenly shouted as loudly as he could, "Shut up!"

This unexpected change of voice mortified the girls.

"I am only following orders," he continued with a similar loud voice. "You either accept my terms or not!"

The girls listened in terror to the terms of the deal, afraid of even catching a breath. However, the Inspector, in control of the situation by then, wanted to appear more humane by talking more softly.

First, they would not be allowed to see the corpses. Then the four of them had to publicly declare that they had been abused and exploited, thus expressing their refusal to see the offenders, even if they were just cadavers. Consequently, they had to produce some physical evidence in support of their affirmations.

Second, their ridiculous online initiative will be shut down without any further questioning or explanations.

Third, Sara had to declare that she was the real author of the two books and have the other girls as witnesses. This way, she would be allowed to claim ownership of the flat and to use the income from the books' revenues to support herself and her mates.

Fourth, all the accusations against them would be removed if the girls behaved, i.e., abstained from getting involved in politics, avoided making any stupid contradictory declarations to the agreement on this deal, and made non-verbal vows to never get involved in similar utopic activities. On top of that, adherence to the imposed terms and conditions would grant them the chance to have normal lives.

Of course, the girls would be monitored. Any trickery would cost them their freedom for a long time.

Two hours later, after giving all the requested declarations and producing the physical evidence by injuring each other, the exhausted girls had no more energy or courage to prepare for the promised "normal" life. Their investigators left, taking away with them all of their computers, the recording of their declarations, and the pictures with their self-inflicted injuries.

They were hungry, but none of the girls had any appetite for eating or any energy to do anything. In fact, they were ashamed to look into each other's eyes and afraid to say anything that might hurt their beloved friends even more.

Their new life that was supposed to be a normal life started with a lot of suffering and despair. They lost almost anything: their friends, their happiness, their smiles, and their courage. What's more, they felt truly alone, defenceless and powerless, at the mercy of an invisible and extremely powerful enemy.

One by one, the girls began sobbing, but it appeared they had no energy left even for this last act of expressing their human feelings. Hugging each other, they found it useless to say anything, and soon all of them began to fall asleep, easy preys to their dreams.

No one kept account of the time, but when the girls woke up, they could see in the window that outside was dark and that night would probably last for a few more hours. Their first thoughts were that they were terribly hungry and needed something to eat. Walking hesitantly and trembling at any single movement, the girls who just two days before were so lively and courageous now appeared terribly insecure and scared of everything. Each of them appeared to be a different version of herself, completely changed and almost unrecognisable. One by one, they went to the bathroom to wash their hands and faces. There was no need for any make-up. There was nobody to see them, and they wanted to see nobody.

The dinner prepared the night before was still there, untouched. They had to discard the food and put away the drinks. There was nothing left to celebrate. Then they put all the plates in the sink to wash later. They would eat something from the fridge, anything that could be found and that didn't require any cooking. None of them had the energy right then.

There was just some cheese, tomatoes and olives, and they put everything on a single plate to share. Julia added some olive oil to the dish and some fresh basil. Fortunately, there was plenty of bread, and the hungry girls didn't bother slicing it but instead broke it by hand, with two girls at a time pulling with little force from a piece of bread.

Meanwhile, Sara prepared the coffee, and she made it very strong in order to regain their forces and to remain awake. For later, each girl would have to decide what to do with her own life, or what was left of it.

However, none of them felt any need to watch the news or to contact anybody from the outside world. They just wanted to be alone, completely alone, with their suffering and the right to mourn for the loss of their beloved "monsters" . . .

Reward for saving the world

Mr Horton was excited as he digested the news that the latest attempted utopia had ended in shame, resulting in a new popular delusion and public outrage.

"Losers should never forget who the boss is," he mumbled.

Now that he was again in control over his media empire, Mr Horton could concentrate on fulfilling his personal ideas about saving the world.

For different people, saving the world could mean very different things. Nevertheless, Mr Horton was clear about it. The world could not be saved unless there was absolute freedom of the media. In other words, this absolute freedom included the right to stalk people, the right to brainwash them as he pleased, the right to create scandals at the expense of their nemesis, and the right to influence and control politicians.

Apart from saving the world, Mr Horton's most important mission was saving the elite and their personal empires. The biggest threat to the world order had been recently eliminated due to Mr Horton's hard work. This had increased his reputation amongst the elite. Although constantly ignored by the triumvirate for a long time, things began to change in his favour. As a result, Mr Horton finally managed to be noticed, and not surprisingly, he received the most important letter ever addressed to him: an invitation to meet the triumvirate.

That day was a great day for him!

Mr Horton left home feeling excited. Taking his private jet, he flew over the huge city to an unknown destination. After a few hours of flight, he arrived somewhere in the mountains and landed on a private runaway surrounded by big well-maintained gardens and exclusive villas. He's never been there before. The place looked somehow similar to his own residential area, although it looked more isolated and far better protected from outside invaders.

As Mr Horton got off the plane, a superstar driver, well dressed and overly nicely mannered, invited him to take a seat in his car. The lavish car drove along the labyrinth of streets at a low speed whilst Mr Horton contemplated—bewildered—all the wonders and beauties of the small remote village. After minutes of amazement and wonder, the car stopped in front of a small yet extremely elegant villa. There were no more fences or gates, just paths connected to the main private road. It appeared that this community had no need to defend themselves from each other. The real enemy had to be outside, and that explained the huge fences, walls, and well-defended gates surrounding the area and giving the impression of delving into a fortress. Mr Horton noticed that all the surveillance cameras were placed in strategic spots and the high numbers of personal guards were placed strategically on the outside walls.

But Mr Horton didn't have to worry about security measures, as he didn't have to worry about what to do next. Everything seemed planned with infinite precision in every minute detail.

As the car stopped, the driver got out of the car and opened the door for him with precise movements and exaggerated politeness. He thanked him cordially for his visit and wished him a great day.

Then another person, similarly well dressed and equally polite and well mannered, took charge of welcoming the honourable guest and invited him to follow him in. They continued walking on a path adorned with statues of lions, tigers, and some other powerful creatures. A few benches were arranged along the path, but other benches and tables could be seen amidst the trees and bushes connected to other pathways.

They finally arrived in front of the exquisite villa, and Mr Horton was invited inside. He walked hesitantly through a series of corridors until a door was opened and he found himself on a terrace behind the house. He had the feeling of walking into another world; everything appeared so magnificent and extraordinary! From the main road, this terrace was completely invisible, well hidden behind the villa, with a small hill linked to the building on its left side.

After a few seconds of contemplation, Mr Horton realised that the terrace was much bigger than previously thought. It was completely protected by the building on one side and the hill on the other. On a third side it had a tall wall, giving it an extraordinary panorama that could be seen on the horizon from far away.

The terrace had a somehow irregular form and was adorned with plenty of ornamental plants and flowers. On the side facing the hill, there was an artificial wall made of big stones. It was built in such a way as to appear natural. There was a path along the hill, with benches and tables placed in strategic places. Mr Horton could see the entrance of a cavern somewhere in the wall, suggesting that there was even more to be revealed . . .

Three men were sitting at a table, and the bewildered Mr Horton was invited to join them. He introduced himself with humility and was thankful for the opportunity to meet the most powerful people on the planet. Having almost perfect looks, the three gentlemen in lavish suits introduced themselves as: the first master, the second master, and the grand master. They welcomed him and shook his hand warmly, and then they invited their fortunate guest to take a seat.

"We would like to express our gratitude for your contribution in saving the world!" said the grand master with a solemn attitude.

"I only did my duty, sir," replied Mr Horton humbly.

He had been instructed in advance to use a submissive attitude with every single question or answer he might address to the great, powerful gentlemen.

In the meantime, Mr Horton noticed a triangular laptop, much bigger than ordinary ones, sitting on the table, and he began staring at it inquisitively. It was not an ordinary laptop. It was more like a triangular desktop attached to a curious keyboard.

Catching the direction of his sight, the grand master began smiling.

"This is the **Game of Power**, and we can watch it instantly," said the first master. "It's so much fun!"

Mr Horton had heard about this game, but he'd never had the privilege of playing it.

"Sir . . ." He tried to continue saying something but stopped in embarrassment.

"Our records shows that you never had the opportunity to play it," said the grand master, showing a generous attitude.

"Yes, sir," replied Mr Horton humbly.

"We have decided to give you a chance," intervened the second master.

"Your name will be on the list for the selection," said the grand master.

"Thank you so much, sir!" replied Mr Horton with extreme gratitude.

They then explained to Mr Horton what this selection meant.

A list containing 240 names, his included, would be prepared for the game. Then the game was to be played according to the rules, and the pyramid was completed with numbers. At the end of the game, half of the numbers would be rejected, the ones that did not find any place on the pyramid. However, the lucky ones would form the audience, and they would have great fun. Moreover, the three numbers at the very top of the pyramid would form the jury. Their duty was to preside over the next **Game of Power** and, most importantly, to decide the fate of the winner.

Later, Mr Horton was invited inside the house. He entered a room that looked similar to a small theatre. However, there was a big difference. On the space that was supposed to be a scene, a huge pyramidal structure made of dots, at equal distances to each other, could be seen on a screen mounted against the wall.

"This is a more comfortable environment for watching the game," he was told.

There was also a huge computer on a desk, and the intimidating grand master took a seat in front of it, inviting his privileged guest to sit close to him on another chair.

"I want to show you something very funny!" said the grand master.

As Mr Horton sat down, his powerful host continued: "This computer contains all the CVs written by the losers on the entire planet. Do you know how many of them call themselves leaders?"

"I have no idea, sir," said Mr Horton, puzzled.

"More than three billion! Isn't this incredible?"

"Unbelievable, sir," replied Mr Horton, still bewildered, taking the chance to show an attempted smile.

Fortunately, the intimidating host began laughing, and Mr Horton had to do the same, abashedly. Nevertheless, he felt more relaxed by then.

"Of course, this number would be much bigger if we counted people who don't have a CV, people who don't need a CV, and people who don't know how to write a CV," continued the grand master, visibly entertained.

"More than three billion leaders?" stressed Mr Horton, trying to be funny. "But what are they leading, sir?"

Such an unexpected question made the three intimidating men descend into uncontrolled laughing.

In the world of losers, everyone claimed to be a leader. Despite the great attributes given to themselves, losers were just leading miserable lives on journeys without destinations.

Leadership seemed to be just one of the great, pompous titles losers used to give themselves significance. But there were plenty of similar incredible and fantastic combinations of curious words, proving that losers didn't lack imagination. They might or might not actually have the skills listed in their CVs, but losers would always have great imaginations.

Losers should be good citizens

By the time the four unfortunate girls finally accepted that their lovers were lost forever, they tried to fill the empty voids left in their lives. For the time being, none of them had any courage or energy to start looking for jobs. Their suffering was still overwhelming.

The unfortunate loss of the four guys was just part of the girls' suffering. An aggressive media campaign to demonise the guys on a daily basis had become unbearable. From a popular hero, Lee had become a ferocious monster in less than a week, and people's outrage reached astronomical proportions. What's more, plenty of people began coming over to declare that they knew in advance the real face of the monster. The same people, who just one week before were asking desperately for his help, shamelessly forgot too soon everything he did for them. Instead, they were to become his most aggressive accusers.

On top of that, some feminist organisations became even more aggressive than all the media combined. Since the most popular words in their agenda included horrific words such as monsters and abusers, they did not bother to check the facts to see what really happened. As a result, plenty of pathetic stories followed, adding more fuel to the fire and creating street protests for the protection of vulnerable women against all monsters.

For the four girls, it was almost impossible to leave home, and they had to order food on the phone. The street was almost always occupied by reporters and activists who desperately wanted to get first-hand interviews with the terrorised victims.

They didn't have to descend into the street to see what was happening. The TV news was broadcasting sequences of events live from time to time. The girls watched in terror all the pathetic declarations and accusations that were made by overly outraged people.

But those relentless people who wanted to offer their terrific help at any cost didn't seem to be happy just invading all the TV channels, the major newspapers, and the quarters where they lived. One day they even managed to invade their flat.

Sara had just ordered some food, and the hungry girls were looking forward it. As the delivery person arrived and asked the porter's permission to go up, news reporters somehow found their way to the street. Consequently, all the terrific supporters, activists, journalists, psychologists, and many other desperate experts specialising in helping people against their will took this opportunity and invaded the building, ignoring the porter's resistance.

The delivery person entered one of the two lifts available, and he was fast enough to close the door and push the button for going up. After a few minutes, he arrived at the right floor and left the door of the lift open for his return. After he rang the bell at one of the doors, a girl answered, looking pale and weak, her entire body trembling. The delivery person gave her a bag with the ordered food. Forcing a smile, she thanked him with an almost inaudible voice.

The other lift arrived before she could close the door. In a blink of an eye, an army of experts were at the door and taking possession of its handle. The unfortunate girl did not have enough force to close it, and in her weak struggle against the invaders, her food fell on the floor. Now that the invaders had scored their first victory, the defenceless girl ran inside screaming, followed by all the angry, zany experts. Plenty of other invaders were coming, taking the stairs. It could be easy to guess their number by the amount of noise they were making.

Soon the terrified girls were assaulted by a huge amount of questions, all being asked at the same time, and the terrible noise made it impossible to understand a word of what they were talking about. As a result, the invaders began shouting even louder, all of them trying to make themselves heard over the others. The girls managed to stay together and to retreat little by little into a narrow corridor, urging their assaulters to leave them alone. Their pale faces were to be interpreted as evidence of the monsters' abuse. The sight of the four girls screaming defencelessly convinced everyone that they definitely needed some expert help. Fortunately, the poor girls managed to find refuge in the bathroom and lock themselves inside. At least those noisy people had the minimum decency to let them enter the bathroom.

During this time, more and more people kept coming up the stairs, flooding the flat, which was already full of people. The ordered food was spread on the floor, and people walked over it rakishly, increasing the mess. The supposed house of horrors shortly became a real house of horrors whilst the invaders kept themselves busy talking pictures, recording and interviewing each other, and adding extra material to their evidence. Some of them went as far as examining and identifying anything that could be used as evidence of the massive crime committed by the monsters.

Some experts with more human feelings tried to show their compassion with the girls by urging them to open the door and accept their professional treatment for post-traumatic stress disorder. Some others suggested plenty of other professional treatments, and they kept shouting desperately and aggressively, giving terrific details about their expertise. However, none of the offered treatments seemed to be more ridiculous than the advice to behave like winners, given by a pathetic woman shouting, screaming, and moving her hands like an orchestra conductor who specialised in horror music.

The four girls seemed to have no other choice but to accept some sort of treatment, but since the offers were so numerous, they were unable to choose the best option. The poor girls only wanted to be left in peace. Unfortunately, the invaders didn't even want to consider this option.

Fortunately, the good porter called the police, who arrived just in time to end the girls' suffering. One by one, the invaders had to leave, disappointed that they didn't get a chance to show their expertise and compassion. As the last of them left, a police officer assured the girls that they were safe and urged them to open the bathroom door. There were many other police officers around, and they watched with compassion as the poor girls came out of the bathroom, walking hesitantly and still sobbing silently.

It appeared that nothing could stop reporters from putting their hands on a shocking story. In a short period, they managed to harass the girls through phone calls, offering their terrorising support. They kept doing that aggressively at any hour of the day or night. Completely exhausted, the four unfortunate girls decided to turn off their phones. This left them with no other alternative for ordering food.

As usual, they gathered in front of the TV—their last connection with the world. Fortunately, there was plenty of coffee and tea. Regarding the food, Julia used her imagination and a few remaining ingredients to make something comestible.

Sara brought the coffee on a tray and put it on the table. There was no more milk left. Julia had made some little cakes out of rice and some other things she managed to find. Minutes later, all of them sat randomly on the sofas. Lisa turned on the TV.

On the news, there were more revealing stories about the four dead monsters. Their anarchic intentions and the danger they posed to democracy had convinced the president that democracy was extremely vulnerable. New measures were to be taken, and the president was going to announce his decisions that evening.

Until then, the four girls had to endure watching people commenting and debating on the declarations they were forced to make against the "monsters". However, those declarations appeared completely different by then, amplified for more effect and modified as to induce the maximum people's outrage.

"Please forgive us, guys!" the girls said helplessly, unable to hide their guilt.

They were well aware that they could do nothing to defend the innocent men.

Mr President was to appear live at any moment. It has been a highly advertised, and perhaps plenty of people were looking forward to such an event.

In the meantime, it started to rain, and the girls had some sort of small relief. Perhaps some of the people occupying the street would decide to go home and to give them a break. All of them were hungry, but there was almost nothing left to eat.

A TV presenter announced the much-expected event, and soon Mr President appeared live. He began his speech, maintaining a serious and professional attitude throughout its duration. He talked about the hard work and commitment demonstrated by the secret police recently, praising them for their impressive performance in unmasking such a horrific threat to democracy and society. Then he expressed his gratitude for the police's hard work, which had ensured that the monstrous evildoers would never be able strike again. He continued assuring the citizens of his protection and outlined what had to be done in order to defend democracy from future threats.

The combination of words concentrating on defending democracy seemed astonishing. The four girls listened to the speech, unable to believe it, especially the fact that it appeared deadly clear that the president was suggesting more spying measures against the citizens. And of course, good citizens had to keep quiet and accept everything with humility.

"Shut the heck up!" shouted Sara, fuming with rage.

The president used a strange combination of adjectives related to democracy, and she couldn't stand it anymore. As the president continued his speech, announcing new tough measures against all enemies of democracy, Sara lost her temper once again and did something she had never done before, which was quite shocking to both her friends and herself. She took the remote control, threw it with all her remaining strength at the TV, and began shrieking in despair.

One of the girls turned off the TV, and all of them gathered around Sara, trying to calm her down.

It was still raining. Sara appeared to have calmed herself, but her state of desperation and worthlessness was still darkening with agony in her soul, and it continued to hurt her gravely.

Soon she made an unexpected decision and ran to her room, followed by the other girls, who were curious to see what her intentions were. Sara began searching desperately in her wardrobe and made signs to her friends not to talk, as they were probably being spied upon. She took a rucksack and began filling it with things, urging her friends to do the same.

One hour later, four girls left the building, each of them carrying a rucksack, and entered one of the cars parked nearby. The car began moving and vanished shortly under the rain and into the darkness . . .

Gambling with other people's destinies

Mr Horton kept watching the selection game with interest and hope. It was the first time that his name was included on the list, and he was particularly curious about it. He took a random seat in the secret private theatre and began to stare at the huge pyramidal structure on the scene that would shape his fate. As he sat down, people he'd never met before filled the seats around him. All he knew about them was that they were some of the world's first-class citizens and that it would be extremely useful to have such powerful and influential people as his friends. He introduced himself to the closest people around and began chatting. Soon the game started and all their attention was focused elsewhere.

As the pyramid was completed line by line, Mr Horton looked forward to seeing the number corresponding to his name. The selection game was somehow different from the **Game of Power**, where losers were involved. They didn't need to make any calculations or speculations. They only needed to see their corresponding numbers on the pyramid. Of course, the top three numbers would form the jury, so people might wish to see their corresponding numbers at the top. However, since half of the total numbers were excluded from participating in the **Game of Power**, some people just contented themselves with any place on the pyramid.

When the pyramid was nearly completed, Mr Horton began to panic. His name had not appeared yet. There was the possibility of getting a place at the top, but he was afraid to consider himself that lucky. He watched in terror at the latest numbers being played, and there was no sign yet of his number. Irrespectively, he was very lucky indeed. The last number was thirty-five red, his number! Mr Horton would therefore preside over the next **Game of Power,** to be played that evening.

A few hours later, Mr Horton sat with two other men in a defined seat closer to the scene, thereby forming the jury. He was the master of the game and gave the signal for its start with utter excitement.

Mr Horton was under no illusions as to what everything was all about. That was definitely a game of chance, and they were gambling with other people's destinies for fun.

They're just losers, he mumbled. Mr Horton was trying to encourage himself in order to feel less guilty. *Those losers should be very grateful to us for giving them a chance.*

After such a conclusion, he felt much better. It was the losers who had to say thanks and to be grateful for the opportunity given.

Lost in his thoughts, Mr Horton did not realise the passing of the time. One hour later, the last piece was played and a winner was announced. It was a certain Mrs Clarke, a jobless young woman studying acting and performing arts. As they went through her CV, populated with plenty of impressive, positive adjectives and a curious combination of her supposed skills, people began losing control of their feelings and started laughing and having fun. There was just so much to laugh about when losers described themselves with such great words!

Mr Horton was having fun too and felt more entitled for doing so now that he considered himself the master of the universe, or at least the master of someone's destiny.

A person he'd never known existed would have a great career due to his decision. Everything was in his hands. Mr Horton would have the chance to play God for the first time in his life.

"Let's make her a famous actress!" he decided.

His decision was received with enthusiasm, and the people present began competing amongst themselves regarding other details. However, Mr Horton was not really amongst them. Intervening from time to time in the debate just to show his presence, he continued to remain lost in his thoughts.

God would have done it differently, he thought.

After the plan of action was presented to him, Mr Horton approved it and then handed it to some other people for its execution. By then, he had a last chance to display his immense power. Taking a serious attitude, he dismissed the audience arrogantly, emphasising his last words: "Let there be a new actress!"

Now Mr Horton considered himself equal to God.

The winner takes it all

Mrs Graham opened the door and was surprised to see the four girls in a terrible status. They were pale and trembling. Each of them was carrying a rucksack that appeared to be too heavy for her fragile body. They looked almost unrecognisable, and Mrs Graham invited them inside out of pity, without asking what had happened. She already knew what had happened to the four guys and followed, without being able to believe it, the aggressive media campaign of demonising them on a daily basis. As she saw them, she suspected that the poor girls had to run away to escape the media pressure and to have peaceful lives.

Claire, her daughter, arrived and welcomed them with a warm hug. "Oh my God! What happened?" she asked, shocked. "When have you last had anything to eat?"

Her friends tried to speak, but their voices sounded almost inaudible. Their mumbling appeared very painful, and Mrs Graham and her daughter decided to spare the poor girls of any inutile effort. Thus Claire took charge of accommodating her friends in some spare rooms, taking off the rucksacks that they could carry no more. One of the two housekeepers came to prepare the rooms for them, and Mrs Graham and the other housekeeper began preparing something for the unexpected hungry guests to eat. It was late, almost midnight, but the girls would have to eat something to regain their strength.

As Claire carried the rucksacks one at a time to the rooms given to her friends, she began to wonder where they wanted to go. The heavy rucksacks were proof that those girls were up to something, but they were not in the condition to travel! Each of them looked extremely weak, and they might need a few days to regain their vigour. She expressed her concerns to her mother, and both of them agreed to give them all the support they may need.

When the food was ready, Claire invited her guests to come to the dining room. They were almost asleep but followed her nevertheless, walking hesitantly and supporting themselves on the walls or anything that came in their way.

Each of them took a seat at the table, and the way they engulfed the food showed just how hungry they were. There was well-prepared fish with a generous sauce made of vegetables, garlic, lemon, and parsley. Mrs Graham and her daughter sat at the same table and offered them anything they might need. One of the two housekeepers brought a bottle of exquisite white wine from the fridge and began pouring the drink into glasses. The girls were encouraged to drink the wine at once in order to relax them.

Half an hour later, the four girls felt much better. Of course, the general conversation was about themselves and about what they intended to do next.

It turned out that they wanted to escape the spying machine and the media pressure, intending to travel around the world. There was no plan yet about their journey, but none of them intended to make one, at least not right then. They just wanted to vanish into the world for a while and try to forget everything.

Mr Anderson had been informed about the girls' decision, and he received the news with the feeling that despite everything, that was perhaps the best decision they could make. He was well aware that the killing of the four guys had had a great psychological impact on the girls; there was nothing they could do to bring them back to life.

Although Mr Anderson lost a significant amount of money in the failed attempt to organise the online revolution, he worried less about the loss of money and more about the way the elite had fought back. If a popular hero could become a monster in such a short time, this was not only worrying but also scary. Perhaps it was time to question democracy itself, its meaning and purpose. Nevertheless, Mr Anderson did not intend to jeopardise his business and financial security for some unrealistic ideals such as equity or fairness.

Damn the political world and their dirty games!

Who cared if a liar was exchanged by yet another liar? Who benefited from this change? Not the majority of people, of course. The majority were always the losers, regardless of who was ruling them. Apparently, everything was about the *winners*—the way they did business with each other and the way they controlled and manipulated the *losers*.

Mr Anderson had plenty of reasons to consider himself a winner, but that didn't make him invincible. Of course, he needed to be in good relations with the bad guys in order to maintain his current social status. Otherwise, he might fall as quickly as the four unfortunate lads, with terrible consequences.

Fortunately for him, Mr Anderson preferred to keep quiet and to avoid challenging the wrong people openly. This was how he managed to survive for so long at the top. Arguing all the time for fairness and other unrealistic moral ideals was akin to nonsense, he thought.

I am a businessman, not a preacher, he concluded.

People, who still believed in such nonsense were free to jeopardise and sacrifice their lives and businesses. At the end of the day, the equation of success appeared to have one single solution only: the winner takes it all! All the rest were just scavengers delighting themselves with what was left over.

This was why society was so ridiculously obsessed with the idea of becoming winners. It was no wonder that so many books and so many movies, in fact too many of them, that appeared on the market over the past few years rotated around the same subject: how to become a winner.

Sadly, there was no victory for the runner-up in any competition amongst humans. Not surprisingly, this was true for the animal world too. However, the funny thing about this philosophy was the speed at which second and third places were forgotten. It was usually up to the losers to do the dirty work of forgetting, and it appeared that losers enjoyed punishing themselves for no apparent gain.

What was so special about becoming a winner? Ironically, a winner was no more a loser, and that was a great achievement. Then there were other advantages and privileges of becoming so, such as social status, reputation, stardom, respect, admiration, financial freedom, and most importantly, more chances to mate.

"That's it!" shouted Mr Anderson, happy about his long expected eureka moment. "Everything is about more chances to copulate!"

He then transposed his idea into the animal kingdom and was not surprised to find a similar pattern. All the battles appeared to be between males in order to control territories, increase their fitness, or to enhance their social statuses and reputations. However, this entire struggle had an ultimate goal: controlling the females. There were a few exceptions when a female could have more males, but that didn't change the general formula of the mating behaviour. Alpha males were the winners, and as such, they deserved everything; damn the losers!

Now, coming back to the human species, why was it so difficult to admit that humans were not different from animals regarding the mating behaviour? Wasn't it true that male celebrities had more females around them, and vice versa? What about kings, emperors, and any other powerful rulers? Of course, this would be a difficult thing to admit since humans are supposed to be equal. Some people might even get upset or outraged just mentioning any kinds of theories that didn't agree with the accepted equity principle. But this implied that there were no winners, therefore no losers.

In a planet without members of the opposite sex, there was no need for social status, money, power, reputation, celebrities, or any other means for impressing each other.

Mr Anderson appeared to be shocked by his findings. Nevertheless, he continued with his philosophising.

Drat it! It was rattling clear to him how ridiculous all the moralists preaching equity were. There was no equity, there had never been equity, and there never would be equity. Life was organised in such a way as to reward winners and punish losers, and it really didn't matter if the rules of the game got broken.

It appeared that all the winners had one important quality: plenty of luck.

In the end, that damned **Game of Power** might not be that crazy. Mr Anderson had finally begun to realise that it was just another tool for creating winners and losers. It was quite similar to natural fights for controlling territories, to doing business and having a career, or to any gambling activities, including playing the lottery.

Life is nothing but a gambling activity! concluded Mr Anderson. *Whether one is looking for the right mate, the right job, the right career, or the right friends, it's all about gambling.* However, the ultimate goal was not money, power, stardom, a great reputation, or a great career. Instead, as shocking as it might be, this entire struggle was only about controlling as many members of the opposite sex as possible.

If that was true, then it explained why so many social networks, instead of building and maintaining relationships, did exactly the opposite. In addition, demonising the members of the opposite sex on a daily basis via the influence of the media could have a similar effect. It was damn clear that creating mistrust amongst both sexes was an effective way of making them feel lonely and vulnerable. Then controlling both genders had to be incredibly easy. And like always, the alpha individuals would be the winners, enjoying all the benefits and privileges resulting from such divisions since the equation of success had one solution only: the winner takes it all!

Conspiracy!

A few days later, the four girls were feeling much better and appeared to be ready to go about their journey around the world.

It was early in the morning, and everyone was awake. The two housekeepers were busy preparing breakfast, the last one their guests would have before vanishing into the unknown. Mr Anderson had promised to join them and was to arrive at any moment.

Sara, Susan, Julia, and Lisa prepared their rucksacks and were almost ready. Claire kept herself busy amongst her friends, moving from one room to another, talking to and encouraging them.

In the meantime, Mr Anderson arrived. At breakfast, the four unfortunate girls were the centre of everyone's attention. Because they would be going forth into the terra incognita for a long period, they received especially friendly and warm treatment. Everyone appeared busy around them, asking if they needed anything and trying to anticipate their movements whilst offering them in advance anything displayed on the table.

This little group of friends was well aware that their common battle for equity and fairness was lost. Revolutions always created winners and losers. Unfortunately, they just happened to be the losers, and the four unfortunate girls had to pay the higher price.

No more revolutions, please! thought Mr Anderson.

None of them, however, appeared to be willing to organise any revolution soon. They had no courage or power for such high-risk activity.

However, Sara had good reason to be upset. It was just too strange that none of the great journalists came to their defence and none of them found it necessary to question the official version of the story! She wondered aloud what the jobs of journalists were, what kind of democracy they were defending.

"It's not about defending democracy," said Mr Anderson. "It's more about defending their own personal interests."

Something didn't make sense. Some of the journalists, such as Mrs Harrison, had openly declared themselves to be their friends.

"That was before the guys were killed," suggested Mrs Graham.

"And before the process of demonising them," continued her daughter.

Mr Anderson believed he had a better answer. "Defending someone against government is simply not practical, and none of the journalists will risk their careers for some utopic ideals. If any of them has the courage to question the official version of a story, they might end up as conspiracy theorists and consequently ridiculed and marginalised."

Apparently, that was the reason such stories were presented in the news with bigger headlines, under the label conspiracy. Any theory challenging governments had to be presented as entertaining news and thus their authors ridiculed.

Sara finally had to accept that any chance of defending the four innocent guys was lost, that there was no hope. The best they could do was hope to find their story under the headline CONSPIRACY! And there were plenty of bored people out there willing to have some fun with it.

In a society so ridiculously obsessed with dancing cats and dogs, where the most important issues facing humanity had to be funny, Sara and her friends could not expect more. And having to face this funny society that seemed to be completely indifferent to its own future, Sara and her friends felt a desperate urge to cry . . .

Two hours later, at a train station, four passengers hugged their friends for the last time and then turned around, trying in vain to hide their emotions. They entered the train with a feeling that everything worth fighting for was lost forever. All of their emotions suddenly decided to betray them, and they began weeping silently.

The signal for the departure was finally given. As the doors closed, the train started moving, slowly at first, then faster and faster. Mr Anderson, Mrs Graham, and Claire kept waving their hands until the train vanished from view, carrying their unfortunate friends to an unknown destination.

Lightning Source UK Ltd.
Milton Keynes UK
UKOW05n1853250214

227134UK00001B/22/P